"I'm getting married."

Maggie hesitated, then added, "And I have to get back to New York to plan my wedding."

Jack couldn't have looked more startled if she'd said she was entering a convent. "You're getting married?" he echoed. "I...uh... Your father didn't say anything about it."

"Well, why would he?" Her voice was curt. Too late she realized she'd introduced the subject of her upcoming marriage in the hope that he would keep his distance since she was having such trouble maintaining hers.

"I guess congratulations are in order then."

"Thank you," Maggie murmured. Then, not trusting herself to say more, she climbed back into the saddle and gave the horse a hard dig with her heel. They raced up the hill and over, thundering down the other side.

Run, run. Go anywhere, Maggie thought, giving Freebie his head. Just as long as I don't have to look back.

ABOUT THE AUTHOR

Risa Kirk's love of animals is very evident in her writing. Her first story, written when she was six years old, was about a fox and a rabbit. The California author belongs to several wildlife organizations and, together with her husband, enjoys riding and training their four Arabian horses.

Risa Kirk has published several mainstream novels as well as Gothic and historical romances. *Worth the Wait* is her eighth Superromance novel.

Books by Risa Kirk

HARLEQUIN SUPERROMANCE

238–TEMPTING FATE
273–DREAMS TO MEND
300–WITHOUT A DOUBT
361–PLAYING WITH FIRE
408–UNDERCOVER AFFAIR
441–SEND NO REGRETS
476–MADE TO ORDER

WORTH THE WAIT

Risa Kirk

Harlequin Books

TORONTO • NEW YORK • LONDON
AMSTERDAM • PARIS • SYDNEY • HAMBURG
STOCKHOLM • ATHENS • TOKYO • MILAN
MADRID • WARSAW • BUDAPEST • AUCKLAND

Published April 1993

ISBN 0-373-70542-5

WORTH THE WAIT

Printed in U.S.A.

CHAPTER ONE

"MAGGIE, you have to come home to Lexington!" Aunt Tilda declared frantically to Margaret Gallagher over the phone one morning. "Your father is—" her voice dropped momentarily with the titillating horror of it "—involved with a younger woman!" Her voice rose. "A Las Vegas *show girl,* no less! She's convinced him to sell the farm and move to Florida. To live on a houseboat! If I hadn't heard him say it myself, I'd think it was a joke. It *is* a joke! The man has never been near the water. He doesn't even know how to swim!"

Tilda gasped to a stop, but Margaret was so shocked she couldn't think of a reply. Her father involved with a younger woman? A show girl? It didn't seem possible. As far as she knew, Dan Gallagher had never even been to Las Vegas. He was a Kentuckian, a Thoroughbred breeder, a horse trainer. He hadn't left home for years!

"Don't say you can't come, Maggie!" Tilda rushed on. "I know you and your dad have had problems, and that there's been trouble between you in the past, but—"

Margaret couldn't let that pass. Reluctantly, she set aside the question of just how *much* younger this friend of her father's was—she, Margaret was thirty-five...did Tilda mean that the woman was younger than she?—and protested, "That's not true, Aunt. We did quarrel the last time I was home, but—"

"And that was two years ago, Maggie. Two *years!* A lot has happened since then, and I think you should come home to see for yourself! I know you've wanted Dan to sell the farm for some time, but you have to admit he shouldn't do something drastic while he's under the influence of this... this *woman!*"

Tilda's tone said "hussy," and despite herself, Margaret smiled. "Aunt Tilda," she said reasonably, "are you sure about this? Since Mom died, Dad hasn't been interested in any woman."

To her surprise, Tilda snorted. "Dan Gallagher might have been a widower for twenty years and more, but he's still a *man,* Maggie, and don't forget it. I know he's always said no one could take his wife's place, and as for selling the farm... well, I myself would sooner believe he'd signed up to be the first racehorse trainer in space. But it's happened, and what are you going to do about it?"

Margaret didn't have the faintest idea. Picturing her rotund aunt, her father's sister, with her gray hair in a tight bun atop her round head, she reminded herself how excitable Tilda was. Then she thought of her father, sixty-some years old, hardworking, lean, devoted to his farm and his horses. No, it just wasn't possible, she thought. Aunt Tilda had been reading the tabloids again and allowing her imagination to run wild.

"So when can you come?" Aunt Tilda demanded in her ear.

"Come?" Margaret repeated, stalling for time. "Home, you mean?"

"Well, of course I mean home! Honestly, Maggie, what do you think I've been telling you here? This is an emergency, a crisis! You have to take the next plane!"

Margaret looked around her office. As executive vice-president in charge of production at Prescott Paper Products here in New York, she had an important job, a demanding job. In fact, this afternoon she was supposed to be meeting with some high-level people from a major lumber company to negotiate a new contract. She couldn't just drop everything and go home. She had responsibilities, duties, more work piled up on her desk than she could get through in two weeks even if she didn't take time off to eat and sleep.

Telling herself that she had to be firm, she said, "I'm sorry, Aunt Tilda, but I can't do it right now. It's just impossible."

"Nothing's impossible! Oh, Maggie, if you don't come home and straighten this out, what am I going to do? Your father's going to ruin his life, and that woman is going to take everything she can get her hands on. Don't you even care?"

"Of course I care," Margaret said. And she did. It was just that right now was a bad time for her. In addition to the workload and the headaches she had with the new computer paper division she'd started, she was engaged to be married to Nowell Prescott, president of the company. And she'd just recently learned that her future mother-in-law expected a big wedding when she and Nowell had planned a small, intimate affair.

But Margaret didn't have time to think about wedding plans, not when she heard her aunt draw breath for another attack. Quickly, she said, "I just can't do it right now, Aunt Tilda. I've got a mountain of work here, and I'm trying to plan my—"

"But your father may sell the farm!"

The farm! How could two simple words cause such conflicting emotions in her, especially after all this time? She tried not to think of it, but the image of home flashed into her mind just the same. As Tilda had said, she hadn't been back in two years, but she knew it wouldn't have changed. From the time she was a child, it had always been the same, the one constant in her life that she'd been eager to leave behind.

Thrusting away memories of rolling green hills and spring air as sweet as balm, refusing to see the big old farmhouse, two stories tall, with the twenty-stall barn looming behind it like a big brother, she said, "Well, I'm sorry, Aunt Tilda, but you know how I feel about Dad selling the place. For years, ever since I can remember, he's just thrown good money after bad. It's taken everything he's had and then some."

"I can't believe you'd turn your back, Maggie," Tilda wailed. "I know you've always wanted your dad to get rid of the place, but are you so anxious to put it behind you that you don't even care?"

"I do care!" Maggie exclaimed. "You know I care about Dad!"

"Then will you come home?"

"I..." Despite herself, despite all the distance she'd tried to put between herself and the farm—coming to New York to go to college, taking a job here, making a life and pursuing a career—for some reason, that damned farm always *would* be home to her. Exasperated with both herself and her aunt, she said, "I told you. I can't!"

There was a short, injured silence. Finally, Tilda said, "Well, I never thought I'd live to see the day when the Gallaghers stopped banding together!"

"This isn't a war, Aunt Tilda!" Margaret said sharply. Now she was even more aggravated than before. She couldn't understand why she was suddenly feeling so guilty. She and her father had had words about this before; he'd made his position very clear.

"I'm not in it for the money, Maggie," Dan had said the last time she'd visited and they'd ended up in another quarrel. "I never have been, and you know it." Then, quick as a wink, he'd changed before her eyes as he always did, a blue-eyed, red-haired Irishman enjoying himself too much to notice how miserable his daughter was. It was always the same; it had been from the time she was small. With a wink and a laugh, he'd added, "I raise and train my horses for the love of 'em, Maggie. There's nothing I like better, or sets my own blood to racing, than to see these magnificent creatures doing what they were born to do, and that's run their fastest."

Margaret had inherited her hazel eyes from her mother, but her auburn hair and her temper came from Dan. "Well, that's all fine and good," she'd told him during that last argument. "The only problem is that Gallagher horses never seem able to run fast enough, or far enough, to win consistently. You might not have noticed, Dad, but I have. And say what you like, you can't feed the stock on air."

Dan's face had changed, and she knew that she'd hurt him. She wanted to apologize, but the temperament she'd gotten from him had also come with a stiff dose of pride. She was silent as he started to walk away, then guilty when he turned back and shook his finger in her face.

"I know how you feel, Maggie, I always have," he said. "You've made it plain enough over the years. But this is my life, and I'll do with it what I choose. Just as you've done with yours. So, go back to New York. It's where you say you belong."

She intended to go, but not before she had her say. "I don't want to fight, Dad," she'd said, although she was aware that they were doing just that. Then she made him even angrier when she tried to smooth things out. "It's just that I'm worried that the farm is getting to be too much for you. After all, no matter what you say, you're no longer a young man."

It was the wrong thing to say. Furiously, he'd declared, "I can work any young whippersnapper you choose into the ground! And on one of my *bad* days, too!"

She knew it was probably true. But in her mind, it hadn't changed the fact that he was getting up in years. In her opinion, there was no reason for him to work so hard, not when he could sell the farm and have an easier life if he chose.

"I don't doubt it," she'd said. "But Dad, you are sixty-two. Don't you..."

"No, I don't!" he'd shouted. "And I'm not in my grave yet, so I'll thank you not to try to put me there!"

She'd been shocked. "I never meant..."

"Good," he'd said, taking his pipe out and clamping the stem decisively between his teeth. He'd given up smoking long ago, but he still carried the pipe from habit. Or maybe because it was an effective means of ending an argument, Margaret had thought. She knew what it meant when the pipe came out: he no longer wanted to discuss it.

"I'm only thinking of you," she'd said, annoyed at being cut off.

"Fine. You've said your piece. Let that be the end of it."

Her temper had flared again. "Why are you so obstinate?"

He'd looked at her over the bowl of the pipe. "Isn't that the pot calling the kettle black?"

Angry that he wouldn't even discuss the matter, she had cut short her visit and left early the next day. Dan had come out of the barn as she was climbing into her rental car to go to the airport.

"This is your home as much as mine, Maggie," he'd said in a conciliatory, if not apologetic tone. "How would you feel if I sold the place and you wanted to come back?"

She'd been too angry at that point to question how she'd feel. Still annoyed, she'd said the first thing that came into her head. "Well, you'd never sell, so the question is academic, isn't it?"

"Maybe now, but not forever, Maggie," Dan had said. His eyes met hers. "Things change, and so do people. You proved that yourself by leaving, didn't you?"

She'd known she had hurt him by leaving home, and she had always felt badly about it. But she couldn't help it, she'd tell herself fiercely. He had his life, and she had a right to hers.

And now what? she wondered, all this time later. She couldn't deny the pang she felt at the thought of Dan actually selling the farm. Yet she'd been after him to do just that for years. Why did she feel this nagging little doubt now?

Irritated, because the last thing she wanted to feel was regret, she said, "Aunt Tilda, I just can't get away right now. I'll tell you what... I'll call Dad and ask him—"

"You know what your father will say if you just phone. Oh, Maggie, can't you come home?"

She was trying to be patient. "Aunt Tilda—"

But as usually happened, Tilda had suddenly become distracted by something else. "It's all going," she said mournfully. "Everything's changing, and after all these years. First the Tidleman place sold, and now this!"

Wondering how they'd gotten so far off track so fast, Maggie sighed. The "Tidleman place," as it was known, was right over the hill from her father's farm. It had been for sale for years, ever since Molly Tidleman had died and her husband, Bert, had decided to move to Baton Rouge to be nearer their daughter who was concerned about his living alone. Reminded that *some* parents worried about what their children thought, Margaret said sharply, "I hope he got a good price for it. It'll make it that much easier for Dad to get a fair amount for the farm."

"Oh, he got a good price, all right. But you'll never guess who bought it, Maggie."

At the moment, Margaret couldn't have cared less. "Who?"

"Jack Stanton, that's who!" Tilda exclaimed, off and running again. "I couldn't believe it when I heard. I always thought that boy would do well, but to come back home and buy that land! Well, it just goes to show, doesn't it? I remember..."

Margaret heard Tilda's voice running on in her ear, but she was no longer listening. She hadn't thought of Jack Stanton in years, but suddenly he appeared in her mind's eye as clearly as if she'd seen him yesterday. At eighteen, when she'd last spoken to him, he'd been a tall, good-looking young man, with thick black hair and blue-gray eyes. A straight nose with a slight bump had saved him from being a "pretty" boy, but in addition to his looks, he'd been a good student and a natural athlete. All the girls had been crazy about him, and she couldn't blame them. He'd been quite a catch, even then.

"You know, his family worked for Leo Castlemaine," Tilda was saying, "and I never thought they'd amount to much, any of them. Why, as I recall, all four of his sisters married young to get out of that two-room shanty they all lived in. And wasn't Jack the only one of the boys to finish high school?"

Margaret didn't know why she felt so unwilling to discuss Jack and his family. "Yes," she said distantly. "His older brother, Floyd, never graduated."

"That's right! Oh, I remember that Floyd now. He was no better than he should be, wasn't he? What a troublemaker he was. And all that carousing around! I'll never forget the night he drove into the window of Spengler's Drug Store. It was a miracle he wasn't killed!"

Margaret had forgotten that incident. It had been all over school the next day, rumors flying that Floyd had been drinking, and that he'd done it purposely to get back at Laura Lee Spengler, the druggist's daughter, because she wouldn't go out with him.

"I never did like that Floyd," Tilda said with a sniff. Then her voice warmed considerably. "But Jack was different, wasn't he?"

Yes, Margaret thought, Jack had been different.

Against her will, a memory of the senior party rose in her mind. As a graduation present, the school had allowed the entire senior class to go to Louisville and hire a riverboat for the night. There was a band, dancing, and the boat had been called... the Ohio Queen.

Frowning, Margaret wondered why she'd remembered that. Then, in spite of herself, she also recalled how full the moon was that night, and how beautiful the water had looked, spangled by the moon's silver light.

Jack had never seemed more handsome, either, she thought, squirming. The senior party was one of the rare times he'd gone on an outing, for usually he was too busy helping out at home. But he'd been there that night, and when he asked her to dance, she refused. Although she'd pretended otherwise, she had always been attracted to him, and she knew he had a crush on her. But she hadn't wanted to get involved with anyone, because as soon as graduation was over, she was going to leave Lexington and never look back. She had planned for too long, and nothing was going to stop her, certainly not Jack.

Jack wouldn't take no for an answer. When the music started—a slow dance, she remembered—he'd reached for her hands and pulled her onto the dance floor despite her protests. He danced as well as he did everything else. Or maybe Margaret only thought so because the instant he drew her into his arms, her heart started to pound. Confused and upset, she had pulled away from him and run out onto the deck. The paddle wheel was sending up sprays of water; she rushed over to it so that the mist would cool her flushed face. She didn't realize Jack had followed her until she looked around and saw him standing there.

He reached for her hand, "Don't go, Maggie."

Trying again to jerk away, she said fiercely, "I don't want to stay. I want to get out of here and *never* return!"

"But why?"

"Why?" she echoed. She'd thought of all the times she'd felt second-rate—an also-ran, like so many of her father's horses. She'd hated the feeling, hated knowing that people looked down on her, hated even more the thought that everyone was snickering at Dan Gallagher and his daughter because they just weren't good enough to reach up and grab that gold ring. Her mouth twisting with bitterness, she'd looked at Jack. "You of all people should know why! We've both been laughed at! We've both lost out because we had to work!"

"Work's nothing to be ashamed of."

"I'm not ashamed!"

"If you're not, why are you running away?"

"I'm not running away from anything!" she cried. "I'm running *to* something, don't you understand? I've scrimped and saved for years for this chance, and nothing—no one—is going to stop me now!"

"And what about your dad?"

"He'll make out." She couldn't keep the acid from her seventeen-year-old voice. What hurt the most, she'd sometimes thought, was that she'd always felt second best to her father's first love, those beautiful Thoroughbreds that took up all his life. Dashing tears from her eyes, she said, "He'll have the horses to keep him company."

"But what about you, Maggie? What company will you have, by yourself in New York?"

She looked at him wildly. "What do you care? Why are you doing this? What could it possibly mean to you?"

His grip tightened. "I've never said this to anyone else in my life, but I... I love you, Maggie. I always have, ever since we were kids."

"Don't say that!"

"Why not? It's true."

She didn't want him to love her. She didn't want him to think a thing about her. She was leaving in the morning, and she wasn't going to look back. "Well, you're just going to have to get over it," she said cruelly. "Even if I wanted to, I don't have time to get involved. I'm going away to make something of myself."

"You already are something, Maggie."

He was confusing her even more now, making her question things she'd thought were settled in her mind long ago. Angrily, she said, "You know what I mean! I won't stay here and live hand-to-mouth! I won't!"

Something changed in his face. She didn't realize that he had misunderstood until he dropped her hand and stepped away from her. His voice low, but hurt and anger in his eyes, he said, "I'll always be a sharecropper's son, Maggie, but I won't always work the fields like my dad. I intend to 'make something' of myself, too."

"I didn't mean—"

It was too late. His jaw tight, he started to turn away, only to look back. With eyes cold as frost, he said in parting, "I wish you luck wherever you go, Maggie. I hope you get everything you want."

Just then, the boat docked. She was so upset by what had just happened that she didn't brace herself. The gentle bump threw her off balance; by the time she righted herself, Jack had gone. She couldn't find him in the milling crowd when everyone got off; he didn't attend the graduation ceremony the next day because he had to be out in the fields. She left right after for New York, as she had promised, and she hadn't seen or heard or thought of him since.

"...couldn't believe that he's returned after all these years," Aunt Tilda was saying when Margaret came back to the present with a start. "He's made something of himself, too. Your dad says he owns some heavy equipment company now, and I guess he must have done well, for he paid quite a price for that Tidleman land. Now Bert's gone, down to be near his daughter, and I'm sorry, but I can't help but be glad. I never did like those people. They just weren't *folks,* if you—"

"Aunt Tilda?" Margaret said.

"Yes, dear?"

Margaret took a deep breath. She didn't like the feelings this conversation had awakened in her.

"What's Jack going to do with that land?"

"Well, isn't it obvious? For heaven's sake, Maggie, he plans to raise and race his own horses, of course!"

Margaret didn't know what to say. Jack and horses? She didn't think he even knew how to ride.

"You remember him, don't you, dear?" Tilda asked.

Wishing she didn't, Margaret closed her eyes. "We went to school together," she said faintly. "But...but that was a long time ago. I doubt I'd know him now."

"Oh, well," Tilda said. Jack Stanton was dismissed as she returned to the original problem. "As for your dad's farm, it makes no never mind to *me* if he sells or not. I just want to make sure he's not under the influence of this...*woman.* I don't trust her, Maggie. So, are you coming down to see what's what, or not?"

Margaret was still preoccupied with a vision of Jack as she'd last seen him—how many years ago? Too many to count, she thought, closing her eyes at the memory of a tight jaw on a handsome face and a blue-gray gaze that had turned hard as glass. "Oh, Aunt Tilda, I don't know—"

"I can't believe you'd let this go!"

Exasperated, Margaret started to refuse. But without warning, Jack's face rose in her mind again, and she hesitated. She told herself she was out of patience, that her aunt had badgered her until she had no choice. But deep down, she knew it was more than that.

"All right," she said severely, to make up for her confusion. "I'll come. But only for a day or so, mind. No longer, I mean it."

At the other end of the line, Tilda sighed contentedly. "A few days will be fine."

Feeling a little dazed, Margaret hung up the phone. Why had she agreed to do as her aunt had asked? And more to the point, she thought suddenly, how was she going to explain it to Nowell?

Deciding she'd deal with one problem at a time, she buzzed her secretary and asked her to make reservations on a flight the next morning. Then, knowing she couldn't put it off, she squared her shoulders and went to talk to her fiancé.

CHAPTER TWO

"HEY, JACK!" a voice called from outside the trailer where Jack Stanton was staying while his new house was being built. "Come on, buddy! You ever coming out? I've got the whole crew waiting on you, an' you said it yourself, time's money!"

Lying in bed, Jack grinned as he heard his construction foreman's heavy footsteps tramp away. It was barely seven o'clock in the morning, but he'd been awake from the instant the crew arrived and the first backhoe was fired up. The sound was a familiar, comforting noise to him; heavy equipment was his business. But as he listened to the roar of the machines as the men outside got to work, he heard a noise from one of the engines that indicated it wasn't firing on all cylinders. Throwing back the covers, he got up, making a mental note to have the noise checked out. Ten minutes later, dressed in jeans, T-shirt and boots, coffee cup in hand, he went outside.

His foreman, Al Watkins, was waiting for him under the tree where they'd set up a makeshift worktable. Stacks of plans were spread over the table's surface, and as he ambled up, Al gave him a meaningful look.

"'Bout time," Al grumbled. "Half the day's gone, and you're just stumblin' out of bed."

Jack smiled. He and Al had known each other since grade school, and there wasn't a better construction man around. After he'd come home and bought the farm from Bert Tidleman, he'd contacted Al to rebuild the place, and they'd had crews working ever since. He didn't have to worry about Al; even though business still took Jack away now and then, he could trust his heavyset old friend to take care of things while he was gone.

Thinking ironically that he could also trust him to speak his mind, Jack said, "Well, I'm here now. What's the problem?"

"No problem. I just wanted to be sure we were of the same mind about these here irrigation lines."

Together, he and the foreman bent over the plans, Al tracing the water lines with a stubby finger. Along with the new house, two big barns were planned, and they had had to dig another well to make sure there was enough water.

Giving his approval to the changes Al had made, Jack straightened and looked back toward the house. Without realizing it, a look of pride stole over his face, and Al, seeing it, smiled.

"You've done right fine by yourself, Jack," Al said. "When we finish, it'll be a showplace, all right."

Their eyes met, and Jack said, "It's a little different from where I grew up, isn't it?"

"It is," Al said with a grin. "As they say, you've come a long way, baby."

Jack couldn't have agreed more. The house behind him had six bedrooms, the same number of baths, three fireplaces, a big living room, family room, office and den. In stark contrast, the place where he'd grown up had been a two-room shanty with a divided loft for bedrooms overhead. His four sisters slept on one side of the wall curtain; he and his brother slept on the other. The single, cramped bedroom below had been reserved for his parents; the space remaining served all the other functions. With eight people crowded around the kitchen table, there wasn't room for much else. The Stantons hadn't owned a television set until Jack was twelve. Even then it had been an old black-and-white someone had given them, third-hand.

Aware that Al was watching him, Jack snapped out of his reverie. "So have you, old friend," he said. "You've done well yourself."

"Yeah, but not as good as you," Al said without rancor. "I always knew you'd be successful one day, but even I didn't think you'd own an international equipment company before you were thirty." He thought a moment, then added, "Of course, you always were good with machines. What an ear you had! Remember auto shop? Man, you could just *listen* to something and know what was wrong with it. And now that I think of it, it was the same for all the farm equipment. When I think of all the money you saved that cheap so-and-so Leo Castlemaine...!"

Jack didn't like to think of those years he and his family had worked for Leo Castlemaine. Even now, he could picture the man: almost as wide as he was tall, with jowls, a balding head and thick lips. Castlemaine had made his money in textiles and tobacco, and Jack still had nightmare memories of working in Castlemaine's tobacco fields. Leo had used people and vehicles until one or the other broke down; then he would grudgingly and angrily order replacements and ignore any problems until the next crisis.

Jack could still recall riding a roofed wooden wagon through the endless fields, cross-pollinating burley tobacco plants to produce hybrid seed. Careful cross-pollination resulted in the most desirable disease-resistant plants, but he hadn't cared about that then, and he wasn't sure he cared now. The thing he remembered most about that time was the hot sun beating down on his sore back, and stiff fingers that wouldn't work after a while. He and his family had worked for slave wages, but an ounce of that hybrid Castlemaine seed had sold for forty-eight dollars, even in those days.

Thrusting the memories away, he looked at Al. "Yes, well, it was a long time ago."

"Thank the Lord," Al muttered. He, too, had worked in the fields and, like Jack, could remember the backbreaking work. In an effort to lighten the mood, he looked down at the picnic table that held all the house and barn plans. Gesturing to the four rocks holding down the corners of the blueprints, he grinned.

"Oh, yeah, buddy, you've really gone up in the world. Didn't you used to have an office somewhere, with a real desk and plush carpets and climate-controlled interiors? And I seem to remember a big mahogany desk and custom-crafted drafting boards—not to mention the three secretaries typing furiously away to log in all the orders."

Jack grinned back. "It is a contrast, isn't it?"

"That's for sure. Man, I don't know how you stood it there."

"I don't know, either. I guess it was because that's where the business was."

"And now?"

"Now the business is where I happen to be."

Smiling again, two old friends who understood each other, they had just started to go over the dimensions for the second barn when they heard a car coming down the road. It was a deep purple '57 Cadillac with big fins on the back, but even if the car hadn't been so distinctive, Jack would have known by the way it was being driven that his brother Floyd had arrived.

As their father had said too many times to count during their youth, Floyd drove as though his tail were on fire or the law was after him—probably both. The years since hadn't made him any more responsible, and the Cadillac crested the last hill as though it were a car on a roller coaster. Bouncing as it came down, it sped through the gates and slid to a dust-raising halt in front of the trailer. Floyd got out of the car before it stopped rocking and looked around. When he saw Jack, he touched the brim of his hat with a sardonic smile.

"Oh boy," Al muttered. He'd known Jack's older brother as long as he'd known Jack, and he made no secret of the fact that he didn't like him. "I think it's time to go check on the crew."

As Al disappeared, Floyd came strolling up. Not quite as tall as Jack's six-foot-two, Floyd had similar coloring with his black hair and blue eyes. Unfortunately for him, the resemblance ended there. Jack had strong features, a direct gaze and a disarming twinkle in his eye. Floyd seemed a pale imitation, his features slightly blurred. Dressed in jeans, boots and a Stetson that had seen better days, he said, "How do, little brother. Here I am, reporting as ordered."

Despite himself, Jack winced. It hadn't been his idea to ask Floyd to be his farm manager; it had been his mother's.

"Floyd hasn't been as fortunate as you," Alma Stanton had said when Jack told her he'd bought the Tidleman land and intended to build a farm there. "After all," she'd gone on with a heavy sigh, "he's never been able to pick a thing and stay with it like you have, Jack."

No one in the family knew all the jobs his brother had tried, but it seemed that he'd been everything from field hand to hashslinger and hadn't been able to find anything he could stay with. Jack hadn't said anything to his mother, but he couldn't help thinking that maybe if Floyd tried a little harder, he would find something he liked and stick with it.

Still, his mother's words rankled, and even though his brother had continually refused to come to work for him at the company, Jack had felt obliged to try one more time. He had bought his parents their retirement home in Arizona, and he had helped all four of his sisters and their husbands obtain homes of their own. He could afford one last attempt to help his brother.

"Hey, I appreciate the thought," Floyd had first said when Jack had approached him with the idea. "I'd like to help you out, but what do I know about running a horse farm?" His voice had taken on a bitter edge he didn't bother to hide. "In case you've forgotten, we didn't quite move in those circles when we were growing up."

"I haven't forgotten," Jack had said. "But we're going to learn together. I plan for Fieldstone Farm to—"

"Fieldstone Farm? Is that what you call it? I don't know, Jack, with what you've got ahead of you, maybe a better name would be Stanton's Folly."

With an effort, Jack held on to his temper. "By whatever name it's called, I'm still going to need a farm manager. Do you want the job or not?"

To his surprise, Floyd had accepted. "Yeah, why not," he'd said. "It might be a kick for a while. When do I start... boss?"

Trying to tell himself he hadn't made a big mistake, Jack had told him to come at the end of the month.

"You're crazy," Al had said flatly when he told his foreman what he'd done. "It'll never work, and you know it."

"It might," he'd said defensively. "And if I hire Floyd, he'll be here all the time—something I won't be able to do. The business is at the point where it doesn't need my constant attention, but even so, there will be times when I have to be away. I'll need someone here to handle things when I'm gone."

"And you think Floyd will be the one to do that? Come on, Jack. Aren't we talking about the guy who can't hold down a job for more'n five minutes?"

Remembering that conversation, Jack had a sinking feeling that Al was right. Well, he was committed now; all he could do was hope.

"You're a tad early, don't you think?" he said easily, as Floyd came up. "I thought I said the farm manager's house wouldn't be ready until the end of the month."

"Yeah, well, you know me. Pack light and travel fast," Floyd said, grinning again. "I didn't have anything better to do, so I came on down."

Jack didn't ask the reason for the rush; he decided it was better he didn't know. "It's okay. You can always bunk with me in the trailer until the house is ready."

"We'll see," Floyd said noncommittally. Lounging against the edge of the picnic table, he glanced idly down at the farm plans and laughed. "What, no manmade lake? No tracks for the train? You're slipping, Jack. I thought this was going to be a showplace."

Determined not to let Floyd get to him, Jack said, "It's not an amusement park. We're going to raise horses here."

"You could have fooled me," Floyd replied, pulling out a toothpick from his pocket and sticking it between his teeth. He pointed. "For instance, what the hell's that thing there?"

Jack turned and looked in the direction his brother indicated. "It's one of the barns—or will be, when it's completed."

"I'll be damned. Let's take a look-see."

Together, they walked over to the half-finished structure. It was the smaller of the two planned barns, this one intended to have eighteen fourteen-by-fourteen-foot stalls, nine on a side, along with a tack room, a wash area, a grain room, space for hay overhead, and a small laboratory and medical area for treatment, when needed. As was typical in the area, the barn was made of oak; not quite so typical were the stainless-steel fixtures: the bars in front of each stall, the water canisters, the handles and locks on the doors.

Floyd whistled. "I didn't believe it 'til now, but it seems you're serious here, Jack. What'd you drop on this thing—half a million?"

"It's not finished yet," Jack said, avoiding the question. "When it is, all the stalls will have rubber mats on the floors, covered with bedding, and in warm weather, the outer wall can be rolled back—see the wire-screen mesh for ventilation?"

"Anything else?" Floyd asked cynically. "Cots for the horses? Television?"

Jack ignored the sarcasm. He'd studied barn designs until he knew what he wanted. He had finally reached a point where he could have the best, and this was it. He wasn't going to apologize, especially to his brother.

"Lord almighty," Floyd said, feigning amazement when they finished the tour. "You can't mean to put *horses* in this thing. I've known *people* who didn't live as well."

"So have I," Jack said evenly. "But times have changed, haven't they?"

"Maybe for you, but not for me. But then, you always were the ambitious one, and I guess this proves it, doesn't it?"

Keeping his voice neutral, Jack said with a shrug, "I guess it does."

Looking disappointed that his brother hadn't taken the bait, Floyd drew back one of the two big doors at the barn's end. The door rolled easily on a steel track overhead, a weight that would have been difficult to move manually, but which seemed as light as a feather on the stainless-steel ball bearings. His expression thoughtful, Floyd pulled out a cigarette and lit it.

"What are you really doing, Jack?" he asked.

Jack turned to him. "What do you mean?"

Floyd gestured with his cigarette. "All this. As far as I know, you know as much about horses as I do—

that they've got four legs and a tail and they eat a lot of hay."

Despite himself, Jack laughed. "I'm not as ignorant as all that."

"Oh, no? Well, when did you learn the horse business? When did you have time between all that travelin' around and making all that money?"

"You know I've always liked horses. When we were kids, I used to sneak over every chance I got to Keeneland or up to Churchill Downs just to watch the morning workouts." Jack smiled with the memory. "And don't forget old Daisy. I used to ride her all the time."

"Daisy?" Floyd frowned, trying to remember. "You mean that ancient plow horse old man Kreiger used to keep next door? She was so old and fat she could hardly walk out of her tracks."

"True. But she was all I had. I used to pretend she was Man-o-War."

Floyd looked at him in disbelief. Then he shook his head. "And we all thought you were the smart one in the family."

"It didn't hurt to have dreams," Jack said casually. He glanced around. "Look what it got me."

Looking at him again from under the brim of his soiled Stetson, Floyd said, "Whatever it is, it's not enough to compete with these elite snobs, I'll tell you that."

Jack knew how resentful his brother was of the people he called society. One of the worst episodes in the family's history was the night Floyd had driven his car through the front window of Spengler's Drug Store in nearby Lexington. Floyd said it had been an accident, that the car had gone out of control when he'd tried to avoid hitting a dog crossing the street, but Jack knew better. Floyd had had a crush on the drug store owner's daughter, a rich girl who had refused to go out with him.

"We'll see if it is or not," Jack said noncommittally.

Sneering, Floyd stubbed out his cigarette. "If you think you're going to beat these people at their own game, you'd better think again, Jack. They'll never let you in, no matter how much money you flash around. Don't forget, they were raising and racing horses long before we were tying tobacco on sticks."

"That's true. But things have changed."

Floyd snorted. "Things haven't changed since cavemen discovered fire, and you know it—not around here, anyway. But it's your business, I guess. I just don't know why you want to drag me into it."

His jaw tight, Jack replied, "I don't want to *drag* you into it if you don't want to be here. If you've changed your mind, it's fine with me."

"Hey, hey! Boy, you always did have a hair trigger, you know that? Did I say I'd changed my mind? I agreed to come—to give it a try," Floyd amended quickly. "Just don't expect too much at first, all right? It's going to take me some time to learn what the hell I'm supposed to be doing."

"Don't worry, you'll have help."

"Who?" Floyd asked. His eyes narrowed. "What's the matter, Jack? I haven't even started, and already you don't trust me?"

"It's not a matter of trust. It's a matter of both of us feeling our way at first. This is new to me, too, remember. I thought it would be easier if I had someone come in—just for a while—to show us both the ropes. Then, when you feel more confident, you can take over completely... if that's what you want." He paused meaningfully. "You did say you'd just try it at first, Floyd. What am I supposed to do if you decide you don't like it here?"

"You think I'd leave you in the lurch?"

"Would you?"

Floyd looked at him a moment longer, then he grudgingly conceded. "I guess I see your point," he said, as they began walking back to his car. Reaching for the door, he opened it. "Well, so long, then. I'm off to Louisville—" he drawled it like the native he was, pronouncing it *Loo-a-vulle* "—to see what's cookin'."

"You're not leaving now, are you? You just got here."

Floyd grinned. "Hey, pretty soon I'm gonna be a man of duty and obligation. I've got to shine while there's still time."

"Wait a minute," Jack said, as his brother got in and started the car. "Where can I reach you?"

"Don't know right now," Floyd said, putting the car in gear. Gunning the engine, he touched the brim of his hat. "I'll be in touch."

Jack's reply was lost in the sound of flying gravel as Floyd took off. Watching the purple Cadillac disappear up the road, he shook his head. His mother thought this was a good idea; his father approved. But they were in Arizona and didn't have to deal with Floyd, like he did. His sisters weren't so sure the new arrangement would work, and neither was he.

"You'll be sorry," his favorite sister, Dulcie, had said, when he'd told her about it. She seemed to speak for all the girls when she added, "Floyd is our brother, but we all know what a trial he can be. He's been in and out of trouble since he was little, and I don't know if there's a thing he hasn't tried. You keep your eye on him, Jack, I'm warning you."

Touched by her concern, he'd said, "You don't have to warn me, Dulcie. I know all about him."

"I don't think you do," she'd said darkly. "I don't think any of us really knows Floyd."

Those words would come back to haunt him later, but today, as he watched the grape-colored Cadillac disappearing over the hill, Jack shook his head. If this didn't work, he wasn't sure what he would do.

One of the men came to ask him about something just then, and after that, it was something else, and then something else again. It wasn't until very late in the afternoon, when the crew was winding down for the day, that he had a minute to himself. With the sun setting in a spectacular sky, he decided to take a walk to clear his mind. But after he had climbed the slope behind the house and looked across the hills to the property next to his, he didn't feel elated, as he had expected. Instead, he was remembering something else from the past.

I won't stay here and live hand-to-mouth, Jack! I won't!

Her voice came to him without warning, making him wince. He had never forgotten Maggie Gallagher, but lately, ever since coming home again, she was on his mind constantly. The last time he'd seen her was the night of the senior party, when the class had gone to Louisville to take a ride on one of the big paddle wheelers. He grimaced with the memory of what a fool he had been.

He was still a fool, he thought, looking somberly down at Gallagher Farm. Why else had he offered to buy Dan Gallagher's land? The instant he'd heard that the farm was up for sale, he'd made an offer. He hadn't even taken five minutes to think about it; he just called up the broker and put in a bid. He'd convinced himself that he needed Dan's twenty-five acres to add to the hundred or so he already had, but was that the only reason?

Standing there with the slight breeze ruffling his hair, he knew that it wasn't. Maybe he'd had a misguided notion he could buy back the past, but too many years had gone by. He might remember Maggie Gallagher so clearly she was like a living, breathing presence to him, but what made him think that she remembered him? Their lives had led them in different directions. He'd learned from Dulcie that she was some kind of executive in New York. And just because he'd taken a path back home again didn't mean she'd want to return to something she'd left behind long ago.

I'll never come back! she had told him that night. *Never!*

He'd been surprised and dismayed by the ferocity in her voice. At that age, it had seemed to him that she hated him, too, but maybe she hadn't been thinking of him at all. In any case, it seemed she had kept her word, for according to Dulcie, she'd made only a few short visits over the years.

Maybe he wouldn't even recognize her now, he thought, then immediately shook his head at the absurdity of the idea. He'd forget his own face before he forgot Maggie Gallagher.

CHAPTER THREE

MARGARET COULD FEEL herself tense as she took the stairs instead of the elevator up to her fiancé's office. She told herself it was because she needed the exercise, but what she was really doing was stalling for time.

"How am I ever going to explain this?" she muttered. She couldn't just walk in and tell Nowell the unvarnished truth; it made her family sound...she didn't know what.

Deciding she'd just have to wing it, she reached Nowell's office and opened the door. His secretary was sitting at her desk in the outer office; as soon as she saw Margaret, she smiled and told her to go right in. Margaret took a deep breath and entered.

Nowell was sitting at his kidney-shaped glass desk, going over some reports. He looked at her but before he could say anything, she said gaily, "Hi. Got a minute?"

Nowell Prescott was tall and slim, with sandy hair and light blue eyes that could be warm when he was pleased, glacial when he was not. She had never meant to become involved with the head of the company where she worked; in fact, for months after he had moved from the Chicago office to take over here when his father died, she had refused even to go for coffee with him. Finally, he'd persuaded her, pointing out that no one could accuse her of dating the boss to get ahead because she was already there.

One thing had led to another, and now, even though they were engaged and by next year would be married, she had never told him of the vague disquiet she'd been experiencing these past few months. It couldn't be her job—at least, she didn't think it was. She loved her work...well, she had at one time. But lately there had been times when she'd wondered if she wouldn't be doing something else by now if she and Nowell hadn't become involved.

Maybe it was the strain and stress of her upcoming wedding, she'd think hopefully. All brides got the jitters. Once she and Nowell were married, she'd be content again, both at home and on the job. This unsettled feeling she had would disappear and she'd be herself again.

"Do I have a minute?" Nowell answered her question with a smile. "For you, I've got all day."

Rising, he came around the desk and grasped her hands. Because they were at the office, where they had both agreed to maintain strict decorum, he gave her a chaste little peck on the cheek before he noticed her expression. "What is it, Margaret? Having a problem with Wagoner down in the new division?"

Gently, she removed her hands so they could sit down. "No, it's not business. This time I'm afraid it's personal."

He frowned. "What is it?" he asked, gesturing to the chairs at one end of the room.

They sat down and she looked at him, mulling over her choices. None seemed good, and she wished she'd just told him the truth long ago and let the chips fall where they may, as her Aunt Tilda would have said.

Now it was more difficult and she had only herself to blame.

When Nowell had first asked about her family background, she'd deliberately been vague, telling him only that her mother had died when she was very young, and that her father kept a few Thoroughbred racehorses on the family farm outside Lexington. She'd felt guilty knowing that she was giving the impression that Gallagher Farm was grander than it actually was, but she couldn't help herself. She and Nowell were just starting a relationship, and she hadn't felt comfortable enough to be completely honest.

Was she ashamed of her father? Her cheeks felt warm at the thought. Of course she wasn't *ashamed.* She loved her dad; it was just that she thought fastidious and proper Nowell might not understand her boisterous, down-to-earth father. She'd told herself she would wait until she and Nowell knew each other better, but as the months passed and they became occupied with other things, she kept putting it off. Waiting for the right moment.

But the moment never came, for whenever she thought of the extroverted Dan Gallagher with his booming laugh, and his sometimes salty language, she cringed at the thought of trying to explain him to her ultraconservative fiancé. It was even worse when she pictured Dan mingling with Nowell's straitlaced family and friends at the upcoming wedding. She knew her father. He'd walk in wearing boots with his tuxedo—if she could get him to put one on, that was—and slap the first person he saw heartily on the back, introducing himself with the sergeant-at-arms voice he had developed over the years from yelling instructions to exercise riders and jockeys at the racetrack.

She could just imagine the reactions of the Prescotts and their refined crowd. She had met some of them before, at the country club Nowell and his mother belonged to. She liked them well enough, she supposed—in any case, she hoped she would, in time. But when she thought of her father in that elite group... well, it just didn't bear thinking about.

Now, the situation had suddenly become even worse. She no longer had the luxury of choosing the moment to explain Dan to her fiancé. How was she going to tell Nowell, who thought her father a gentleman farmer, that her aunt was in hysterics because Dan had gotten himself involved with a young Las Vegas show girl? It sounded unbelievable even to her, and she'd had time to think about it.

She couldn't lie but perhaps she needn't tell the whole story. She took a deep breath and began. "I've got to go home for a day or so, Nowell," she said. Seeing a look of concern on his face, she went on quickly before he could respond. "It's not serious, just a little family problem, nothing to worry about." She smiled, getting to her feet. "I'll be back before you know it."

"Wait!" he exclaimed, as she turned toward the door. A gentleman always, he had risen with her. "What do you mean, nothing to worry about? Is it your father? Is he ill?"

No, according to my Aunt Tilda, he's just lost his mind, she thought, and said hastily, "No, no, nothing like that. It's just something I have to fly down and see about. I'll be back as soon as I can."

"Margaret!" he exclaimed again, as she started toward the door once more. He looked confused and worried. "Margaret, you can't just leave like this, without any explanation. It isn't like you. What's going on?"

Turning to look at him, tall and meticulously groomed, with that unconscious patrician air that had first attracted her, she knew she absolutely could *not* tell him about the show-girl business... not until she knew for sure if it was true, and probably not even then.

"It seems that my father has decided to put the farm up for sale," she said carefully. "And my aunt is worried that he's being... influenced by someone else to do it. She called and asked if I could come down to talk to him about it."

"Oh." As always when he was confronted with something unexpected, Nowell paused a moment and frowned, thinking about it. "Well, in that case," he said finally, "I definitely think you should go."

Stifling a retort that she hadn't asked his permission, she smiled faintly. Her face felt stiff enough to crack. "Thank you. As I said, I'll be—"

But to her horror, he'd come to another decision. "And I think I should go with you."

She was so appalled at the idea that she blurted out, "Come with me! No, absolutely not!

He looked surprised by her outburst. "There's no need to shout. For heaven's sake, Margaret, what's the matter with you?"

She knew she had offended him. Nowell was in control at all times; it was part of his attraction. Still, letting him come with her would be disastrous. Hoping she didn't sound as frantic as she felt, she said, "I'm sorry. I didn't mean to say it like that. It's just that my father can be... difficult at times. You understand, don't you?"

Nowell's father, Donald James Prescott, had been a tyrant of the first order. He never shouted, he never even raised his voice. But Margaret, who had worked for him, had often wished he had; that would have been easier to deal with than his renowned frigid looks of displeasure.

Her reference to a difficult parent made Nowell pause. "Yes, I understand," he said, but then held up a warning finger. "I'll accept your decision, this time. But you know how anxious I am to meet your father, Margaret. I've been trying for months to arrange an introduction, and I absolutely insist on getting together before the wedding."

"Yes, yes, I know," she agreed, cringing despite herself at the thought of Nowell and Dan together. One reason she'd resisted taking him down to the farm was that she knew Dan would probably hand Nowell a pitchfork and expect him to help with the chores.

Forcing away the image of Nowell faced with the prospect of mucking out a stall, she added quickly, "You two will get together—soon, I promise. Just let me get this other business straightened out first."

"All right, my dear, whatever you say." Clearly, he didn't like the compromise, but he was too polite to argue further. He was just bending to give her another chaste peck on the cheek when, without warning, the door opened and Olivia Prescott, Nowell's mother, walked in.

"Darlings!" Olivia cried. "How fortunate I am to find you both here!"

The last person in the world Margaret wanted to see right now was Nowell's mother. Trying to hide her dismay at her future mother-in-law's unexpected appearance, she went dutifully forward with Nowell to greet Olivia.

"How are you, Mrs. Prescott?" she murmured.

"Mother, how nice to see you," Nowell said.

Olivia Prescott was in her sixties, a formidable woman who looked at least ten years younger than she was. Under her expertly tinted silver-blond hair, she had a smooth complexion she regularly tended at an exclusive European spa, a figure women years her junior envied, and sharp blue eyes that didn't miss a thing. Invariably she wore Chanel-type suits and even in this casual day and age, always carried gloves with her purse. She disliked driving, so she kept her own chauffeur, and, no matter what the weather was doing, she walked two miles every day for exercise.

Margaret hated to admit it, but she was in awe of the woman, who seemed so sophisticated and elegant. It had taken all her courage to stand up to Olivia about the wedding, insisting as tactfully as she could that she and Nowell had agreed on a small, intimate ceremony.

Not that it had done much good. Olivia immediately began pressing for a much more elaborate affair. Nowell was her only son; she wanted him to have a wedding she—and her society friends—would always remember.

Protests were useless, not even heard. It was Margaret's first experience with someone like Olivia Prescott who was totally accustomed to getting her own way—and who managed to do it without turning a hair. There were plans to be made, Olivia would say serenely, arrangements to consider. What Margaret wanted wasn't even considered, but she was ignored so politely that she didn't know how to take charge.

So far, Margaret had managed to avoid a showdown, but she knew she was going to have to talk to her mother-in-law. She just didn't want it to be today, when she had so many other things on her mind.

Unfortunately, she didn't have a choice about that, either. Before she could caution Nowell not to mention that she planned to be away for a day or so, Olivia turned to her son.

"Hello, Nowell, dear. I hope I'm not interrupting, but I simply had to come. We *must* decide on the caterer. If we don't, Andre will be taken by someone else, and then where will we be?"

"Without the watercress truffles and the cream of rutabaga soup, I hope," Nowell said dryly. He caught Margaret's amazed eye and smiled slightly. He rarely made jokes, and as he bent to give his mother a kiss on the cheek, Margaret was even more astounded to see him wink at her.

"Don't make fun, darling," Olivia chided, giving him a reproving pat on the arm. "Andre is one of the best caterers in Manhattan. Everyone is *dying* to get him. It would be a real coup!" She turned again to Margaret. "Don't you agree, dear?"

Margaret had never heard of Andre. Furthermore, she didn't care to meet the man. She didn't want a caterer; she wanted a few friends to share a little cake and some champagne. "Well, I—" she started to say.

"Oh, now, don't tell me you don't want a fuss," Olivia said airily. "We really don't have time for that. We must discuss this now, or lose Andre forever. Time's wasting, you know, and we have to clear up these little details."

Margaret knew that if she didn't take up the reins right now, Olivia would turn into a runaway coach. "I think the first detail we need to clear up is the size of the wedding, Mrs. Prescott," she said carefully. Aware of Nowell's quick look, she went on, "You do remember that Nowell and I want a *small* affair."

"Of course I remember," Olivia said blithely. "You've told me so a dozen times. But whether you have ten guests or a hundred, or *five* hundred and ten, you still need a caterer, and Andre is the best."

"Yes, you're right, of course, Mother," Nowell said, before Margaret could reply. Ignoring her indignant look, he went on smoothly, "By all means, see if we can book this Andre fellow. Just make sure he understands that it isn't going to be a lavish affair."

"Yes, and that's another thing I want to talk to you about," Olivia said. "I've been thinking about it, and I really feel—"

Margaret knew what was coming, but she didn't have time to deal with it right now. "I'd love to discuss it, Mrs. Prescott, but I have so much work to do before I leave. Perhaps we can meet later—"

"Leave? You're not going on a business trip now, are you?" Olivia looked shocked, immediately turning to her son. "Darling, you have to reschedule things. We simply can't have Margaret off on some meeting or other when there's so much to do. You're the president of the company. Do something!"

"It's just a quick trip home, Mrs. Prescott," Margaret said.

Nowell tried to help out. "Yes, when she returns, we'll come over for dinner, and get everything straightened out."

"You're going home?" Olivia said, diverted. She turned to Margaret again. "Do you mean, to Kentucky?"

"Yes, to Lexington," Margaret said, mentally crossing her fingers and hoping that Olivia would just leave it at that.

But Olivia wasn't ready to abandon the subject. "Your father still lives there, isn't that right?"

Unwillingly, Margaret admitted that he did.

"Oh, dear. I do hope he isn't ill."

"No. It's just a...family matter. Nothing serious."

"I'm so glad," Olivia murmured, looking thoughtful. "You know, I've always wanted to visit a real Kentucky horse ranch."

"Farm. We call them farms, Mrs. Prescott."

"Farm, ranch, what's the difference," Olivia said, waving her hand. Before Margaret could answer there was quite a *big* difference, the older woman went on. "You *do* plan to invite us there soon, don't you, dear? As I've told you before, I'm so eager to meet your family." Smiling, she added, "And if you put us off much longer, Nowell and I are going to wonder if you have something to hide."

"What makes you think I have anything to hide?" Margaret exclaimed guiltily, before she realized that Olivia had been making a little joke. Embarrassed, she immediately apologized. "I'm sorry. I don't know what—"

"Well, it's no wonder," Olivia soothed. "A wedding is always a strain, even under the best of circumstances. Perhaps it would help if, instead of going to Kentucky, you invited your father up here."

"No, I don't think that will do," she said. "But I know how anxious you are to meet him—as he is to meet you," she added. "And I promise, as soon as I get this...other business cleared up, we can all get together for lunch, or something."

"That would be lovely, dear," Olivia said, but clearly her thoughts were now elsewhere. "I've been meaning to tell you this for quite a while now, Margaret, but I think, since you're going to be Nowell's wife, you don't need to call me Mrs. Prescott any longer."

Thinking that she wasn't sure she could ever bring herself to call this formidable woman "Mom," Margaret was trying to think of a response when Olivia went on graciously, "I think the time has come for you to call me 'Mother Prescott.'"

Margaret didn't know how to reply to that. "That's very nice of you...Mother Prescott," she said tactfully. "I'm...touched."

Olivia patted her on the arm. "Well, you *are* going to be my daughter-in-law, and I think it's only right. Now. About the wedding—"

Here they were again. Wondering if she was ever going to escape, Margaret looked again to Nowell for help. He rescued her once more. "Mother, we told you that Margaret has to be on her way," he reminded her.

"Yes, but the wedding is *important,*" Olivia insisted. She turned to Margaret. "Don't you agree?"

"Yes, I do," Margaret said, although right now, it was the last thing on her mind. She was anxious to get going, to meet this show girl her aunt had told her about. The more she thought about it, the less she liked the idea of her father's being influenced by a woman who, she was sure, had been around the barn more than once.

Then, too, Margaret thought, there was this business about Jack Stanton buying the land right over the hill from her father's farm. She didn't like that idea, either. But why? Irritably, she realized that she didn't understand Jack's motives any more than she could suddenly comprehend her own. Why should she care where he bought property, or what he intended to do with it? She hadn't seen him for years; until her aunt had mentioned him, she hadn't thought of him in all that time. What was he to her?

"I'm sorry, Mrs.—Mother Prescott," she said, realizing suddenly that Olivia was staring at her, waiting for her to continue. "This trip can't be avoided. But when I get back, I'll call you, and we'll...get together."

Before Olivia could protest, Margaret turned to Nowell. He disliked public displays of affection, so she gave him a brief smile. "I'll be back as soon as I can."

"Well, if you *must*," Olivia said, distressed. Nowell took Margaret's arm and went with her to the door. In a low voice, he said, "Don't worry, I'll handle Mother."

"Thanks," she said. "I owe you one."

"Just make sure you take her to lunch when you return," he replied. "And call me when you get to your father's farm."

Promising both, Margaret went back to her office, made arrangements for the time she'd be gone and then went home to pack. The next morning, she was on her way.

CHAPTER FOUR

DESPITE HERSELF, Margaret had to admit Bluegrass Country in early spring was one of the most beautiful sights she had ever seen. The Ohio River flowed serenely in the sunlight, and once out of Louisville, the greening, rolling hills seemed to go on and on. Aunt Tilda had offered to come and pick her up, but she preferred her own transportation, so she rented a car at the airport, and soon after landing, was on the highway home.

The closer she came to the farm, the more tense she felt. At first she had been tempted just to show up at the house, but then she reconsidered and called from the airport. To her relief, her father had answered the phone; to say the least, he was surprised that she was in town.

"But why didn't you tell me you were coming?" he asked. Then, quickly, "You're okay, aren't you, Maggie? Nothing's wrong?"

"Nothing that you can't fix, Dad," she answered, glad to hear his voice in spite of herself. She hadn't been sure of his reaction; she remembered all too well the last time they'd quarreled.

"What do you mean, nothing I can't fix?" he demanded. Then, "You've been talking to your Aunt Tilda, haven't you? I swear to blazes, that woman is going to drive me stark raving mad yet!"

"Aunt Tilda called me, yes, but only because she was concerned, Dad."

"Yes, well, she has no cause to be. Things here are just fine."

Margaret didn't want to get into it, not over the phone. But she couldn't help asking, "If that's so, why are you selling the farm?"

There was a brief silence. "So she told you that, too, did she? I suppose she also told you about Belle."

"Belle?"

"Oh, don't play the innocent with me, darlin' girl. If she told you about the farm, I know she told you about Belle. That's really why you're here, isn't it?"

"I think we should talk about it when I get there, Dad."

"Well, come ahead, Maggie. But I'm warning you, nothing you can say is going to change my mind."

"About the farm—or about . . . Belle?"

"About both," he said firmly. But then his voice softened. "I'm glad you came, Maggie—for whatever reason. I've missed you, girl."

"I've missed you too, Dad," she said, and hung up.

The drive from Louisville to the farm on the outskirts of Lexington took just over an hour. As she came close to the road that led to the house, Margaret looked around. The place hadn't changed; it was as if it had been frozen in time. She hadn't realized until now just how much she had missed these gentle, sloping hills with the fences marching off on either side in militarily straight lines. Of course, now more of the fences were painted charcoal-brown instead of the famed white they'd been in the past. But that was because white paint was so dear these days, and no more so than at Gallagher Farm, she thought, where things had always been tight.

As she came to the gates with the small brass nameplate hanging to one side, she turned in and drove past the big front paddocks. Even though she'd been gone a long time, she could still identify the yearlings and the two-year-olds, one group to each enclosure; farther on was the broodmare pasture. One horse stood out from the rest, a big, blood bay, who looked up at her as she passed. Even at this distance, the mare showed quality, and she stopped the car a moment to stare.

It was rare that a horse like this graced Gallagher Farm, and when she saw that the mare was heavy in foal, she wondered if her father had taken in a boarder. For some reason, she found herself hoping the horse belonged to Dan. Putting the car into gear, she drove quickly up to the house.

As always, the rambling farmhouse was in need of painting; she had barely driven into the big front yard before she saw bare spots in the siding and worn places in the front porch steps. A shingle or two was missing from the roof, and the sagging screen door stood open as it usually did, ready to admit visitors—or more likely, insects.

With a sigh, she stopped the car and got out with her suitcase. The barn was about fifty feet away, big, dim, the interior shadowed. At this time of day, the horses were out, and as she looked around, one of them nickered from the closest paddock. As though the sound had alerted him, her father's aging retriever, a good old dog named Skeet, came around the corner of the house and offered a token bark before he realized who it was.

"Hi, Skeet," she said, smiling as the dog came up to her and wriggled in greeting. His tail thumped against her legs, and she bent down to stroke his silky ears. "Where is everybody, huh?" she murmured. "Did they hear I was coming and all skedaddle, leaving you behind?"

Skeet butted against her again, as though to tell her he, at least, was glad she had come.

Smiling again and giving the dog one last pat, she went up to the porch steps and into the house, calling, "Anybody home?"

She could hear her father talking to someone on the phone in the office, just off the kitchen. Hearing her voice, he hurriedly ended the call and rushed out to greet her.

"Maggie!" he exclaimed, his face lighting up when he saw her standing there. He crossed the kitchen to give her a big bear hug that left her breathless. "Oh, it's good to see you!"

"It's good to see you, too, Dad," she said, smilingly trying to extricate herself. She looked at him more closely. "You look great."

He did; she had to admit it. Dan Gallagher might have the weathered skin of the outdoorsman, the rough hands and the lean physique of the perennial hard worker, but his hair was still more red than silver, and his blue eyes were bright and merry. He looked young, content . . . happy. Grabbing her hand, he gave it a squeeze, obviously delighted to see her.

"How long can you stay?" he asked.

"I don't know. It depends."

"Now, Maggie—"

But he didn't have a chance to finish, for just then they both heard quick steps on the back porch. Margaret turned toward the sound, but before she had time to prepare herself, a woman she judged to be in her mid-forties came rushing in, her face pink with excitement. Dressed in a cotton skirt and simple blouse that flattered her full figure, she had short brown hair, wide brown eyes and a beautiful smile. She wasn't wearing any makeup; her face was scrubbed as fresh as a young girl's. As soon as she saw Margaret, she came forward, her hand out.

"I was out in the barn when I heard the car and saw you come in," she said breathlessly. "Oh, of course you're Maggie! You look so much like your mother's picture. I'm so pleased to meet you. My name is Belle—Belle Wallace. I'm a friend of your father's."

Belle was so different from what Margaret had pictured that she was thrown completely off balance. Returning the handshake, she said a little blankly, "How do you do?"

"Let's not be so formal, Maggie!" Dan boomed, reaching out for Belle and putting an arm around her waist to draw her closer. Proudly, he looked at his daughter. "She's something, isn't she?" he asked, giving Belle a kiss on the cheek, making her blush. "I can't tell you how lucky I am to have found her."

"Now, Dan," Belle protested. "Let's not overwhelm her. After all, she just got here." She looked at Margaret with twinkling eyes. "You'll have to excuse him. Ever since you called from the airport, he's been so excited. I hope you can stay for a while. Dan's told me so much about you that I already feel as though we're acquainted. But I would like to get to know you, Maggie—or do you prefer Margaret?"

"Margaret is the name I usually use," she said faintly, although now she wondered why. When she'd left here, she thought it was more sophisticated to use her full name, but now it seemed a little pretentious. Thinking that this wasn't going at all as she expected, she forced a smile. "But you can call me Maggie, if you like."

"You'll always be Maggie to me," Dan said. Reaching out, he drew Margaret to his other side. With an arm around each of them, he beamed. "This is the life! My two favorite women in the whole world, right here in my own kitchen. What more could a man ask for?"

"Other than his dinner?" Belle teased.

Dan roared with laughter. Letting go of Margaret, he swung Belle around in an exuberant dance around the kitchen table. Beginning to feel like a fifth wheel, Margaret said, "I think I'll get my suitcase. I left it by the car."

"This one you mean?" said a new voice from the doorway.

Surprised, they all turned around. In all the excitement, no one had heard another car drive up, and when Margaret saw who was standing on the threshold, she felt her heart stumble.

It was Jack Stanton, and he was holding the suitcase she'd left outside. He was taller than she remembered him, broader, older, but even so, she would have recognized him anywhere. He was a year older than she was, she suddenly remembered, because his birthday was in January, and he'd started school late. But other than a new air of maturity about him, he looked almost the same as he had in high school.

With one difference, she thought distractedly. Back then, working as much as he had, studying hard, playing basketball on the school team and working with his father in the tobacco fields, he'd worn his hair short, almost in a butch—or was it called a buzz? She wasn't sure, and it didn't matter. Now his hair was longer, just as black, waving back from his strong face and curling slightly over his ears.

But it was his eyes that held her. More blue than gray, his glance met hers across the kitchen in the old farmhouse. He'd always had a twinkle, as though he found life endlessly delightful, but today there was something else in his gaze. As they looked at each other in the sudden quiet, Margaret felt something stir inside her. She didn't see her father look at her quickly; she didn't notice the sudden knowing expression in Belle's wise face.

Without warning, she was smelling the damp breeze off the river, and feeling the mist from the churning paddle wheel as it cooled her hot face the night of the senior dance. She even fancied she heard the soft tinkle of music from the band below-deck, as the *Ohio Queen* made its way back toward Louisville the night before graduation.

Shaking her head to clear it of memories she thought she had left behind, she made herself step forward, her hand out.

"Hello, Jack," she said, willing the shakiness out of her voice. "It's... been a long time."

He put the suitcase down. "Yes, it has," he agreed, taking her hand. His fingers felt strong, his palm slightly calloused, as though he was still no stranger to hard work. His deep voice striking another cord in her, he added, "It's good to see you home again."

Home? Maggie thought, confused. But home was New York, not this broken-down old farm that had seen better days. She was about to say something more when she suddenly realized that she couldn't remember what Nowell looked like. Her own fiancé! she thought in panic. Why couldn't she picture his face?

As though she'd been burned, she quickly withdrew her hand. Jack was still staring at her, and as she looked up at him in total confusion, the years seemed to fall away, and they were teenagers again. Her heart sinking, she suddenly knew that, for more reasons than one, it had been a mistake to come home.

"Coffee, anyone?" Belle said brightly.

The last thing Margaret wanted was to sit down with Jack and be forced into polite conversation, but it seemed she had little choice. Before she could say a word, Belle had settled everyone at the kitchen table, set out a plate of cookies, and was busy making a fresh pot of coffee. All too conscious of the fact that refreshments were only going to prolong this unexpected reunion, Margaret could have throttled the happy hostess.

"I hear you're an executive in New York," Jack said, sitting back easily in his chair and fixing those intense blue eyes on her face.

"Yes, I'm with Prescott Paper Products," Margaret answered stiffly, trying to throw Belle a look that indicated she wanted to cut this short, but only receiving a cheery smile in return.

"Maggie's a vice president," Dan put in helpfully, sounding proud as he added sugar to the coffee Belle was pouring for him.

As distracted as she was, Margaret didn't miss the affectionate arm he put around Belle's waist. She frowned slightly as she turned back to Jack.

"Only in charge of production," she said, and then immediately wondered why she'd added the qualifier.

It had been a silly thing to say, unnecessary and awkward. She'd worked hard; she had a right to be proud of what she'd done.

"Only?" Jack said, sounding amused and making her feel—if possible—even more inept. "It sounds like an important position to me."

"Oh, it is," Dan said. He was still being earnest, and Margaret glared at him. Blithely ignoring her, he went on. "Maggie's in charge of an entire division. They couldn't run the company without—"

"Dad, I don't think Jack is interested in all that," she interrupted. She didn't want to talk about herself, and she didn't want this meeting to go on longer than necessary. She didn't know if it was because she felt defensive or vulnerable... or both.

Summoning all her fast-disappearing poise, she gave Jack what she hoped was a sophisticated smile. "You're the one who's accomplished so much. Aunt Tilda tells me that you own your own company now and that you've bought the Tidleman place."

Jack seemed amused again, this time by her obvious changing of the subject. "Yes, I do," he said agreeably. His eyes crinkled at the corners as he smiled. "But how would your Aunt Tilda know about that? I can't imagine heavy equipment is one of her interests."

Margaret was so flustered that she laughed, shrilly. "Oh, you know Aunt Tilda. I love her dearly, but she is a bit of a busybody."

"I remember," he said, and laughed, too. But unlike the nervous cackle she had emitted, his laughter was such a rich sound that she felt something stir deep inside her even before his eyes met hers again. "How is your aunt? I haven't seen her in years."

Margaret had to look away; she was being mesmerized by that blue gaze. Her eyes dropped to his hand, tanned and strong and square, curled casually around his coffee mug. Against her will, she found herself imagining his hands caressing her, and she was appalled.

"Aunt Tilda's fine," she said, swallowing. She had to get control of herself or they would all think she was a fool. What was this breathless feeling, this sense of being off balance? It had to be her imagination that was making her feel the heat of his body. Maybe the kitchen was warm. Yes, it must be that, she decided, clutching at straws. It *was* hot for this time of year.

Jack hadn't taken his eyes off her face. "I remember that Tilda used to be your housekeeper," he said. "Do you think she might still be interested in that line of work? Or know someone who is? I'm going to need someone at Fieldstone Farm."

"Fieldstone Farm?" Margaret echoed. Making an effort, she snapped out of her trance and reached for her coffee. She was so unnerved by him that she nearly dropped the cup. "Is that what you've renamed the Tidleman place?"

Lifting his own cup with a hand that was as steady as a rock, Jack took a sip of coffee, gazing at her over the rim. "Yes, it is. Why? You sound as if you don't approve."

Absurdly, she had to steel herself to meet his gaze. "Of the farm or the name?" she asked, and with a supreme effort, gave an indifferent shrug. "Either way, it's none of my business."

"I see," Jack said. He looked over at Dan, who for once in his life was listening avidly instead of spouting off himself. His eyes returning to her face, he said calmly, "Is it your business if your father sells Gallagher Farm to me?"

Margaret wasn't sure she'd heard right. When she looked at her father, he suddenly seemed very interested in the dregs of his coffee. But his expression told her everything she wanted to know, and without realizing what she was doing, she turned fiercely back to Jack. "Why are you interested in Dad's farm when you've just bought a hundred acres of your own?"

If he was surprised at her tone, he didn't show it. "It never hurts to expand, and if the place is for sale, someone has to buy it. Since it's right next door, it might as well be me, don't you think?"

She didn't know what to think. Sensing trouble brewing, Belle picked up a plate. "Cookies, anyone?" she said brightly.

Jack hesitated, but seeing Margaret's stormy expression, he shook his head and stood. "No, thanks, not for me. I really should be going. I didn't mean to interrupt a family reunion, but it was nice to see you again, Maggie."

"And you," she said stiffly. She wouldn't look up at him.

"Er. . . Jack, you don't have to go," Dan said, with a quick glance in his daughter's direction. "Did you want to talk to me about something?"

"It can wait," Jack said easily. Smiling at Belle, he added, "Thanks for the coffee."

"Any time," Belle said with an answering smile.

Watching them all, Margaret wondered why they were all *smiling*. Was she the only one feeling the tension here?

Wishing Jack would just go, she sat still while Dan went outside with him. Belle was just about to say something when the phone rang. She was closest, so she answered, and after a moment said, "Yes, she's here. Would you like to talk to her?" Holding the phone out to Margaret, she said, "It's Tilda. She'd like to speak to you."

Thinking blackly that she'd like to speak to her aunt, too, Margaret excused herself and took the call in Dan's office. She hardly noticed all the familiar clutter of stud books and registration forms and pedigree charts and sales catalogs that were strewn all over the desk. Sweeping everything aside, she sat down in the cracked old leather chair her father had had for years, only to spring up again because she was too agitated to sit still.

"Why didn't you tell me that Jack Stanton was the one who made an offer for Dad's farm?" she demanded as soon as she picked up the receiver.

"Didn't I?" Tilda tittered. "Oh, I'm sure I must have!"

"Well, you didn't."

"Oh, really, Maggie, what does it matter? Besides, the point isn't *who* might buy the farm, but *why* your father is selling it!" Tilda's voice dropped into a conspiratorial tone, as though someone might be listening. "You've met her, Maggie. What do you think?"

Margaret wasn't thinking of Belle, who she had liked immediately despite her aunt's warnings, she was thinking of Jack and the effect he'd had on her. She hadn't felt so unsure of herself in years. For those awful first few minutes until she got herself under some semblance of control, she had actually stammered!

"I don't know what to think," she said crossly. "I've just met the woman. I'm more interested in the fact that Jack has apparently made an offer for the farm. And you knew it, Aunt Tilda! Why didn't you tell me?"

Tilda seemed taken aback by the unexpected attack. "Why, I—I don't know, Maggie," she stuttered, sounding tearful. "I didn't think it would matter. Does it, so awfully much?"

"I don't know. I'll have to think about it."

"But in the meantime, what about Belle?"

"What about her? Honestly, Aunt Tilda—"

"Oh, I *knew* she'd get you on her side!"

"I'm not on anyone's *side!* For heaven's sake, I just got here!"

"But you'll stay until we get this all sorted out, won't you? Oh, please say you will, Maggie! I'm counting on you."

Margaret couldn't imagine what for, but in any case, it was Jack she was more concerned about. Why had he made an offer for Gallagher Farm, and why did it bother her so much? If the farm was for sale, did it matter if Jack was the one who wanted to buy it? Maybe the point she should really be addressing was why, after all these years, she still felt attracted to him.

I'm not attracted, she told herself fiercely. *For heaven's sake, I'm going to marry Nowell! How can I possibly even think of looking at another man?*

She was making too much of it. Seeing Jack so unexpectedly had simply thrown her off-balance for a while. That was all there was to it.

But she couldn't stop thinking of him that night when she finally excused herself and went up to bed. And all through a sleepless night—when she should have been sorting out her thoughts about her father's involvement with Belle and why it bothered her *now* that he was going to sell the farm—all she could think about, as she pounded the pillow, was Jack. She didn't know him anymore; she didn't *want* to know him, so what was the problem?

The problem was that the past seventeen years or so had been good to him, she thought. Well, more than good, she had to admit. In addition to the fact that he was obviously successful, he still had the body of an athlete and the good looks to go with it. And he still had that damned twinkle in his eye, as though he found life endlessly fascinating and exciting.

What she couldn't understand was why she hadn't remembered how deep his voice was, how full-bodied and rich. Or his laugh, she thought. It was too infectious. Had he been that way in high school? She couldn't be sure. In fact, she thought grouchily, she couldn't be sure of anything about Jack Stanton, except that she wished they hadn't met again, not after all this time.

"Blast it all, anyway," she muttered, somewhere around six o'clock the next morning. Forced to admit she was wide awake, she sat up against the headboard of the bed with an exasperated sigh. There was no way she was going to sleep now. The internal alarm clock that had been set in her youth when she'd had to get up so early for the horses had never been readjusted. Even now, no matter what time she went to bed, she was usually up by six or six-thirty, at the latest. It was great when she had a lot of work to do or a hard day ahead of her, but not when she hadn't slept the night before.

Trying to distract herself, she glanced around. She'd taken her old room as a matter of course when she had excused herself the night before, and it was almost the same as when she'd left it, years earlier. She had never been a frilly type of person—even as a girl she had disdained ruffles and bows. A good thing, she used to think, since she never had time in those days to fiddle in front of the mirror. But she had liked the pictures—her father had never taken down the framed prints of famous racehorses she'd put up.

Her favorite was a portrait of the brilliant black filly Ruffian, who had been put to sleep after breaking her leg during the famed match race with her rival, a colt called Foolish Pleasure. Said by many to be the best distaff runner of her time, possibly even of her decade, Ruffian's death had hit the entire racing community with the force of a blow. Margaret remembered mourning the loss of that great racehorse with everyone else. Even now, she felt sad thinking about it, and she switched her glance away from the picture.

Her ancient teddy bear was sitting on the chair by the bed, and when she saw it, her expression softened. She knew her father had left her old friend sitting on the pillow to welcome her, and when she'd first seen it last night, she was touched. Picking up the threadbare stuffed animal, she had held it tightly for a moment before setting it carefully down again. Why was it, she wondered, that the simplest things could stir such poignant memories—like a ragged stuffed toy...or the sight of moonlight on water?

Frowning at the thought this morning, she threw back the covers and went to the window. The early-morning sun gilded the roof of the barn and touched the pastures beyond with gold leaf, making everything seem bright and new. As a child, she had loved this view. From the window she could see most of the farm, and she used to stare out for hours. Once, she couldn't wait to spring out of bed and run out in the morning to visit with the horses, and just for a moment, as she stood here now, she felt the same sense of excitement and anticipation she'd had as a child.

Displeased by the feeling, she moved away from the window. As she straightened the rumpled sheets and drew up the blankets, she told herself it was absurd for her to feel so nostalgic. She didn't even want to be here, and horses hadn't been a part of her life for longer than she could remember. In fact, she hadn't even made time to go visit the barn yesterday after she had arrived.

But then, she really hadn't had time, had she? Before she had been able to think of any excuse to get away, even one that was rude, Belle had invited Jack to stay for coffee.

Remembering the scene around the kitchen table, her mouth tightened as she pulled the bedspread over the pillow and gave it a last tuck. She was glad that they had never returned to the subject of Dan's selling the farm last night. She wanted to discuss it privately with her father, but as she hesitated about what to wear, her hand hovering over a pair of slacks before finally reaching for an old pair of jeans she'd thrown into her suitcase at the last minute, she felt tense again. She and Dan were always at odds over things, and she suspected that they were going to quarrel again over this.

Nothing was right, she thought as she jerked a brush through her hair. Everything seemed topsy-turvy, herself most of all. Belle didn't seem to be the hardened floozy she had imagined, out to take Dan for all he was worth. And, she asked herself again, why she,

Margaret, felt so resistant to her father's selling the farm? She'd been after him for years to get rid of it; now that he seemed ready to do so, she was suddenly doing an about-face. Two days ago, everything had been so clear.

Yes, but two days ago, you'd forgotten that Jack Stanton ever existed.

Squirming at the thought, she threw down the hairbrush, put on some lipstick and went downstairs. She didn't want to think about Jack; she wanted to confront her father so she could leave Kentucky and get back to New York, where she belonged.

But Dan wasn't in the kitchen when she came in. Belle was there alone, sitting comfortably at the table, drinking a cup of coffee and reading the paper.

"Good morning," Belle said, smiling. "Did you sleep well?"

"Oh, yes, fine," Margaret lied. Although she knew Belle was living here now, she hadn't expected to see her. Feeling awkward, Margaret looked around. "Is Dad here?"

Belle put the paper aside. "No, he went into town to get some hay and run a few errands. I'm glad in a way. It'll give us a chance to talk—just us women."

Margaret wasn't in the mood for girl talk. Feeling wary, she went to the stove to pour some coffee. "Talk about what?"

"Oh, about me...and your Dad," Belle said. "But first, can I fix you some breakfast? If you don't mind my saying so, you're a little on the slender side." She grinned. "But then, I could just be jealous. I used to have a pretty good figure, if I do say so myself, but once I left Vegas and all that dancing, I just couldn't keep my weight down." Her eyes sparkled. "Thank goodness Dan likes me this way, or I don't know what I'd do.'' She saw the look Margaret couldn't hide and smiled again. "I see you know about my sordid show girl past."

Margaret despised herself, but she couldn't meet Belle's eyes. "My aunt mentioned it, yes," she said. "But as you said, it's in the past. I'll understand if you prefer not to talk about it."

Belle laughed outright. "Not talk about it! It was one of the most exciting times of my life! Not that it was *all* good, mind you, but I had some times, all right. In fact—" Suddenly, she stopped and looked at Margaret. "You really *do* think it's a bit squalid, don't you?"

"No, of course not," Margaret lied again. She could feel herself getting red and reached for more coffee. Trying to muster some composure, she said, "It's just beyond my experience, I guess."

"Well, it was beyond mine, until I did it, I'll tell you," Belle said. She shook her head. "But when you're sixteen and look twenty-five, and you can't go home because your dad won't let you alone, well, honey, you do what you have to. And I never went topless, I'll tell you that." She laughed again. "Not that I wasn't asked! You won't believe it now, but I was quite a looker in those days. I could have done a lot of things I didn't."

As Margaret came to the table and sat down, she realized she hadn't even questioned the reason Belle had become a show girl; in fact, she thought, it hadn't even occurred to her to wonder. She and her father hadn't always gotten along, and there were still some things she resented, but she couldn't imagine him ever...well, she just couldn't imagine it.

"I'm sorry," she said. "I didn't realize—"

Belle patted her hand, comfortable with herself even if other people weren't. "Heck, honey, not many people do. It's not something that's dinner table conversation, after all." Her warm brown eyes met Margaret's hazel, and her voice softened. "Your dad knows, bless him. He knows it all, and it doesn't matter to him. Does it to you?"

Margaret hesitated. But Belle had been honest with her; she had to be truthful, too. "Not in the way you mean. Your past is none of my business. All I really want is for my father to be happy."

"And you don't think he'll be happy with me?"

"I don't know. I don't know you well enough to say. It's not up to me, anyway. Dad's an adult. He has to decide."

"But you're family, too, Maggie. And even though I love your dad, and he loves me, we both want your blessing." Belle paused. "Is it the age difference, or the difference in our backgrounds?"

Again, Margaret hesitated. But she'd come this far; she might as well go all the way. "Both," she said unwillingly. "Oh, not your...er...former profession. It's not that. I can see that you...well, you're not what I expected at all, I admit it. It's just that, except for his time in the service, Dad has lived here all his life. Horses are the only thing he knows."

"Don't kid yourself, honey," Belle said dryly. "Dan might know everything about horses, but horses aren't everything he knows."

Margaret reddened. "I didn't mean that. What I meant was..." She hesitated, but then it all came out in a rush. "I just can't see his selling the farm and moving to Florida. And this houseboat business, that's the most surprising of all. It's just not like my father. I'm sorry, Belle, I can't help but think you're influencing him. There. I've said it. I'm sorry, but that's the way I feel."

She thought that the other woman would be angry, defensive, hostile. What she hadn't expected was that Belle would laugh—a great, big belly laugh, the kind that makes a person throw her head back and roar with mirth. Feeling somewhat bewildered, Margaret stared at her while Belle tried to get herself under control.

"Oh, I'm sorry, I am!" Belle finally gasped. "I'm sorry, but that's so..." She was nearly off again but managed to stop herself in time. Merrily, she looked at Margaret. "You thought the houseboat was *my* idea?"

Her face stiff with embarrassment, Margaret said, "Of course I did. As I said—"

"Aw, honey, don't be angry with me. It's just..." Wiping her eyes, Belle composed herself. "I didn't mean to laugh, but it *is* funny. Moving to Florida and living on a houseboat wasn't *my* idea, it was your Dad's. If I had my druthers, I wouldn't get near the water. I'd never leave dry land. Why, I can't even swim. Every time I try, I sink like a stone!"

Margaret didn't know what to make of this new information. "But...but Dad's never been near the water—not the ocean, I mean. Except..." Her voice trailed away as she thought of something she'd forgotten. "Except for the time he was in the service," she said faintly. "He was stationed in Corpus Christi, Texas." A thought occurred to her, and she looked quickly at Belle. "Don't tell me he's harbored a secret love of the sea since then!"

Belle's eyes sparkled. "Yes, indeed. Hard to believe, isn't it?"

For Margaret, it was impossible. Her face blank, she sat back against the chair. Until this moment, she thought she knew her father, but after this revelation, she wondered if she knew him at all. "But why didn't he ever say anything?" she asked, almost plaintively.

"I don't know, honey. You'll have to ask him."

Margaret's mouth tightened. She felt excluded. "I will."

Belle reached out and touched her arm. "Maybe this isn't the right time to say it, but then, I always did believe in taking the bull by the horns, so I'll just come right out with it. I love your Dad, Maggie, and he loves me. I plan to spend the rest of my life with him."

Margaret couldn't help her sarcasm. "On a houseboat, instead of dry land, where you said yourself you'd rather be?"

"If need be. I'll go wherever he goes, a houseboat, an igloo, a tepee. I want to be with him, that's all that matters."

Before Margaret could reply, the telephone rang. Because she was closest to it, she picked it up. The greeting left Margaret's lips as though it had been just yesterday she had answered this phone.

"Gallagher Farm."

"Maggie?"

It was Aunt Tilda. Reminded that she was still upset with her aunt, Margaret said, "Yes, it's Maggie—Margaret. How are you today?"

Tilda's voice dropped to a whisper. "She's there, isn't she?" she breathed.

Margaret glanced across the table at Belle, who was gathering the newspaper together and picking up her coffee cup. "Yes, she's—"

"Shh! Don't say anything to make her suspicious!" Tilda exclaimed. "For heaven's sake, Maggie, I don't want her to know we're talking about her!"

Obviously realizing the call wasn't for her, Belle carried everything over to the sink, waggled her fingers in Margaret's direction and went outside.

"It's all right, Aunt Tilda—" Margaret started to say.

"Just answer yes or no, okay?"

Rolling her eyes and thinking that her aunt was definitely watching too much TV, she said, "It's not really necessary."

"Why not?" Tilda demanded.

Smiling, she said, "Because she just went outside, that's why." Then she couldn't help it; teasingly, she dropped her voice. "So it's okay if we just speak right up."

"Why are you laughing? This is *serious!*"

Her smile vanished. "I know it's serious, Aunt Tilda. But I really don't think Belle is going to spy on us. From what I've seen so far, she's a lovely woman."

"How can you say that?" Tilda demanded indignantly. "She's put all sorts of crazy ideas into your dad's head!"

"According to Belle, Dad's done just fine thinking up these crazy things all on his own."

Tilda was outraged. "You mean she's blaming him?"

"She's not blaming anyone. But we were just talking about this houseboat business, and she said it was all Dad's idea."

"And you believed her?"

Margaret thought about it. "Yes, I did."

"And you think he's the one who wants to sell the farm?"

"He can't do both, Aunt Tilda—keep the farm and move to Florida, too."

"Aha! You see?"

"See what? Don't you think you're overreacting?"

"No, I do not. And furthermore, I can see that I'd better come over there right away. If this...woman has charmed you with her wiles the way she has your father, you both obviously need my help!"

After Margaret's mother died, Tilda had come to live at the farm to take care of them, but for years now, she'd had her own little apartment in town. Picturing the tiny place, crowded with the figurines Tilda painted, every available surface covered with hand-crocheted antimacassars and doilies and little statuary, Margaret said, "Well, you're certainly welcome to come. But I should tell you, Dad's not here right now."

"Oh, if I know him, he's just gone down to the tack store to talk about horses. He'll be back before long, and in the meantime, you and I can get a few things straightened out. I'll be there just as soon as I put Chester out—" Chester was her cat "—and stop at the store for more bird seed." Tilda also had a canary named Jenny. Sniffing, she added, "And you can tell that woman not to bother to bake, not that she knows how, I'm sure. I'm bringing a pie I made, and a tin of cookies—oh, and some cinnamon rolls, just in case."

"In case of what?" Margaret asked, trying not to laugh. "Do you think we're in danger of starving here?"

"You can joke all you like, but you never did eat right, and heaven knows what that woman is feeding your poor father," Tilda said ominously. "Well, don't worry, I'll come and we'll have a nice long talk."

Touched and exasperated at the same time, Margaret said goodbye. She'd barely hung up the phone before it rang again. Once more, she said, "Good morning, Gallagher Farm."

"Margaret?"

Margaret's hand flew to her forehead. Nowell! How could she have forgotten to call him? Oh, good Lord, she thought, horrified. What was he going to think?

"Hello, Nowell," she said.

"'Hello, Nowell'? That's all you can say? Margaret, where in the world have you been? Don't you realize I've been worried sick? I thought you were going to call me as soon as you arrived. Is something wrong? Is your father ill?"

"No, no, he's not ill," Margaret said, her hand still to her head. She couldn't believe she had completely forgotten to call him! "Everything's fine. It's just... well, things have been a little hectic."

"Hectic? Something *is* wrong."

"No, no, it's not," she reassured him. "And I meant to call, really I did. But with one thing and another, well, it's been difficult."

"Difficult? Margaret, it's not like you to be obscure. Just what is going on down there?"

Wishing she knew, she said, "I don't mean to sound cryptic, Nowell. But I... I think I'm going to need a few more days to get everything straightened out."

"A few more days!" He couldn't have sounded more appalled had she said *she* intended to go live on a houseboat. "But, Margaret, I need you here!"

She misunderstood. "I'm sure the office can get along without me for a day or two."

"It's not the office I'm worried about!" he exclaimed, then immediately added, "Although, I really don't like the idea of your being gone so long at this particular time. We are trying to sign Disrud Industries, you remember, and I do need you here for the meetings. Oh, never mind, that's not the real problem at the moment."

She sat up. "What do you mean, not the *real* problem?"

There was the tiniest of pauses, then he said reluctantly, "I might as well tell you. I was going to wait until you got back, but if you aren't coming right away, you probably should know. It's... Mother."

Her fingers tightened involuntarily on the phone. "What do you mean? Has something happened?"

"She's not ill, nothing like that," he assured her hastily. Margaret was about to sigh in relief when he added, "It's the guest list."

She closed her eyes, feeling disaster rushing at her. She and her future mother-in-law had already gone a few rounds over the guest list. Olivia wanted to invite everyone the Prescotts had ever known or spoken to; Margaret wanted to include twenty-five people at the most. She thought they had compromised; she had believed the worst was over. Now something in Nowell's voice warned her, and it was all she could do to ask calmly, "Are you trying to tell me that your mother has added to the guest list?"

There was an ominous silence. Then, he said, "It won't be so bad, Margaret...."

Realizing her fingers were cramping from the death grip she had on the phone, she made herself relax. He was right, she tried to tell herself. It couldn't be that bad. After all, she'd only left—was it just yesterday? How many more people could Olivia think to invite in such a short time? Already, one hundred names were on the list, and even though she'd thought that was about seventy-five too many, she had agreed on that number to please Nowell. Thinking she should have stuck to her guns, as her father would have said, she asked, "What does that mean exactly, Nowell?"

"It means that she's added a few people—"

"A few?" Relieved, she continued. "Well, that's all right. How many is a few?"

"Only about a hundred."

She bolted upright. "A hundred!"

Obviously deciding just to get it over with, he added, "And fifty."

Margaret shot to her feet. "A hundred and fifty! Your mother added a hundred and fifty people to the guest list? My God, Nowell, that makes two hundred and fifty people!"

"I can count, Margaret."

She barely heard the sarcasm. Immediately, she declared, "You're just going to have to tell her it's impossible! We agreed—"

"I can't tell her that," he interrupted.

She thought she hadn't heard right. "What? Why not?"

"Because these are her friends, her close friends."

"No one in the *world* has that many close friends!" she cried.

"Margaret, there's no need to shout."

"I'm not shouting! I'm just—" she made herself calm down "—I'm not shouting," she repeated, her lips stiff. "But you have to admit, I have a right to be a little...upset. We agreed—"

"I know what we agreed, Margaret, but as I said, I just couldn't tell her she can't have her friends at our wedding. I *am* her only son, after all...her only child." His voice took on an injured tone, as though it were her fault. "And I really can't help but think that if you had been here, we could have worked out a compromise."

Direly, Margaret doubted it. "Fine," she said between clenched teeth. He knew how she felt about a big wedding, and she wanted to throttle him. Why hadn't he stood up to his mother? Was this the way it was going to be after they were married? Thrusting away the horrible fear that it might be, she said tersely, "We'll discuss it when I get back."

Her tone had obviously offended him. Coolly, he asked, "And when do you think that might be?"

"I told you, I'm not sure. A day or so more, at the most." She couldn't help adding, "Surely, you can avoid discussing our wedding plans with anyone else until then, can't you?"

Nowell hated conflict. "You're angry, aren't you, Margaret?"

Damned right, I'm angry! she thought. But then she realized it really wasn't his fault. Her jaw tight, she said, "No, I'm not angry. I suppose I'm just disappointed. I really thought we could keep our wedding simple."

"And it will be," he assured her. "You'll be home soon, and we'll be able to present a united front."

"Do you think it will do any good?"

There wasn't a smile in his voice as she'd hoped. "We can try, anyway."

Gloomily, she hung up the phone. Two days ago, her life had been calm, ordered, serene. The future had beckoned politely; she'd known where it led, and she'd wanted to go there. Now, in the space of forty-eight hours, everything seemed to have turned upside down. Her father, who had never professed a love for the water, wanted to sell the farm and buy a house-boat; the woman he wanted to share it with wasn't a floozy as Margaret had been led to believe, but a warm, caring person who loved him so much she was willing to follow him anywhere.

Margaret, on the other hand, didn't feel quite so warm about the man she planned to marry, and the wedding she wanted to be a small, intimate, private affair had suddenly blossomed into a gala crowd of her mother-in-law's closest friends. Worse, while her fiancé waited back home for her to remember his existence, she couldn't stop thinking of a man she hadn't thought of in years.

"What next?" she muttered wearily. Then, before the phone could ring again with news of another crisis, she got up to wash the breakfast dishes.

CHAPTER FIVE

WHEN DAN WASN'T HOME by eleven, Margaret went out to the barn to wait. She'd been inside trying to do some of the work she'd brought with her, but she felt too restless and unsettled to concentrate. Finally, she gave up and went outside. Even though horses were a part of her life she had put behind her, she assured herself it wouldn't hurt just to have a look at the latest stock.

The interior of the barn was cool when she entered, the first ten of the twenty stalls along the aisleway empty now that their occupants were out on pasture for the day. But one stall held the beautiful mare she had seen yesterday while driving in, and she stopped to take a better look.

Dan had always said she had an unerring instinct where horses were concerned, and if it was still true, she knew she was viewing the best animal on the place. It was also obvious that the mare was due soon, if Margaret knew her horses. But as swollen and misshapen as she was, this mare was one of the loveliest creatures Margaret had ever seen.

A dark blood bay, the color of cherries, the horse was big, over sixteen hands, Margaret thought, with wide-spaced, large eyes, pricked ears, and a coat that shone from good care and good health. From the slight sway to her back and the way she carried the unborn foal, this wasn't the mare's first pregnancy.

"How did Dad get hold of someone like you, eh?" she murmured, reaching in through the stall bars and scratching the mare behind the ears. "Are you a visitor, or do you belong to Gallagher Farm?"

The horse nuzzled her hand a moment, not by way of introduction, Margaret knew, but because she was searching for a treat. Disappointed when she didn't get anything, the mare moved away and Margaret murmured, smiling, "What a spoiled, pampered creature you are!"

She was about to leave when a noise from a stall farther down made her turn and head in that direction. She laughed aloud as she saw the cause of the sound. An obviously unhappy equine was running his teeth across the grill in front of his stall, just like a convict might move a tin cup along the bars of his cell for attention. When the horse saw her coming down the aisleway, he stopped for a moment to peer through the grill to make sure he'd been noticed. He looked so silly that she had to laugh again. She'd been away a long time, but not so long that she didn't recognize her father's old "pony" horse, a demanding, obnoxious brute called Freebie.

Freebie wasn't his registered name, of course; it was the name Dan had given him when he'd found the horse in one of his stalls at the track one cold morning. The big colt's former owner had abandoned him in disgust because it seemed that while Freebie loved to run, once he was out in front he ignored the urgings of his jockey and allowed all the other horses in the field to catch up to him so they could all amble up to the finish line together, in a friendly pack. This behavior was frowned upon by anxious owners who preferred their horses to win, so Freebie had been left behind.

Everyone at the track knew about Freebie, so it was impossible for Dan to give him away. Stuck with the unwelcome responsibility, Margaret's father had decided that if the horse didn't want to run, he could earn his keep another way. Six months later, gelded and retrained, Freebie had become a "pony" horse, the horse the trainer or his assistant rides when he's leading a running horse out onto the track for a race.

To Dan's surprise and subsequent delight, Freebie turned out to be good at his new job. Because he was big and just as stubborn as his high-spirited former colleagues, he just forged ahead, pulling even the most ill-tempered racehorse along in his wake. It wasn't long before Dan was refusing offers for him. A good pony horse was worth its weight in gold; with a mount like Freebie, calm, strong, able to keep his mind on business, an outrider only had to worry about the runner he was leading, not the horse under him.

Margaret was still laughing when Freebie bared his teeth and ran them over the bars again. Clearly, he was upset at not being let out, and she was just taking his halter from the hook outside his stall, intending to do just that, when she had another idea.

"Are you up to a ride today, Freeb?" she murmured. She hadn't ridden in years, and she would probably be sorry when she tried to walk tomorrow, but suddenly she longed for a quick gallop.

In the past, whenever something was bothering her, she'd go for a ride to clear her mind, and as she found some tack and saddled Freebie, she hoped the same tactic would work today. Wondering if she still remembered how to ride, she led him out into the sunshine. He jigged a bit when she first climbed aboard, and hopped around when she picked up the reins, but she remembered his antics from long ago and actually laughed when he tried to buck. Even at twenty years old, he was still full of himself, but she was confident she could handle him.

It felt good to be on a horse again, and as she turned him toward the track that led through the back pasture and up the hill, she shook her hair back and lifted her face to the sun with pleasure. Now that Freebie had tried his bag of tricks, he settled down into the good horse she knew him to be, and they began cantering easily along. With his long legs, he soon reached the top of the hill and Margaret could see the construction going on at the old Tidleman place. Pulling back on the reins, she stopped to watch.

Jack had mentioned that he was rebuilding the farm next to Dan's, but he'd been so low-key about it that, looking at it now, she could hardly believe her eyes.

The fact that money was being spent in a big way was evident. There was no sign of the old house. In its place rose a giant structure of wood, limestone and glass. Two tall windows met in front like the prow of a ship. It had to have six bedrooms at least, she thought, and felt a jolt. Jack hadn't said anything about a wife, or the prospect of one, but she knew a man didn't build a house this size without having the future in mind. Telling herself it was none of her business, she jerked her eyes away from the house to the barn.

Or rather, *barns,* she amended, counting two, one looking almost finished, the other still under construction. Each looked as big as, if not bigger than, the one at Gallagher Farm, and her eyes narrowed as her glance went beyond the structures to the new fences going up behind them. Jack hadn't been kidding when he'd said that he intended to get into horses; obviously, he was going to do it in a big way.

With a frown, she turned and looked back at her own home. From this vantage point, she could take in the entire farm, and to her eyes, it looked even more shabby and forlorn than it ever had before. The fences needed to be painted again, and there were those shingles missing on the roof. Two of the pastures obviously needed reseeding, and from what she had seen of Dan's tack this morning, practically everything should be replaced.

Now that she was seeing it in such stark contrast to the newness going on over the hill, she knew that it was time for her father to sell. Refurbishing the place would take more money than Dan had—more than he'd accept from her, even if she could save it herself. It was clear from the condition of things that it was getting too much for one man, even for Dan, with his boundless energy, and since she didn't want it, there was no one else.

Uneasily, she turned back in the saddle and looked down at Jack's new place again. An old hurt flared as she studied the farm below. This was the place, not the one behind her, she had always dreamed about, she thought. When she was a girl, she had fantasized that one day Gallagher Farm would take its place beside its more elegant cousins—Greentree, Claiborne...oh, even the names had sounded glamorous!

Even now, she could recall dreaming about white, well-kept fences and a house that was a showplace where all visitors would be welcome. The freshly painted barns would be home to stakes winners and broodmares who had retired with blazing track records as long as her arm. Expensive foals and yearlings and two-year-olds would dash about in the lush pastures, sold almost before they were born.

Then she became angry with herself. Her dreams had been those of a child. Reality was spread out in front of her, first-class on Jack's side, Dan's second-best on the other.

I hope Jack does buy it, she thought defiantly. Then he could raze the entire place and start over again, as someone should have done long ago!

But that wasn't what she wanted, either, and as she sat there with the restless horse pawing under her, she felt frustrated and irritated. She couldn't understand what was wrong with her. What had happened to the take-charge Margaret Gallagher she'd been only yesterday?

Freebie started pulling against the bit, anxious to move on, and because she didn't want to sit here any longer, either, she gathered her reins. Just then Jack came out of the house trailer below her. Before she could turn her horse around and disappear, he looked up and saw her.

"Maggie!" he shouted. "Hey, Maggie, come on down and visit!"

She didn't want to visit. She didn't want to see Jack up close. Even from this distance, the sight of him made her pulse race a little faster, and after her inexplicable reaction to him yesterday, she didn't know what would happen if they were in close proximity.

"Oh, for heaven's sake!" she muttered angrily. She was being absurd. Why shouldn't she ride down and see Jack? As awkward as the situation was, he was still a neighbor, and couldn't be avoided. Shouldn't be avoided, she told herself contemptuously. She was no schoolgirl with a first crush; she was a grown woman, a professional engaged woman, an executive vice president of a successful company. She could handle her feelings for Jack Stanton. She could handle anything. Lifting her chin, she put her heel into Freebie's side and cantered him down the hill to where Jack was standing.

"Good morning," she said, after she'd pulled Freebie to a stop.

"Hi," Jack replied, squinting up at her. "I was surprised to see you up there."

"I was out for a ride."

He grinned at the obvious. "Curious, eh?"

She tensed. Was he making fun of her? "Not in the slightest," she said haughtily. "I've seen the old Tidleman place before."

"But not like this."

She couldn't very well deny it. "No... that's true."

"What do you think?"

She felt like being difficult. "I don't know. What should I think?"

Placing his hand on Freebie's neck, he looked up at her. "Why are you being this way, Maggie?"

Her entire face felt like a mask hiding her feelings. Why was she so attracted to him? Why did she feel this... this *pull* toward him, as though it was time to finish something they'd started long ago? Annoyed by the thought, she looked away, trying to get herself under control.

"I'm not being any way," she said. "You asked a question, and I answered it, that's all."

He was silent a moment. She could feel the heat of his gaze on her even though she wasn't looking at him. At last, he said, "Has New York changed you so much, or is it just that you dislike me?"

Involuntarily, her glance went back to his handsome face. "I don't dislike you, Jack. What a silly thing to say!"

"Not so silly. The way you're acting—"

"I'm not acting any way! Will you stop saying that?"

He looked at her a moment longer, then he smiled suddenly, shaking his head. "There's one thing that hasn't changed about you, I see."

"And what's that?"

"Your temper. You always were a firecracker."

Embarrassed at the reminder of those days and the realization that she wasn't acting any more mature now, she said, "I'm sorry. I didn't mean to sound abrupt. I guess I've just got a lot on my mind."

"I understand. Say, are you in a rush, or can you stop in for a cup of coffee?"

It was one thing to carry on a conversation—stilted as it was—from her safe position on the horse; quite another to go inside where she'd be face-to-face. "Oh...I'm sorry, but I don't have time," she said. "I'm waiting for Dad to get home from the feed store."

"Knowing your father, he'll be there until noon. Please, Maggie, I wanted to talk to you alone."

She didn't want to be alone with him. Warily, she asked, "About what?"

"About your dad. Come on, Maggie. I won't bite. We can put your horse in a stall if you like. One of the barns is finished now."

She couldn't think of another excuse. Besides, what harm would it do just to talk? Freebie was used to standing for hours with the reins hanging over the most convenient snubbing post. Sometimes at the track it had been a hitching rail, at others, a mirror on the side of the closest truck. She was about to say that he didn't have to be put into a stall, but as she hesitated, she just knew this would be the day the horse would prove her wrong. She could imagine him running for home the instant he was left alone.

"All right," she agreed reluctantly, kicking out of her stirrup irons and dropping lightly to the ground. "Where do you want him?"

"Anywhere, it doesn't matter. I wanted you to see the barn, anyway."

She didn't want to see the barn; in fact, now that she and Jack were standing side by side, she was beginning to wish she'd just ridden away. He was wearing jeans and a plain white T-shirt, but even casually dressed he was still far more attractive than any man had a right to be. His wavy black hair glinted in the sun, and she caught a whiff of his after-shave—a scent of spicy lime that made her want to breathe more deeply.

Trying to distract herself, she looked around. It was certainly impressive. "You told me you were remodeling, but I had no idea how much. I have to say I didn't even recognize the place."

Together, they started walking toward the nearest barn. "It has changed," he said. "I felt badly about tearing down the old house, but I wanted to start over."

"Well, you certainly have. By the time you're finished, this will be quite a showplace."

"I hope so. That was my intention."

She couldn't help herself; she had to ask. "What else do you intend?"

"What do you mean?"

Deciding she might as well just come right out with it, she asked, "Why do you want to buy Dad's farm?"

He looked down at her—he was at least half a foot taller. "As I said—because it's for sale."

They both stopped, the horse between them. She searched Jack's face. "And if he sells, are you going to raze Gallagher Farm, too?"

He returned her look with a direct one of his own. "I don't know. I haven't decided yet."

"But you've thought about it."

"Of course. But I guess in the end, it depends."

"On what?"

He looked at her again, his eyes more blue than gray, the slight breeze lifting a lock of his hair and blowing it across his forehead. Quietly, he said, "I guess it depends on you."

It was the last thing she had expected him to say. "On me! What do I have to do with it?"

"Isn't that why you came—to convince your father not to sell?"

She didn't like him second-guessing her motives. Maybe because she herself was no longer sure what those motives were. "Why do you say that?"

"Then you do want him to sell?"

"Of course I want him to sell. I've told him so for years."

"So the problem must be that you don't want him to sell to me."

She backed away a step. "Why should I care who buys the farm?"

"I don't know. You tell me."

But she couldn't. And she didn't want to think about it now. "I don't think I'll have time for coffee, after all. I'm sure Dad's home by now, and we have—"

"You're angry again, right?"

"I'm not *angry!* I just don't have much time. I'm only here for a day or two, and I have to get things settled and get back to New York." She hesitated. Then, almost defiantly, she added, "I'm getting married, and I've got a wedding to plan."

Jack couldn't have looked more startled if she'd said she was entering a convent. "You're getting married?" he echoed. "I...uh...your father didn't say anything about it."

"Well, why would he?" Her voice was curt. Too late, she had realized why she'd introduced the subject of her upcoming marriage. It had been in the hope that he would keep his distance since she was having such trouble maintaining hers.

Clearly, Jack was better at retrenching than she was. His expression once more under control, he said, "I guess congratulations are in order then. When's the happy day?"

"I don't know. We haven't decided yet," she said belligerently.

"Who's the lucky fellow?"

Sorry that she'd brought up the subject, she shook out the reins she'd been gripping. "His name is Nowell Prescott." Then, before he could make the connection, she added, "His family owns the company where I work."

Without waiting for his reply, she climbed back into the saddle. "I should congratulate *you,* I guess. Your wife must be thrilled with this place."

"I'm not married—anymore, I mean. Connie and I were divorced a few years ago."

She felt an unexpected stab of satisfaction at the news, but made herself say, "I'm sorry. I didn't know."

"No reason that you should. It was for the best. She accused me of being more married to my work than I was to her, and she was right. By the time I realized what was going on, it was too late."

Margaret couldn't think of anything more to say. She muttered a goodbye, and was just turning Freebie toward home when Jack put his hand on the bridle. "Maggie—"

The way he said her name made her feel . . . strange. Closing her eyes briefly to regain her control, she looked down at him. "What?"

He seemed about to say something, then changed his mind. "I see you haven't lost your touch with horses," he finally said. "It's too bad you won't be here very long. I could use someone like you to advise me."

She didn't know what he was talking about. All she could think about was how blue his eyes looked in this light and how much she suddenly wanted to put her fingers in his hair to see if it was as thick as it looked.

"Advise you?" she repeated blankly.

"I'm not building this place to stay empty, Maggie. I'm going to start buying horses as soon as I can." He smiled, a self-deprecatory little smile that made him seem even more devastating. "I'm going to need all the help I can get."

Her lips felt stiff. Suddenly, she thought of Nowell and couldn't remember the color of his eyes. "You can always hire a bloodstock agent," she heard herself say.

"Maybe you can recommend one."

"I... I've been out of the business too long, Jack. You'll have to ask my father."

He looked at her for a long moment. Was that a flash of disappointment she saw in his eyes? She couldn't be sure, for he backed away just then, saying politely, "I'll do that. Goodbye, Maggie."

She didn't trust herself to say more. For a horrible moment, she wanted to get down out of the saddle again and...

"Goodbye, Jack," she said, giving Freebie such a hard dig with her heel that he shot forward, nearly unseating her.

She didn't look back. Thinking how glad she was that they were so close to home, she gave the horse his head and they raced up the hill and over, thundering down the other side. Free to run, Freebie was having the time of his life. Margaret let him go where he wanted—anywhere, she thought, urging him forward—just as long as she didn't have to look back.

DAN WAS BACKING the hay-filled truck into the wide main aisleway of the barn when Margaret finally came trotting in. She and Freebie had covered a lot of ground before the horse had grown tired. When Dan glanced up and saw her in the saddle, a look of amazement, quickly followed by one of pleasure, crossed his face. Jamming on the truck's brakes, he stuck his head out the window.

"Hey! It's been a long while since I've seen a sight like that!" he shouted. "What put you in the mind to ride again?"

Despite the differences they'd experienced, Margaret was aware that her father knew her better than anyone else in the world. She didn't want him to guess how her visit with Jack had disturbed her, especially now when she wanted to talk to him about Belle and the houseboat and Gallagher Farm. With this in mind, she put on a good face and said with a laugh, "It was either that, or have him chew the barn down!"

"Oh, he was after those bars with his teeth again, was he?" Exasperated, Dan shook his fist at the horse. "You'd better watch it, Freebie, or one of these days, you'll be gumming your hay because you'll be toothless!"

Laughing again, Margaret guided Freebie around the truck toward the other end of the barn. By the time she had untacked him, brushed him off and let him out to roll in his pasture, Dan was unloading the hay. Watching him covertly as she walked toward him, she was concerned again.

"Dad, why don't you hire someone to do that?" she asked. She knew his pride, and she didn't want to start off by alienating him before they'd had a chance to talk.

Gripping hay hooks in each hand, he wrestled another bale off the truck. "What for?" he grunted, pausing to wipe his arm across his forehead. "You think I'm too old to do this?"

"No, I just think you've reached a point in your life where you don't have to work so hard."

"Nuts," he said succinctly. To demonstrate his ability, he reached down and picked up a big bale, tossing it to the ground. Frowning, Margaret ducked out of the way.

"Dad—"

"Watch out, Maggie!"

Again, she had to sidestep quickly in order to avoid being flattened by another bale that came flying by.

"Dad!"

"I don't have time to talk now, Maggie. Can't you see I'm busy?"

"All right, then, if you won't stop and talk to me, we'll talk while we're working. Where's the other pair of hooks?"

Walking back along the bed of the truck, he stopped in midstep. "You're not going to come up here and unload this hay!"

"Yes, I am. I used to do it, and it's not something a person forgets how to do. Now, just tell me where—" But just then she spied the extra pair of hooks by the tack room door. She didn't take time to look for gloves, but grabbed the implements and jumped up onto the bed of the truck.

"Maggie," he protested angrily. "Is this really necessary?"

"You tell me," she puffed, tugging at the next bale and trying to get it in line. "You know that old saying—if the mountain won't come to Mohammed..."

"I never did understand what the hell that meant." Reaching out, he grabbed her arm. "Here, now. You stop that, Maggie. You'll hurt yourself!"

She looked at him. "And you won't?"

"I'm used to this, you're not." Fiercely, he jabbed his hay hooks into another bale and threw it off the truck as if to prove his point.

Not to be outdone, she maneuvered her bale toward the edge and shoved it off. Triumphantly, she looked at him. "And I told you, it's not something you forget how to do."

They glared at each other for a moment, then she straightened. As she did, she thought of Nowell and his mother. What would the Prescotts think if they could see her now? Grimacing at the thought, she decided she couldn't worry about that at the moment, and demanded, "Are you going to talk to me or not?"

In answer, Dan turned toward the hay that was still stacked at the back of the truck. "I told you, I'm busy."

Exasperated, she exploded, "You are the most stubborn, bullheaded, intractable man I've ever met!"

"And you're the most meddlesome, hot-tempered, tenacious daughter a man ever had the misfortune to have!" Dan shot back. Reaching out again, he tugged at a bale that seemed to be caught. "What do you want to talk about, anyway?"

"I want to talk to you about this houseboat business, Dad. I want to talk to you about selling the farm—"

He looked over his shoulder, his face red—with effort, or anger, she couldn't tell. "What about it? Why do you care? You're never here, and you've been after me for years to sell the damned place!"

She could feel herself growing red, too, but in her case, she knew it was temper. "Yes, but not to the first person who asked!"

He was still pulling ferociously on the recalcitrant bale that wouldn't come loose from the others. "What difference does it make who I sell the farm to? You don't want it!"

"That's not—"

She never got a chance to finish the sentence. With a last mighty heave, Dan finally pulled the big bale free. As he did, his face contorted, and he grabbed his back.

"Dad!" she cried. She started forward, but just then the stack of hay above him shifted. In a flash, she saw about ten bales start to fall and she screamed a warning.

"Dad! Look out!"

It was too late. Like giant green building blocks, the stack tumbled down onto Dan, burying him beneath a mountain of hay.

"Dad!" she screamed again, throwing herself forward. All she could see of him was a scuffed boot. Terrified, she began frantically pulling at the stack, but the bales were wedged so tightly, she couldn't make anything move.

"Help!" she shouted. *"Belle, help!"*

Half crying, perspiration rolling down her face with her frantic efforts, she shouted again, tugging and jerking at the heavy bales with her hands until she remembered the hay hooks. She was just reaching for them when Belle came running into the barn.

"I heard you call—" she started to say, and took in at a glance what had happened. "My God," she whispered, clambering immediately up onto the truck. "Dan? *Dan!*"

"Here—" Almost sobbing, Margaret thrust one of the hay hooks she'd retrieved into Belle's hand. Together they reached for the nearest bale, and with the extra strength that came from desperation, they managed to jerk it free. They could see Dan underneath, saved by a pocket that had been formed when the stack had fallen.

"Dad!" Margaret cried.

"Dan, say something!" Belle shrieked.

"Well, I will if you two will stop hollerin' like banshees," Dan groaned. "Here, get these things off me. I think I twisted my back before they fell."

"Your back!" Belle cried. "Oh, Dan—"

"Stop carryin' on, woman," he commanded. "It's gettin' hot in here."

Somehow they managed to get him free. With Belle practically holding him down to make sure he wouldn't injure himself further, Margaret leaped off the truck and raced to the phone. Although the ambulance arrived in spare minutes, it seemed to take forever. Finally, Dan stowed carefully inside on a flat board, his head and neck protected by an inflatable air splint, the ambulance took off and the women followed the vehicle to the hospital in Margaret's rented car.

"You drive," Belle had said. Her voice was shaking as badly as her hands, her face was absolutely white.

Margaret wasn't sure she was in any better shape, but somehow she managed to get them there safely. As soon as they arrived, they raced into Emergency, where Dan was already being examined and x-rayed. An hour later, a doctor came out to tell them that, miraculously, nothing was broken, but that Dan had strained his back and would have to lie flat for a while. He also intended to keep him overnight for observation.

"How long will he have to be in bed?" Margaret asked, after Belle had collapsed in teary relief.

"Too soon to tell," the doctor said. "It could be a couple of days, maybe a week or two. It all depends on the patient."

Relieved, Margaret said, "Well, if I know my father, he'll be up and around by tomorrow."

The doctor smiled briefly. "I hope you're right. But his age is against him, so I wouldn't be quite that optimistic."

Suddenly frightened again, she grabbed his arm. "But he will get well!"

"Oh, yes, he'll be fine. It'll just take some time."

"Can we see him?" Belle asked.

Despite the seriousness of the moment, humor glinted in the doctor's eyes. "I think you'd better. He's already insisting he's going to walk out. Maybe you two can talk some sense into him."

Belle looked grim. "Oh, don't worry about that," she said. Taking Margaret's arm, they went in together.

Looking a little pale, Dan was lying on one of the gurneys in Emergency. As soon as he saw them, he said, "Get me out of here. I hate hospitals, and I won't stay in one!"

"It's just for a night," Belle said, taking his hand. "Then you can come home."

"I want to go home now! Who's going to care for the stock? Who will—"

"I will, Dad," Margaret said quietly.

He turned and looked at her in surprise. "You!"

She was so relieved that he was going to be all right that she wanted to hug him tightly. She didn't dare. He was wearing a neck brace, and she was afraid she'd hurt him. Right now she would have done anything for him, and she reached for his other hand and squeezed it, telling herself she wouldn't cry.

"Don't sound so surprised," she said shakily. "I've done it before, you know."

Dan squinted. "Yeah, but that was a long time ago."

She took a deep breath. "I'll manage. Besides, you'll be home tomorrow and able to supervise."

"From bed," Belle put in firmly.

Agitated again, he said, "I can't stay in bed forever! Besides, that mare is about due to foal, and I have to be there."

Belle was adamant. "She'll get along fine without you."

"No, she won't. You don't understand, Belle!" Impassioned, Dan turned to Margaret. "Will you stay, Maggie—until the mare foals?"

She fought to hide her dismay. "Well, Dad—"

"Please, Maggie. You do this for me, and I'll never ask another thing of you, I swear. I've got everything tied up in that mare and her foal. She's bred to that stakes horse Worth Waiting For II, so you know what we're talking about here."

Margaret might have been away a long time, but she recognized the name of the stallion who had sired the foal, and her eyes widened. "His stud fee is in the thousands, Dad," she said. "How did you ever—"

"It was my nest egg," he said, gripping her hand tightly. Like any good breeder, even in pain, he could reel off the statistics without pausing to think. "The mare's name is Never Forget, and aside from her own career—twelve starts, eight firsts, in the money the other four—she's a daughter of Knight Music out of another stakes winner First Love. I knew she'd be a good cross, so I sold practically everything on the place to get her and pay that stud fee. Maggie, you know how valuable the foal is going to be."

Margaret knew, all right. Knight Music had won the Derby and the Preakness before being retired with a stress fracture. Never Forget's dam had won practically every big race in California before shipping east and being bought by Grover and Annabelle Sheffield of nearby Finish Line Farm. She had no idea how her father had gotten his hands on Never Forget, but she knew what this meant to Dan.

She had to help, she thought; she owed her father at least that much. Besides, she told herself, it would only be a day or two longer, at most. Trying not to imagine Nowell's reaction to hearing she had to stay longer than she'd planned, she said, "Of course, I'll stay. When is Never Forget due to foal?"

"Oh, soon, soon," Dan said, avoiding her eyes.

Margaret knew that look. "*How* soon, Dad?"

He looked at Belle before he glanced back at her. "A couple of weeks."

"A couple of weeks!"

"At most, Maggie—at most. We bred her late. We couldn't get her in foal, and well, you know how it is. But she's had babies before, and she was always early, so it could be any day now, any minute!"

And it could be a month, Margaret thought. When in foal, mares were like the proverbial pot that wouldn't boil no matter how carefully watched.

"Dad, I—"

"Please, Maggie," Dan said. "You know I wouldn't ask if it didn't mean everything to me."

She tried one last time. "But Belle—"

"Belle's a wonderful woman, but she doesn't know beans about horses, do you, darlin'?"

Reluctantly, Belle shook her head. "I'd like to help, Maggie, but Dan's right. I wouldn't know what to do."

Dan's blue eyes were guileless as could be. "There's no one else, Maggie."

About to mention that a veterinarian would be a good bet, Margaret hesitated. Was that a gleam she saw in his eyes? It couldn't be tears, she thought. But it could be a ploy to make her stay longer.

Immediately, she dismissed the notion. Was she really going to believe that her father had deliberately strained his back because he didn't want her to leave? She was getting as bad as her Aunt Tilda, letting her imagination run away with her this way. Obviously, whatever she'd *thought* she'd seen in her father's eyes was the result of medication, or shock, or pain.

But she still couldn't help sounding reluctant when she finally agreed. "All right, Dad," she said. "I'll stay until the mare foals."

"Good girl, Maggie! I knew you wouldn't let me down!"

She gave him a warning look. "But only until then, Dad. Then I *have* to leave. Is that a deal?"

"Deal!"

Her father looked delighted, and Belle was pleased. But Margaret still couldn't quite shake the feeling she'd been manipulated. With dragging footsteps she went to call her fiancé.

CHAPTER SIX

FLOYD STANTON BRAKED his purple Caddy to a stop just before he reached the crest of the hill leading down to Fieldstone Farm. Opening the door, he got out and walked to where he could look down on his brother's place without being seen himself. His eyes narrowed as he stared at the newly completed big house, the barns, and the construction still going on over at what Jack had said would be the farm manager's—his—house.

"Damned charity, that's what it is," he muttered. Taking out a crumpled pack of cigarettes, he lit one with an angry snap of a throwaway lighter. Then he squatted down on his heels to smoke it, the smoke wreathing his head for a moment before it dissipated in the breeze.

For as long as he could remember, he had hated the kind of person his own brother seemed to have become. Growing up in a poor family, Floyd had learned early on that those who made it had two things: money and power.

He'd never had either, and the way his luck ran, it didn't seem likely that he ever would. He was forty years old, and what did he have to show for it? Three marriages, three divorces... a string of jobs, half of which he couldn't even remember now. The only things he owned were the Caddy behind him and the clothes in the trunk. Not much to show for all those years, was it?

He'd been down to pretty near his last buck when Jack had tracked him to Amarillo, where he was living with a waitress named Maizie, who, for some crazy reason, wanted to marry him. Thinking of it, he shook his head. What a scene she'd made when he told her he was going to work for his brother and that she couldn't come with him.

She'd clung to him. "Just let me go along! I won't be any trouble, I swear! I'll get a job, and you won't even know I'm there!"

He could just imagine what his brother would say if he showed up with a woman. "No. I told you, I'm going alone."

Her face contorting, she'd flung herself away. "I don't get it," she'd cried. "I thought you hated Kentucky! You told me so, often enough! You said you'd never go back there!"

"So I did say those things, and more," he'd admitted, while Maizie sobbed. "But that was before little brother grew up and decided to become a farm owner. Now, I think it might be interestin' to go, that's all."

"Interesting!" Maizie had looked at him as though he was crazy. "To work for your brother? I thought you hated him most of all!"

What's the matter with you? Why can't you be more like Jack?

His father's words echoed in his mind. From the earliest he could remember, he'd been compared to his sterling, never-put-a-foot-wrong younger brother. According to his parents and just about everyone else he'd ever met who knew the two of them, Jack never made a mistake. He never did anything wrong. He was perfect. By the time Floyd had finally left home—for good, he'd thought—he was so sick and tired of hearing about Jack that he was glad to go, just so he wouldn't have to listen to the inevitable comparisons anymore.

And now he was going to work for his brother. Even to himself, he couldn't explain why he'd agreed to go. It wasn't because he was broke; he'd been down on his luck before, much worse than this. And it wasn't because he had any great love of horses, that was for sure. In fact, what he knew about the big, dumb creatures could fit on the head of a pin, with room left over for the Salvation Army marching band.

Maybe it was curiosity, he thought. When Jack had called, someone could have knocked Floyd over with a feather, that's how surprised he'd been. He'd never thought about Jack owning a horse farm; he'd totally forgotten how horse-crazy Jack had been as a kid. But now that he thought about it, he could still see those cheap prints of racehorses his brother had tacked up over his bed in that damned loft they'd slept in as kids. And he could vaguely remember Jack sneaking away as often as he could to watch the workouts at the racetrack. But own his own farm? When had he made that decision? For years he'd been obsessed with his heavy equipment business. That was what had made Floyd decide maybe this was something he'd have to see for himself.

And now he was here. Finishing his cigarette, he ground it out under his heel in the dirt. He was just straightening up to go back to the car when he saw Jack come out of the house below and walk toward the barn.

His eyes narrowed as he watched his brother's confident, long-strided gait. Although he'd tried not to, he'd always envied that about Jack. As foolish as it sounded, he used to try to imitate Jack's walk just to see if he could do it. But on him it didn't feel right, so he'd taken the opposite tack and, depending on his mood, either swaggered or slouched.

As Jack disappeared inside the barn, Floyd's glance went to the manager's house again, and he frowned. What was he doing here? Why had he agreed to come? He didn't know beans about horses, and furthermore, he didn't care. Jack might have a fondness for the creatures, but for him it had always been fast cars—and women. Take the past couple of weeks, for instance, he thought with a sudden grin. He'd been having a hell of a time in town.

His smile faded. All that was about to change, though, and pretty soon he'd be walking the straight and narrow. Jack might have reached out a hand here, but he knew his brother, and this wasn't going to be an easy gig. Jack would expect him to do more than put in his time, and even now he felt resistant and resentful at the thought.

Why was it that people like Jack, who succeeded because he'd had all the damned breaks, always felt that everybody else should work as hard as they did? It wasn't so easy to prosper, especially when all your life things went against you. But did his brother understand that? Hell no. Worse, he knew from experience that if he complained about never having any luck, Jack would give him that *look* and say, "The only luck I know of is where opportunity meets hard work."

Thinking of it, Floyd snorted. If that were true, then it was obvious that opportunity had always just passed him by. Besides, people like Jack liked to work; it was almost a religion with them.

"Self-righteous bastard," he muttered. "It's a good thing we all don't feel that way or there'd be no fun at all in the world."

Still, as he went back to the car, he consoled himself with the thought that managing a farm with no horses on it yet couldn't be too hard, even for him. He could sleep 'til noon, quit about three, he thought.

Hell, he could go out every night if he wanted, or maybe—his eyes gleamed—have someone in if he chose. He'd have a *house,* after all; he wouldn't be taking them back to a hotel, as he had so often in the past. And later on, when the horses started coming, Jack had said he'd have help. As manager, he could delegate, couldn't he? Of course he could, he decided with another grin. It would be his duty.

And there were always other alternatives, if things just didn't work out. He'd heard of something going on in Miami, and California was always ripe. He hadn't checked yet, but there might even be a few opportunities around here if he looked. Jack was paying him good, but he was always open to making a little money on the side. It never hurt.

But that was still in the future; in the meantime, now that he was here, he might as well go down and say hello. Climbing into the Caddy, he switched the engine on and leaving it in neutral, he pressed the accelerator to the floor just to hear the resulting roar. Money and power, he thought, putting the car in gear and starting down the hill in a blur. There were times, like this, with the big engine throbbing around him and the wind whistling in the window, that if he'd been given a choice, he'd take the women and the fast cars over money and power any day.

DOWN IN THE BARN at Fieldstone Farm, Jack was feeling depressed as he and Al discussed a swinging wall for the new tack room door. He tried to keep his mind on what his construction foreman was saying, but when Al had to repeat something twice, he muttered a curse.

"Sorry," he said. "I guess I'm somewhere else today."

"I'll say," Al said, giving him a curious look. "You want to talk about it?"

Jack wasn't sure. He knew where his mind was, but did he want to discuss it, even with an old friend like Al?

"I don't know," he said. "Do you remember Maggie Gallagher?"

"Maggie?" Al's eyebrows shot up. "Who wouldn't? Her dad still owns the farm next door, doesn't he? But I thought she moved to New York, or someplace, years ago."

"She did. But she's here for a visit, and I saw her the other day—"

"And?" A knowing smile crept across Al's broad face. "Are you telling me that even after all these years you still got a thing for her?"

They'd been friends too long for Jack to hide it. "Yes, I guess," he said gloomily. "I thought I was long over it, but..." He shook his head. "I can't get her out of my mind."

Al laid a sympathetic hand on his friend's shoulder. "Boy, you sound like you've got it bad."

Jack sighed. "When she came over, riding that horse, it was like I was eighteen all over again, going to the track and watching her exercise her father's runners. I always thought there wasn't a more beautiful sight than Maggie Gallagher on a horse. I remember they used to say at the track that it was a pity she wasn't a jockey, because she sure had the touch."

Seeing the look on Jack's face, Al grinned. "She's got the touch, all right, old buddy. It looks like she's put a spell on you for good."

Jack couldn't deny it. He hadn't been prepared for it at all, but he realized now that he'd fallen in love with her all over again the moment he'd seen her in the kitchen at Gallagher Farm. He'd hoped it was an aberration, something he'd conjured up because he'd been thinking about her so much since he'd been back, but the other morning when she came riding in, he knew he'd been fooling himself.

It had been all he could do to keep his hands off her. The touch of her arm made his pulse jump; the sight of her long legs in those tight jeans, the sparkle in her eyes, her face flushed from her ride, made him want to grab her and kiss her until they both gasped.

Thrusting away the images, he said, "A lot of good it will do me. She's getting married."

"Yeah? Who told you that?"

"She did. And you know what I said? *Congratulations. When's the happy day? Who's the lucky guy?* I sounded like a complete idiot."

"Hey, you were taken off guard, that's all," Al said stoutly.

"Yeah, but I shouldn't have been. A woman like Maggie, as intelligent and beautiful as she is? I should have been more surprised that she *wasn't* married."

"So what are you going to do?"

Jack didn't know. "I guess I should just forget her."

"Well, I'd say so, since she's engaged to someone else."

Jack didn't want to talk about it anymore. "You're right," he said, determined to get down to business once more. He forced a smile, a laugh. Slapping Al on the back, he said, "Thanks for setting me straight."

Looking relieved, Al started discussing the new changes Jack had asked for in the tack room. But a few minutes later, after the foreman had gone off to another job, Jack sat alone in the new office in the barn, his head in his hands. Despite his outward show for his old friend, he couldn't get Maggie out of his mind. She'd been there ever since he'd seen her the other day.

He stopped. Who was he kidding? He'd never forgotten Maggie, ever. She'd been at the back of his mind for years, a constant ache, a never-forgotten longing, a reminder of what he could have had if only things had been different. Was that why he'd offered to buy Gallagher Farm the moment he'd heard Dan had put the place up for sale? Maybe he'd had some foolish hope that Maggie would hear about his offer and come home—out of curiosity. Maybe what he'd thought was that once she was here...

And then what? he asked himself scathingly. Had he honestly thought she'd take one look at him and realize what she'd been missing all these years? If that was the case, he'd stumbled right out of the gate, hadn't he? Far from bowling her over, all he seemed to have done was alienate her. For some reason he couldn't even begin to fathom, she resented the fact that he'd made an offer for the farm—she, who claimed that she'd been asking Dan to sell the place for years. "Forget it, just forget it," he muttered. He hadn't settled anything; he was still just as frustrated and baffled as he'd been before. If he didn't put Maggie out of his mind, at least for a while, he'd drive himself crazy.

That resolved, he was reaching for one of the sales catalogs on the desk when he heard the car. Lifting his head, he listened to the sound of the engine only a moment before he knew who it was. Wondering what his brother was doing here, he came out of the barn just as Floyd came flying into the yard.

"Hi, little brother," Floyd said, after he'd screeched to a halt in a swirl of dust and gravel and got out of the car. He looked around. "I'll say one thing for you, you know how to get things done. From the looks of things, the place has progressed like a house afire." Realizing what he'd said, he grinned. "Oops. Wrong metaphor. What did you do? Hire crews around the clock to finish?"

"Almost," Jack said. He wasn't in the mood for Floyd right now, and his tone was curt. "I hired some extra people because I was tired of living in the trailer."

Glancing in that direction, Floyd snorted. "You're tired of it, huh? Some of the places I've lived in make that look like a palace."

Telling himself again that he was not going to be goaded, Jack said, "In that case, would you like to move into the trailer? I'm going to be living in the house from now on, so the trailer is yours if you want it."

Floyd looked at him speculatively. "You know, I think I might just take you up on that. If, that is, I can have a guest or two now and then. You wouldn't object to that, would you, Jack?"

It was a test and Jack knew it. "As long as you do your job, your private life is your own business, Floyd," he said. But then, because he knew his brother, he added, "Just don't show up drunk—or stoned, that's all I ask."

"Would I do that?"

"I don't know. Would you?"

Floyd shrugged. "Well, I admit in the past, I haven't exactly been a sterling character—not like you," he added maliciously. "But even I can turn over a new leaf."

Jack nodded. "Fine, then. I'll be getting the rest of my stuff out today, so you can move in when you like. The other house will be finished in a week or so, and you can switch over then."

"Oh, I don't know," Floyd said thoughtfully as he took out a cigarette. "I might just stay in the trailer. It suits me better than a house, I think."

"Please yourself," Jack said, watching Floyd pull out a battered lighter. "By the way, I don't care if you smoke, but not around the barn, all right?"

"Don't want all that expensive horseflesh going up in flames, right? Say, when are the pampered critters going to make their appearance, anyway? I got to gear up for this, you know."

"I'm not sure. I've been looking through catalogs, and there are some sales coming up, so I'm hoping to find something then."

"And when you do, what are you going to do with them? You don't expect me to actually *touch* the beasts, do you?"

"Well, it would help, Floyd," Jack said dryly. Then he shook his head. "But no, I don't expect that. I hired a barn crew, and they'll be going to work just as soon as the horses start coming in."

"Another crew, eh?"

"Yes, some people to groom and feed the horses, muck out the stalls, that sort of thing."

Floyd blew out a fat smoke ring. "Top drawer, huh? Nothing but the best for our Jack."

Jack had schooled himself to have almost unlimited patience with his brother, but sometimes enough was enough. His voice hardening in a way Floyd knew all too well, he said, "Let's get one thing straight. I told you when we first talked about it that I intend to do this the right way. If you have a problem with that—"

"Hey, hey, what are you getting all worked up about, anyway? All I said was—"

"I know what you said, Floyd. It's—"

But just then they were interrupted by the sound of another car. Both men turned as a brilliant red sports car turned into the long driveway. The top was down, and they could see the driver's mane of blond hair blowing in the breeze. The car was a Ferrari, and Floyd glanced across at Jack.

"You expectin' anybody?" he asked.

Jack shook his head. "No, I—" he started to say, then he drew in a sharp breath. "I can't believe it. Is that Lilah Castlemaine?"

"Lilah?" Floyd repeated, his eyebrows lifting. "I don't think—"

But it was. As the Ferrari braked to a stop practically on top of where they were standing, Leo Castlemaine's daughter, Lilah, waved and called out a greeting.

"Hi," she said gaily, getting out of the car and slamming the door. Her long, red fingernails glinted in the sunlight as she waggled her fingers at them, and she sashayed—there was no other word for it, Jack thought—around the front of the car wearing high, high heels, skintight pants and a formfitting halter top. It was an outfit calculated to show off her assets, and it succeeded. Jack had to jerk his eyes away from the sight of her full breasts almost bursting out of the halter, but Floyd felt no such compunction. He was openly staring, his cigarette hanging from his lips.

"You remember me, don't you, boys?" she purred, posing against the hood of the car. "Lilah Castlemaine? As I recall, you used to work for my father."

That brought Floyd back to life. Both brothers remembered all too well having to toil in the Castlemaine tobacco fields. Sensing Floyd tensing beside him, Jack shot him a quick look. "Don't start anything," he muttered. "Let's find out what she wants first."

Floyd hesitated. But then he said, "You're the boss," and took a deep drag off the cigarette.

"Hello, Lilah," Jack said.

"Hello, Lilah?" she echoed mockingly. "Is that all you can say to me, Jack Stanton, after all these years?"

Still wondering what she was doing here, he said, "It has been a long time."

"Indeed. And what about you, Floyd?" She laughed, making a coy little face. "Cat got your tongue?"

"Not at all. I'm just surprised to see you, that's all. What are you doing here?"

Flirtatiously, she took off her designer sunglasses. Jack saw then that she hadn't aged as well as he'd thought at first. She looked hard and...used, he thought; there was no other word. He was thinking of Maggie, who looked so fresh and vibrant and beautiful, when she said, "Why, I came to see Jack, of course. I had no idea you'd both be here, but then, who would have dreamed the gossip was true?"

"What gossip is that?" Jack asked.

"Why, that you bought the old Tidleman place and intend to convert it to a horse farm," she said throatily. Glancing around, she added, "You seem to have done very well for yourself, Jack."

"I've had some opportunities," he said neutrally.

"And made the best of them, it's clear."

"Things are shaping up."

"Yes, and so have you."

Her knowing eyes came back to him. Almost insolently, she looked him up and down, running the tip of her tongue sensuously over her top lip as she did. He couldn't imagine Maggie doing something so obvious. Lilah was inspecting him, categorizing him, deciding whether he would be interesting as a future sexual partner. For once, Jack knew just how women felt when a man did the same thing to them. He didn't like the feeling and he spoke abruptly.

"If that's meant as a compliment—"

"Oh, it is," she said huskily, her eyes finally making it up to his face. "It definitely is. If I'd had any *idea*..." Deliberately, she allowed her voice to trail away. Then she smiled her catlike little smile. "Well, it's obvious that we need to reacquaint ourselves, and

I did have another purpose coming all the way out here besides satisfying my curiosity. I came to invite you to the Kentucky Horse Breeders' annual fund-raiser next Saturday. You'd be my escort, naturally, and I can introduce you to all Daddy's friends."

"Daddy's friends" that Lilah so casually mentioned were Kentucky's racing elite. Jack knew how difficult it was to be admitted into that charmed circle—and yet how necessary it would be, if he was to succeed. When he had decided to buy the farm and start raising and racing his own horses, he knew entry into those ranks would be the biggest stumbling block he'd face. To have Lilah offering it to him was an opportunity not to be passed up. Still wondering what she was really after, he said, "I'd like that."

"So would I," she purred. "Oh, by the way, it's black tie. You do own a tuxedo, don't you?"

"I'll dig something up," he said, as she straightened from her seductive pose against the hood of the Ferrari. A gentleman to the last, he stepped forward and opened the car door. She paused a moment before she got inside, twirling her keys and looking speculatively up at him.

"I'm so glad I decided to drop by," she murmured, pressing her body briefly into him. He felt the thrust of her breasts, and despite himself, some treacherous part of him responded. As though she sensed his reaction, she smiled again as she backed away and climbed into the leather seat. "I'll look forward to Saturday, then, Jack. Eight o'clock. They're going to have a buffet, but I'd prefer a quiet little supper somewhere after. Just you and me. Wouldn't that be nice?"

Jack had an idea that a "quiet little supper" wasn't exactly what she had in mind, but he decided to play her game. "Fine. I'll make reservations."

She arched an eyebrow. "Where?"

"I'll think of a place," he said casually, slamming the car door shut.

She laughed, and as she started the powerful engine, she glanced coquettishly up at him. "Just make sure the restaurant's dark," she said, and blew him a kiss as the car roared off.

Neither brother said anything as the red Ferrari flashed up the hill again and was gone. Then Floyd let out a low whistle. "Boy, she hasn't changed, has she? Except to get older and more worn around the edges, she's still the same stuck-up bitch she always was. Why in hell did you say you'd go to that fund-raiser with her?"

His eyes still on the place where Lilah's car had disappeared, Jack said, "Because she knows people I want to know."

Floyd looked at him contemptuously. "Well, I'd advise you to wear your armor, boy. Women like her eat guys like you for breakfast."

Floyd left soon after, and Jack went inside. The red light was blinking on the answering machine, so he idly switched it on. When he heard Maggie on the recording, he tensed. Something was wrong; he could tell it from the sound of her voice.

"Hello, Jack, this is Maggie—Margaret," she said, correcting herself. "I'm just calling to tell you that there's been an accident. Dad strained his back when we were unloading hay. It's not serious, or so the doctor says, but he's going to be in bed for a few days, maybe a week. Dad wanted me to call and tell you that you'll have to put off discussing the sale of the farm until he gets back on his feet. In the meantime, I'll be staying this week until, hopefully, Dad's prize mare foals. So if you have any questions, just call."

The machine switched off, but Jack just stood staring at it. He was sorry Dan was hurt, but all he could think of was that Maggie was going to stay for a while longer. A few days, he thought. Maybe a week.

Suddenly—and totally without substance—he felt as if he'd been reprieved. He knew she was engaged, knew he should just put her out of his head. But he couldn't help think that a lot could happen in a week. A *lot.*

A wild surge of elation rose in him and he grabbed his keys and raced out to his car. If Dan was hurt, it was only right that he offer his help, he told himself, and was halfway to Gallagher Farm before he remembered that he hadn't even closed the front door.

CHAPTER SEVEN

"WHAT DO YOU MEAN, you'll be tied up for a few more days?" Nowell demanded when Margaret finally got hold of him and relayed the news of Dan's accident.

She had tried calling from the hospital, but couldn't reach him. It wasn't until the next day that she got through, and at first he was horrified by the news. That was before she told him she couldn't come home right away.

"Well, it's sort of complicated," she said unhappily.

"Maybe you should try to explain, then."

She'd known he wouldn't understand, and he didn't. But why should he, she asked herself despairingly, when she didn't understand it herself? Her explanation sounded absurd even to her own ears, and she couldn't blame him for being upset.

"The problem," she said, "is a broodmare Dad has. She's due to foal—to have her baby—very soon, and Dad wants me to be here to make sure nothing goes wrong."

"I see," Nowell said, in a tone that indicated he would have understood her running off with another man more than he understood this. "Am I then to assume that the entire state of Kentucky has no equine veterinarian?"

Wearily, trying to control her temper, wondering what else could go wrong, she rubbed her forehead. "It's not that, Nowell. It's just that Dad trusts me—"

"Only you? There's no one else? Really, Margaret, I find that difficult to believe. If that's true, how did he get along without you all these years?"

She'd started by being almost apologetic for inconveniencing him, but now she was getting annoyed by his tone. "This is a special case, Nowell. I'd hoped you would understand."

"Well, I don't," he said flatly. "I'm sorry, Margaret, but you have to understand that I need you, too. Apart from my requiring your presence at the office, we do have wedding plans, you know."

Wishing she could forget about the damned wedding, she said, "I know, but what can I do? My father wouldn't have asked if it wasn't important to him, and I can't refuse."

There was silence. Then he said tersely, "All right, Margaret. It seems that your mind is made up on this, so I'll give you until the end of the week."

Tempted to tell him she really didn't need his permission, she held back the words. Telling herself he was *trying* to be fair, she said, "Thanks. I'll keep you posted."

NOW IT WAS A WEEK since Dan's accident, and Margaret was exhausted. It wasn't so much because of the hard work involved in running the farm; it was because her father was such a difficult patient. He tried; it was just that he seemed constitutionally unable to sit—never mind *lie*—still for days at a time. He was too filled with nervous energy. *Too determined to have his finger in every pie,* she thought in exasperation.

"Did you put those yearlings out in the west pasture?" he'd call from the bedroom after she got back from doing just that.

"Yes, Dad," she'd say, collapsing into a chair. She took aerobics classes when she was in New York, but she had quickly realized jumping around in a studio was no preparation for wrestling excitable young horses out to the paddock in the mornings. There was one filly in particular, coal black but hot as fire, who was a real pistol. Margaret knew that if she hadn't been able to draw on past experience, that filly would have dragged her all over the farm. As it was, she thought wryly, some days it was touch and go.

"And what about the two-year-olds?" Dan would shout when she staggered in for lunch. "Sam Emmons is going to call soon about one of them, and I—"

"It's taken care of, Dad," she'd say. "I called him and told him about your accident and he'll wait."

Another time, it would be, "What about getting someone in to help with the barn?"

She knew he was worried that she was working too hard, so she tried to be patient, even when he asked her the same thing every day. "I already found someone, Dad—a boy named Yates," she told him. "He's going to come before and after school just as long as we need him."

"Well, you be sure he doesn't waste straw," Dan would order her. Raising his voice, he'd call, "Do you hear me?"

Thinking it would be hard not to, since he was yelling his head off, she'd say, "Yes, Dad, I hear you. He's doing just fine, trust me."

And no matter what else he wanted, he always asked about Never Forget, the broodmare that was the cause of Margaret's putting all her plans—her *life*—on hold. Sometimes when her father kept calling from the bedroom, Maggie wondered if the foal was worth the wait. Plaintively, Dan would ask at least a half dozen times a day, "Did you check Never Forget, Maggie?"

"Yes, Dad," she'd say resignedly. The mare was beautiful to be sure, and no doubt would have a wonderful foal. She just wished the horse would hurry up and deliver; then Margaret could leave and go home to New York where she belonged. She had nightmares about the size of her wedding growing like Topsy the longer she was gone.

Now the week was up, and she still hadn't heard from Nowell since their last phone call. She debated, but then decided not to call him herself. They both needed time to cool off, and she had enough problems at the moment without trying to deal with Nowell. One of her problems was Aunt Tilda, who came every single day to make sure she and Belle were taking proper care of the reluctant and recalcitrant invalid.

"I just don't understand you, Maggie," Aunt Tilda had said in a pointed aside the first day. Balefully, she glared in the direction of the bedroom, where Belle was keeping Dan company. "How can you allow that... that woman to stay here? I thought you were on *my* side!"

Margaret knew Tilda was genuinely concerned about Dan, and that her aunt probably felt left out now that Belle had come into her brother's life, but she couldn't allow the remark to pass.

"It's not a matter of *sides,*" she said quietly. "We both love Dad, don't we?"

Tilda grasped her big patent leather purse more tightly over her ample stomach. "You know we do," she sniffed.

"And we both want him to be happy, don't we?"

Another sniff. "Well, of course. But you can't honestly believe that... that woman—"

"Her name is Belle, Aunt Tilda," Margaret said firmly. "And I have to tell you that I've never seen Dad so happy as he's been with Belle around. She's good for him, I've seen it myself. I didn't want to believe it at first, but the more I get to know her, the more I think they really are right for each other."

For the first time, Tilda looked uncertain. "You... do?"

"Yes, I do."

"But what about the age difference?"

Margaret had already come to terms with that. "If it doesn't bother them, I don't think it's any of our business."

"I don't know, Maggie," Tilda said sorrowfully. "I'm beginning to think she's dazzled you just like she has Dan. I still believe she's out for what she can get. This houseboat business, for instance—"

"I told you, that was Dad's idea."

"Dan wants to live on the water? Oh, no, I don't believe that for a second, Maggie."

"It's true, Aunt Tilda. Didn't you ever ask him?"

Tilda drew herself up. "Well, I would have, Maggie," she said loftily, "but I just didn't figure it was any of my business!"

Margaret gave up at that point; she had horses to take care of and a farm to run. She knew how her aunt felt, but during those first couple of days especially, she was glad Belle was there. It took a while to get back into the rhythm of things, and if she'd had to do all the chores and keep the impatient patient occupied as well, she felt she would have lost her mind.

But there was yet another problem she faced, and that was Jack. Even though she had called and told him about Dan's accident, saying that her father would get in touch when he could, Jack had come roaring over the very same day she'd left the message for him. Margaret, still upset about what had happened, had gone out to the barn after she and Belle brought Dan home the day after the accident.

Dan was a pack rat where his tack was concerned, keeping everything he'd ever bought just in case he ever needed it. Margaret planned to straighten up the room—she needed time to think. Plunging in, she started folding blankets and hanging up bridles and checking that halters and lead ropes matched, even lining up the grooming brushes all in a row. When there wasn't anything more to do, she'd decided to work on one of the saddles, and she was just getting out the saddle soap when she heard a car outside.

She couldn't see who it was, but she knew by the way Skeeter barked that the visitor was a friend, and she came out to the yard just as Jack climbed out of his car.

Immediately, she became conscious of her appearance. Her jeans were dusty and her blouse mussed. A kerchief covered her hair, and she was sure there was a streak of dirt across her face.

"What are you doing here?" she demanded, her embarrassment making her sound abrupt. "Didn't you get my message?"

Jack turned toward her. He was wearing jeans, too, but his were so old they were practically white—and tight enough to define the muscles in his long legs. His checked shirt was open at the throat, and under his short shirtsleeves, his arms looked tanned and powerful.

"Yes, I got it," he said. "That's why I came over. I wanted to make sure Dan was all right."

Thrusting away a sudden mental picture of those hay bales falling, she said, "He's going to be fine. He hurt his back, and he'll have to have bed rest for a while, but other than that, there's no damage."

"We can be thankful for that. Is he up to having visitors, do you think?"

"I don't know. We just brought him home, and the doctor gave him something to help him relax, so he'll probably be pretty groggy."

Jack smiled suddenly. "Too bad it won't last," he said wryly. "Knowing Dan, he's going to be a tough patient."

She had to smile at that. "You know him well, I see. We're probably going to have to tie him down before long."

They laughed together, then Jack turned serious again. "I came to see Dan, but I also wanted to offer my help. If you need anything—anything at all, you'll let me know, won't you?"

"Oh, I don't think—"

"I know you and Belle will be able to manage, but just in case, remember, I'm just across the hill."

How could she forget? She knew she sounded stilted and awkward, but even when he was just standing there, he had the ability to make her heart race. She didn't like being so affected by him, but what she disliked even more was that she couldn't seem to control her feelings. After all, she ran an entire department at Prescott without a qualm; she chaired board meetings without losing her composure even in a roomful of demanding males. And more to the point, she remembered guiltily, she was engaged to be married—to another man. What was it about this one that made her feel she was tumbling head over heels?

"Well... thank you," she said. "I'll remember that."

His eyes held hers. "I hope so."

It was then she knew that no matter what disaster or crisis occurred, Jack would be the last person on earth she'd call. It wasn't that he couldn't be relied on; the painful truth was that *she* couldn't be trusted. When Jack was around—even when he wasn't, she thought hopelessly—she had a disturbing tendency to forget everything else... like Nowell, waiting for her back in New York.

No matter what, she told herself, she had to remember that she and Nowell were getting married. She was committed to him; she wanted to be his wife. So she couldn't recall at this particular moment which side he parted his hair on, or remember how his voice sounded—but those were small details, easily excused because she was still so upset about what had happened to her father. She was sure that once she had a chance to calm down she could remember Nowell down to the last particular.

And anyway, she told herself defiantly, it didn't matter because soon she would be going home and Jack would be part of her past again.

"Maggie—" Jack started to say.

But just then Belle came out of the house and saw him. "Jack!" she exclaimed in delight. "Why, how nice to see you. I think you're just what the patient needs! Did you come to see Dan?"

Jack turned to Belle at once. "Yes, I did. When I got the message that he'd been hurt, I came right over."

"Well, come in, come in. How thoughtful of you."

Together, Jack and Belle went back inside, leaving Maggie alone in the yard. Skeeter came and sat down beside her, thumping his tail on the ground. Distractedly, she looked down at him and was sure he was smiling.

"A lot *you* know," she muttered, and went back to finish up in the tack room.

SOMETIME DURING the rest of the week, Maggie gave up being called Margaret. Up at dawn and ready to fall into bed at dusk, running around in jeans and T-shirts and the boots she had hastily bought in town, she bore little resemblance to the sophisticated Margaret Gallagher of New York. Every time she looked in the mirror, she saw good old Maggie.

Even if she'd wanted to, she didn't have time or energy to do her face, or her hair, or her nails. The most she had time for, or interest in, was scrubbing her face clean and brushing her hair back into a ponytail to get it out of the way. Then it was on with the gloves and out to the barn. By Friday, she felt she was getting the hang of it, enough to take a little time after lunch to talk to Belle.

"You're working too hard, Maggie," Belle said worriedly, as they sat at the kitchen table. Clasping her hands together, she looked distressed. "I wish I could be more help!"

Smiling, Maggie reached across and patted the older woman's arm. By this time, they had become friends, and she said honestly, "You're more help than you realize, Belle. If Dad didn't have you, he'd go out of his mind." Shuddering at the thought, she added, "And so would I. He's driving me crazy as it is."

Belle laughed, then she turned serious again. "Thanks, Maggie, but still, I can't thank you enough for staying on and helping like you have. If you hadn't agreed, I don't know what I would have done."

"Hired someone, I expect."

"I'm not sure it would have been as easy as that. You know how particular Dan is, and Lord knows, I don't know anything about horses. It's been difficult enough keeping him in bed now. If he had to worry about a stranger handling the place, I know I couldn't keep him down."

"I can't stay forever, Belle."

"I know. Dan knows it, too. But if you stay just until that mare foals, things will be all right. He's counting so much on that little horse, I know he'd be out in the barn day and night no matter what the doctor ordered."

Maggie had been thinking about that. "I've never seen Dad so anxious about a particular foal, Belle. We've had babies here before and he was never quite so intense."

"Yes, but this one is different."

"Different? Why?"

Belle looked down at the table. She seemed about to say something, then changed her mind. "It just is," she said. "Maybe because it's the last."

Maggie didn't know what to say. She glanced toward the bedroom door. "Maybe Dad shouldn't sell the farm."

"Oh, it's time, Maggie, you know it is. You've said so yourself."

"Yes, I have. But maybe I was wrong."

"Why? You don't want it. You made that clear."

Frowning, Maggie said, "I know. It's just that... well, this place has been home all my life, you know. And when I think that soon it won't be here..."

Belle looked up. "You haven't changed your mind, have you, Maggie?"

"No, no, I haven't changed my mind." Her voice became more brisk. "No, of course not. Why would I change my mind? I've been after Dad to sell this place for years. It'll be the best thing for everyone."

"You don't sound so sure."

"Of course I'm sure. It's silly. I don't know why we're even talking about it."

"I don't, either. You're the one who brought it up."

"Well, I didn't mean to." Restless, she got up. "It's time to get back to work."

Dark clouds were massing overhead when she came out of the house, but she hardly noticed. Still frowning in thought, she crossed the yard and entered the big barn. The first thing she did was check on Never Forget.

Because it was so close to time, she was keeping the mare inside this week, in one of the two foaling stalls built to give restless mothers-to-be plenty of room to move around. On the bigger and more modern farms, a camera would be set up in one corner so the barn manager could monitor the broodmares from the office. The Gallaghers didn't have such luxury; at this farm, she had to do it the old-fashioned way, in person.

Never Forget seemed quiet when Maggie peeked inside at her, and she stood for a moment looking at the mare before she impulsively opened the stall door and went inside. This close to term, the mare was huge and ungainly, and as Maggie gave her a comforting pat, she checked her over to make sure everything was all right. She didn't like the fact that the foal seemed to have changed position, and was now resting sideways, causing the mare to bulge out on both sides, but she'd seen this before and wasn't particularly worried—yet.

"Well, what do you think, sweet?" she murmured, stroking the mare's glossy neck. "Will it be tonight? Come on, you can tell me. I won't tell anybody else, I promise."

But in the time-honored tradition of broodmares who keep such things to themselves, Never Forget just looked placidly at her and moved closer so her ears could be scratched. With a sigh and a last pat, Maggie left the stall. Carefully closing the door behind her, she went on to the myriad other chores she had assigned to herself.

It was late afternoon by the time she finally emerged from the barn again. She'd been so preoccupied that she hadn't noticed the gathering storm, and when she stepped outside, she was surprised to see that it looked almost dark. As she stood there, the wind suddenly came up, and with it, the scent of rain.

"Swell," she muttered. Now she was going to have to run around bringing all the barn horses in from their paddocks. She knew better than to dally; even as she stood there, her father called from inside the house.

"Maggie! You'd better bring in those horses, do you hear me?" Dan shouted from his bed. "It's going to rain to beat the band, and they should be in by now!"

"Keep your shirt on!" she shouted back. "I'm way ahead of you!"

"Don't get cheeky with me, girl," he yelled, "or I'll come out and give you what-for!"

Maggie smiled. She knew Belle was in there to hold him down, and she had heard the smile in his voice. Shaking her head, she grabbed a coat and headed toward the nearest paddock. The high school kid she'd hired to help clean stalls and do other work was peddling in on his bike when she reached the gate, and she stopped to tell him he'd better get on home before the storm broke.

"I'll help you get these horses in before I go," he said, forced to shout a little above the rising wind.

"That's not necessary!" she shouted back. "If you don't go now, you'll get wet!"

"That's okay," he yelled with a grin. "I won't melt!"

Maggie didn't argue; she was glad of the help. As they'd stood there talking about it, the first drops of rain began to fall, and she knew by their size that they were in for a deluge. She was right. By the time she and Yates got all the horses in, the storm had arrived with a vengeance. As they stood in the doorway of the barn catching their breaths, she looked out at the sheets of rain coming down and said, "I'm going to drive you home. You can't ride your bike in this."

"Oh, shoot, I don't want you to bother. You've got that mare to watch and everything."

"She's not going anywhere," Maggie said firmly. "Here's what we'll do—you put your bike in back of the truck while I get the keys and tell Dad and Belle where I'm going. Okay?"

"You're sure? It's so much trouble."

"It's no trouble, not when you've been such a big help to me. Now, go on, scoot."

Scoot? she thought, as she ran toward the house. She hadn't used that expression in years. Either she hadn't really left home at all, or this place was rubbing off on her again. Startled, she realized she didn't mind. Now what did that mean? she wondered, and decided she didn't have time to think about it now. Grabbing the truck's keys from the board near the kitchen door, she shouted to Belle and her father that she'd be back, then she ran out to the truck again. Yates had already wrestled his bike into the back, and moments later, they were off.

It was dark by the time she got home, and, far from showing signs of abating, the storm seemed to have worsened. The yellow gleam of the windows was a welcome sight, and as she parked the truck in its customary spot in the yard, she longed for a hot cup of tea. She'd gotten wet while bringing the horses in and hadn't had time to change; even with the truck heater going full blast, she was feeling chilled.

But before she did anything for herself, she was obliged to check on the mare. She knew it would be the first thing Dan asked when she went back inside, so with a sigh, she decided she might as well get it over with. She was just heading into the barn when she heard a strange noise and she stopped to listen.

It can't be, she thought blankly. *That sounds just like water running.*

Galvanized by the thought, she ran inside, switching on the lights as she went. Her foot hit something sloshy and wet, and she slid to a stop, horrified by the sight of the aisleway awash with water.

At first all she could think was that the roof was leaking. A quick visual check of the beams overhead didn't reveal anything, and she looked down again. Following the stream to its source, she realized that the water was coming from the grain room. Running in that direction, she threw open the door, took one look and groaned.

Water was everywhere, gushing from a broken pipe directly above the grain barrels, flooding the place right before her eyes. Wildly, she looked around for a wrench, a shovel, a tool to stem the flow, but all she could find was a towel, which she hurriedly wrapped around the broken pipe. She might as well have used a tissue. Water immediately started spurting out again, and as she held the soaked cloth with her hands, she tried to think. What was she going to do?

Then she remembered the cut-off valve—at the other end of the barn. Slipping and sliding on the wet floor, she floundered her way out of the grain room and skidded down the aisle. The valve was located an impossible distance above her head; she couldn't reach it even by jumping. She knew she had to do something fast, so she raced down to the tack room, snatched up a footstool and dashed back. The valve resisted her frantic efforts for a moment, then to her relief, it finally turned. But once the water was off, she still had a job to do, and she ran back to the grain room again.

It took another ten minutes to wrestle the heavy grain barrels away to a dry spot on the floor, and by that time, she was in a sweat, covered with dirt and grime, completely soaked. She still had to sweep the water off the floor or everything would grow mold, but when she looked around for a broom, naturally none could be found.

"What else can go wrong?" she moaned as she dashed toward the house to get the kitchen broom.

"Oh, Maggie, I'm glad you're home," Belle said, when Maggie came running in the back door, breathless and disheveled. "I—" She stopped, agog at Maggie's appearance. "What in the world?"

"Shh!" Maggie said desperately. "I don't want Dad to hear!"

"Hear what?" Belle exclaimed, then she dropped her voice. "What is it, Maggie? What's wrong?"

"A pipe burst in the barn, but I'm going to fix it, so everything's all right," she explained hurriedly. "I just need the broom—"

"You're going to fix the pipe with a broom?"

"No, no, I—"

She was interrupted by the ringing of the phone. She was closer than Belle, so she answered it. The instant she heard the voice on the other end, she wished she hadn't.

"Margaret?" Nowell said, sounding puzzled. "Is that you?"

The last person in the world she wanted to talk to right now was Nowell Prescott. "Yes, yes, it's me," Maggie said hurriedly. "Listen, Nowell, I can't talk right now. I have a little—"

Nowell was at his labored best. "Well, really, Margaret," he said, miffed. "The least you could do is say hello. It *has* been more than a week, you know."

"Really?" She felt like laughing hysterically. "Has it been that long, already? I've just been so busy—"

"Margaret, I hate to keep interrupting, but haven't you forgotten something?"

"Forgotten something?" She couldn't imagine what.

He sounded injured. "You promised to be home by now. What, may I ask, are you still doing there?"

She couldn't remember promising to be home by a particular day. "I don't recall—"

"Margaret, I've tried to be as understanding as I can, but really, this is too much. In addition to the fact that I need you at the office, Mother has been waiting to discuss the new wedding plans with us."

"Nowell, I—" She'd been about to say she'd called the office and spoken to the people she'd left in charge of her division. After issuing more orders and reassuring them that she'd be back soon, she'd felt they could take care of things a little longer without her. But Nowell's mention of his mother and the wedding plans alerted her and she tensed. "What do you mean, the *new* wedding plans?"

"Oh, this is most inconvenient. I'd thought we'd be able to discuss this face-to-face."

"I think we'd better discuss it now!"

"All right, if you insist. The thing is, we have a slight addition to the guest list."

Her eyes narrowed. "Perhaps you'd better be more specific."

"Only if you promise you won't be upset."

"Just tell me what we're talking about."

He sighed. "Well, if you must know, Mother has now invited three hundred people—"

For a second, Maggie thought he was joking. "Three hundred?" she repeated. Then she realized that Nowell didn't joke. "Three *hundred!*" she cried. "Is she out of her mind?"

"Well, *really,* Margaret! What a thing to say!"

"That's not *all* I'm going to say! Nowell, if you—"

"It's obvious you're going to be difficult about this, so I might as well tell you that we now have twelve bridesmaids, two flower girls, a ring bearer, and a ten-piece band. Oh, and by the way, she was successful in signing Andre to cater. It was quite a coup, she tells me. I didn't know what to say, myself. I thought you'd be home long before now, and you could deal with it. So, really, Margaret, it's all your fault."

"*My* fault!" She was still reeling from the latest statistics. Princess Diana hadn't had a wedding like this, and the whole world had been invited to hers!

"Yes, if you'd been home where you belonged, this wouldn't have happened. I just hope you're happy, having the time of your life in Kentucky, while I'm trying to deal with this . . . this *travail!*"

"The time of my—" She looked down. Shivering, dirty and cold, she was standing there in muddy boots, her hair clinging to her neck in wet tangles, rain gear dripping all over the floor. In one grubby hand she was holding the broom; in the other, the telephone. Outside, the rain pelted down, she had a flood in the barn and any second her father was going to shout at her and ask if she'd checked on his mare.

"Oh, yes, it's just been one picnic after another!" she shouted. "And you might as well know right now that I couldn't come home even if I wanted to. Never Forget hasn't foaled yet, and I can't leave until she does!"

"Well, really, Margaret!" Nowell exclaimed. "Are you trying to tell me that a . . . a *horse* is more important than our wedding?"

She didn't know what possessed her; it was as though a demon had her by the throat. "Yes!" she cried. "Now, listen, I'm sorry to cut this short, but I've got a few problems of my own right now, and I can't talk anymore."

Hanging up on his outraged sputter, she gripped the broom more tightly and slogged over to the back door. Belle was still there, and she took hold of Maggie's arm. "Is everything all right?"

Nothing in her entire life was right at the moment. "Yes, everything's fine!" she exclaimed. "Just keep Dad out of my hair and—"

At that moment, all the lights went out.

"Oh, no!" Maggie groaned.

From the bedroom, Dan shouted, "What in the hell's going on?"

"I'll take care of Dan," Belle said hurriedly. "You do what you have to, all right?"

Maggie didn't argue. Belle knew where the flashlights were and handed her one. Leaving the other woman to deal with Dan as best she could, Maggie took the light and started out to the barn again. She wouldn't have believed it possible, but the storm seemed to have increased in intensity, and the wind almost knocked her down before she was halfway across the yard.

Gasping, trying to get her hair out of her eyes, she finally made it to the barn door and flung herself inside. The calm warmth was welcome after the driving rain, and she stood there for a moment, panting, trying to get her breath. Remembering that she still hadn't checked the mare, she headed in that direction. The broken pipe would just have to wait until she had lights again; at this moment, the horse was more important.

"Here, girl," she murmured, as she came up to the stall. She didn't want to frighten Never Forget, and she carefully shone the flashlight through the bars. When she couldn't see the horse, she began to panic until the beam picked out the swollen form lying on the straw. In another time-honored tradition, the mare had decided to foal at the most inconvenient, inopportune moment possible.

"Oh, no!" Maggie exclaimed. Jerking open the door, she went in and gave the horse a quick check. The mare's sides were heaving, and when she felt the sweat along the flanks, she was even more alarmed.

Maggie had helped her father foal out a lot of broodmares over the years, and she knew instantly this one was in trouble. She'd been so preoccupied with everything else that she had no idea how long the horse had been down, but if it had been longer than thirty minutes, she needed a vet right away. Carefully getting to her feet, she tiptoed out of the stall and then dashed for the nearest phone, in the office at the other end of the barn.

Like the lights, the line was dead. "Damn it!" she cried. Was nothing going to go right tonight?

Banging the receiver back down in the cradle, she thought quickly. Hoping this was the only phone that had gone out, she raced back to the house again. Rain pelted against her, the wind tried to drive her back, but she flung herself up the porch steps and in through the back door with a gasp. Grabbing the phone by the wall, she put it to her ear, but to her dismay, it was dead, too. All the lines must be down, she thought. What was she going to do now?

Longingly, she looked toward the bedroom. Just for a moment, she was tempted to call Dan. He had forgotten more about horses than she had ever learned, and he would know what to do for the mare. Panicked, she took a step in that direction, then she stopped, biting her lip. She couldn't ask him; he'd get up and do whatever was necessary to help, even if it meant injuring himself again.

"You'll just have to do it yourself," she muttered, trying not to think how afraid she was. The horse meant so much to her father, the foal even more. What if something went wrong? She didn't have any lights, no power, no help. How could she handle it alone?

"Stop it!" she told herself. She was starting to panic again. Before she could think about it, she jerked open the back door and headed back to the barn. She was in the middle of the yard, slipping and sliding in her muddy boots, leaning into the wind, when headlights stabbed the darkness. Startled, she turned around just as Jack came driving up in a truck.

"We're out of power," he said, getting out. "I figured you were, too, and I thought you might need some help."

She was never so glad to see anyone in her entire life. For a weak moment or two, she nearly threw herself into his arms, but there wasn't time. Grabbing his arm instead, she hauled him behind her, explaining things as she went. She was in such a rush that she didn't even think to thank him for coming; it was enough that he was here, offering to help.

"One of the pipes broke in the grain room, but I've turned off the cut-off valve, so it's not an immediate concern," she said hurriedly, holding her wet, blowing hair back from her face. "More important, Never Forget has gone into labor, and the phone lines are down so I can't call the vet. We're going to have to foal her out ourselves, Jack."

She looked up at him, close to panic again. "I think she's in trouble, and I'm not sure what to do. Oh, Jack, if she dies... if we lose the foal...!"

She heard the hysteria in her voice, but she couldn't control it. Jack heard it, too. Calmly, he took her by the shoulders, forcing her to look into his face. The storm howled around them, the rain beat down. The world was dark except for the fragile beam of the flashlight, but she saw the strength in his glance, the absolute assurance in his eyes.

"She won't die," he said quietly. "You won't lose the foal. You know what to do, Maggie—you've done it dozens of times before."

She wanted to believe him, but she couldn't. "But I think this is a breech birth!"

His hands tightened on her shoulders. "It doesn't matter," he said in that same quiet, strong voice. "You know what to do, and you'll do it."

"But what if I can't?"

"You can," he said, with all the confidence in the world. "And you're not alone, Maggie. I'm here to help."

She searched his face a moment longer, trying to gather in the strength he was offering her. Shakily, she said, "I'm glad you're here."

"So am I," he said, and put his arm around her. Then, together, they went into the barn to help foal out her father's prize mare.

CHAPTER EIGHT

NEVER FORGET was on her feet again when Maggie and Jack crept up to the stall, but it was obvious when they shone the flashlight on her that she was restless. Pacing back and forth, she occasionally reached around to nip at one flank or the other—not a good sign, especially with sweat shining along her neck. Clearly, something was wrong, and Maggie bit her lip, trying to think.

"Do you have a lantern?" Jack murmured quietly, so as not to upset the mare any further. "I think we're going to need more light."

She didn't take her eyes off the horse. "There's one in the office, and another in the tack room on the top shelf. Here, you take the flashlight—"

"I know where the office is," Jack said. "I don't need it."

"Yes, but I want you to try the phone in there again," she told him. "The line was dead before, but maybe they've got it working now. We need to call the vet. Her name is Dee Quinlan, and her number's right by the phone."

"Got it," Jack said. Briefly, he touched her arm. "Will you be okay?"

"I'll be fine. Go ahead, I'm going inside the stall."

"Be careful. You know how nasty some mares can get at this time."

She was grateful for his concern, but she didn't need the reminder; she knew all too well the dangers. Sometimes broodmares completely changed personality at foaling time, charging those who were trying to help them, kicking, laying back their ears, baring their teeth even if nothing was outwardly wrong. There was no way to tell which horses would behave this way; Maggie had seen some of the quietest, sweetest mares turn into hellions in the blink of an eye.

Sometimes this aberrant behavior ceased as soon as the foal was born; sometimes it didn't. Although it was rare, there were mares who had to be physically restrained to prevent them from kicking their foals to death, or tied up so that the baby could nurse. Usually such problems resolved themselves in a few days, but with everything else going on tonight, Maggie hoped that was one more thing she wouldn't have to deal with.

Murmuring soothing sounds, she slowly opened the stall door as Jack disappeared into the darkness, then she slipped inside. The mare was so anxious that she didn't even notice someone had come in with her; she continued to pace, stopping to paw the trampled straw before she tried to lie down—only to change her mind and get up to start the restless process once more.

Maggie watched worriedly, reluctant to interfere unless it was necessary. As uncomfortable—and incredible—as it sounded, she knew that some mares foaled standing up, but she hoped this one wasn't one of them. Usually nothing happened to a foal born that way, but Never Forget's baby meant so much to Dan that Maggie didn't want to take any chances. Catching a newborn one-hundred pound foal in midair was no easy task, although she'd done that in the past, too.

But with the lights out, the storm still raging and the mare clearly in distress, she didn't want to do it tonight.

"Easy girl, easy," she murmured as she cautiously approached the horse. She could barely see the big shape in the darkness, but she knew where the mare was by the sound of her breathing. She'd brought a halter with her, and she quietly slipped it on the animal, buckling it blind from years of experience. She felt better once she had Never Forget under control; now there was nothing to do but wait. She couldn't make the mare lie down, but it didn't matter. Even if Dee were here, she doubted that the veterinarian would give the restless mother-to-be anything to calm her. A tranquilizer might interfere with the birthing process, and that was the last thing they needed.

Maggie was standing beside Never Forget, trying to soothe her with words and the touch of her hand, when the comforting glow of light pierced the darkness. Jack had found the lanterns, and he brought them both, along with an armful of other equipment. She looked at him hopefully as he came up to the stall, but he shook his head.

"The lines are still down," he said, slowly lifting the lantern so the light would flood into the stall without scaring the horse. "How's she doing?"

"She's restless. If you'll hold her, I'll go down to the tack room and get the stethoscope to check—"

He held it up. "I brought it. I knew you might need it, along with a tail wrap and a blanket from the tack room. Oh, and some palpating gloves I found. Do you need anything else?"

"A vet," she said, reaching out to take the items from him when, one eye on the restless mare, he carefully came into the stall.

The gloves she shoved into her pocket; they were sterile plastic mitts that reached all the way to the shoulder, used in emergencies for a physical check of the mare's genital tract. Hoping she wouldn't have to use them, she busied herself with the stethoscope while Jack set the two battery-powered lanterns down, one at each end of the stall, so they had some light.

As she listened to the mare's increasing heart rate with a sinking heart of her own, she glanced at Jack. He had gone around to the back of the mare and without being told, was wrapping the tail. He looked competent and confident, as though he'd done it a million times, and as Maggie watched him, she felt something more than gratitude that he was here. With him beside her, things didn't seem so bad, and just watching the way he worked, his hands sure and steady, made her feel that as long as they were together, nothing could really go wrong. Disturbed by the feeling, she straightened and took the stethoscope from her ears.

Jack's eyes met hers over the mare's back. "How is it?"

She shook her head. "It doesn't look good, Jack. Maybe I'd better warn Dad."

"Can't we wait a—" he started to say, but just then the mare went down. Folding her legs under her, she collapsed with a heavy grunt, stretching her head and neck out. A contraction, like the ripple of a violent ocean wave rolled down the length of her side, and her legs stiffened like posts as she strained.

For better or worse, Maggie knew the time had come. There wasn't time for niceties; she immediately took charge. Grabbing the blanket, she said, "Hold her head, Jack. I don't want her to get up again."

The next few minutes were the most harrowing of Maggie's life. Again and again, she blessed Jack's strength; if he hadn't been there to help, she didn't know what she would have done. The mare labored and strained, but without result: the foal was caught in the birth canal and couldn't be born. Maggie watched in tense silence for as long as she could, but when it became obvious that Never Forget needed help, she took a deep breath, removed her coat and put the palpating gloves on.

To his credit, Jack didn't offer to take over. They both knew she was more experienced in these matters than he was, and she was grateful when all he said was a quiet, "What can I do?"

"Just make sure she doesn't get up," Maggie said, getting to work before she lost courage.

Kneeling behind the mare, her position was awkward, and despite the chill from the storm, sweat began to soak her hair and run down her cheeks in rivulets. With her arm buried almost to the shoulder as she tried to feel what was wrong, she had to trust Jack to hold the mare's powerful hindquarters; one kick and the horse could kill her.

"The head's turned backward..." she panted after an endless few seconds. Her seeking hand found the foal's front legs, then the neck, following the curve upward to where the head should have been. "I'm going to try to turn it."

The birth canal was only so big, and there wasn't much maneuvering room. By some miracle, she got her fingers on the foal's nose, and with a feat of strength that would have astounded her if she'd had time to think about it, she managed to move the head a little.

Inch by inch, while the mare grunted and thrashed, Maggie forced herself to pull slowly and steadily. When the head caught again, she nearly burst into tears; every muscle in her body was screaming from the effort, but she couldn't let go, not now, when they were so close. Finally, she managed to bring the head around to the proper position.

"I think I got it," she panted. Slowly pulling her arm out, she waited tensely for Never Forget to do her part. When, interminable seconds later, one of the foal's forefeet emerged, followed by the other, she would have cheered if she'd had the breath. Then the nose appeared, right where it should be, and with a final massive contraction, the mare expelled the rest of the baby, and it fell, right into Maggie's lap.

The foal was covered by the protective sack, a whitish, opalescent membrane that Maggie immediately ripped away so it could breathe. Quickly, she checked, then looked up at Jack with shining eyes. "It's a colt!"

The umbilical cord was still attached, but she left it alone; rich, antibody-laden blood was still flowing from the mother to the foal, and the cord would stay in place until the mare stood and broke it herself.

That was, if the mare stood. Now that she knew the baby was all right, Maggie quickly looked to the mother. Never Forget hadn't moved since giving birth, not even to lift her head. For a terrifying instant, Maggie thought she was dead.

"Jack!" she cried, panicked.

He already had the stethoscope in his ears, checking the mare's heart rate. Maggie waited an endless moment, her own heart in her throat, until he nodded. She felt almost weak with relief.

"I think she's all right. Do you want to listen?"

But before she could reach for the stethoscope, Never Forget lifted her head, then sat up. Exhausted from her ordeal, she folded her legs under her, looked around to where her baby was lying on the straw and whinnied softly. Maggie glanced at Jack.

"Let's move out of the way," she whispered.

Nodding, he reached for her hand and pulled her to her feet. Together, they tiptoed over to one side of the stall just as, with a mighty heave, Never Forget stood up. The umbilical cord broke when she did, and as though that were a signal, the foal tried to stand, as well. His coat was still wet from birth, his long, spindly legs looking too wobbly to hold him up. But after a few false starts, he managed to get all four tiny feet under him—for a grand total of five seconds. He was just whinnying shrilly in triumph when he lost his balance, took two steps forward, four back, and promptly fell down on his rump. He looked so indignant and embarrassed and startled that Maggie laughed.

Jack laughed, too. "Welcome to the world, little fellow," he said. Looking down at the ecstatic Maggie, he put his arm gently around her. "And congratulations," he added admiringly. "You were wonderful."

Feelings of relief and exhilaration sweeping through her, Maggie looked up at him. Her hair was still wet at the temples from both rain and sweat; she had a streak of dirt across one cheek. But her eyes were aglow and her face was flushed a vibrant pink, and to Jack, she had never looked more beautiful.

"Thanks," she said. "But I had help. If you hadn't been here, I don't know what I would have done."

He couldn't seem to look away from her face. "Exactly what you did, I think."

"No, I—" she started to say, then stopped. "Are we going to argue about this like we do about everything else? I'm trying to give you a compliment!"

He didn't know what made him say it, but the words were out before he thought. "I'd rather have something else."

"What's that?"

"This...." Before Maggie could react, he bent down and kissed her.

The second his mouth touched hers, she realized she'd never been kissed like this. Or maybe, she thought dazedly, she'd just never felt this way during a kiss. When she felt the warmth of his lips, it was as though something blossomed inside her. A thrill raced through her all the way from her head to her toes, and without realizing it, she raised her arms and put them around his neck.

How well they fit together! she thought distantly. Even through the bulk of their outdoor clothes, she had the fleeting thought that it was as though their bodies had been made for each other. For an instant, she could feel him trembling as he held her, but then reaction overtook her, too. Her legs would hardly support her, and she clung to him tightly, pressing against him, yearning to feel completely enclosed. He smelled like rain and clean sweat and another scent that was indefinably his own, and when she opened her mouth and their tongues met, it was as though fireworks exploded.

Then, from some depth of sense, she realized what she was doing, and she jerked away, appalled. "I'm sorry," she gasped. "I shouldn't have done that!"

He looked just as dazzled as she felt. For a moment, he didn't say anything, but shook his head as if to clear it. "No, it was my fault," he said. Obviously trying to get himself together, he muttered, "What the hell happened?"

She wanted to say that nothing had happened, but she couldn't form the words. Something *had* happened, and she didn't want to think about it, maybe not ever. How could she have done such a thing? she asked herself in a panic. She was engaged to be married; she was supposed to love another man!

Confused and upset, she reached for the stall door. She knew she had to get away from him before she did something even more rash. The taste of him was on her lips; her legs were still trembling from the effect of his kiss. She was horrified at herself, and yet...

And yet, she didn't want to leave him. Incredibly, she wanted to be back in his arms, wanted to feel his body against her, his thighs on hers, his chest crushing her breasts. Oh, how she longed to be in his strong embrace! When his arms had gone around her just a few moments ago, she'd felt as though nothing could hurt her, that he would protect her from all the evils in the world, that everything—no matter what—would be all right.

Such thoughts shocked her even more. How could she think these things about Jack, when it was Nowell she loved, Nowell upon whom she depended?

She hardly knew what she was saying when she said, "I...I think I'll see if the phone lines are fixed yet."

"Wait!" Jack said, as she turned to go. Running his hand through his hair, he started to take a step toward her, then stood still. "I'm sorry, Maggie," he said, looking miserable. "I know I shouldn't have done that. You're going to be married...I had no right."

She took a shaky breath. "It was my fault, Jack. I shouldn't have...put us in the position where something like that could happen. I'm the one who's sorry."

"Maggie—"

She didn't trust herself to talk about it anymore; already she couldn't bear the look on his face, the pain in his eyes. "Don't, Jack. Please."

"You're right. It wouldn't serve any purpose, would it? You...you go ahead and I'll stay here with the horses." He glanced at the foal, who had been up to nurse and who was looking for a place to lie down. "He's a fine little fellow, isn't he?" Jack said softly.

"Yes, he is," she said, watching the foal herself because she didn't want to look at Jack. Tired out, the baby had plopped down on the straw and was instantly asleep. His coat had dried, and she could see that he was going to be the same beautiful blood-bay color as his dam, except that he had a star marking on his forehead, followed by a small blaze and a snip. When the colt sighed in his sleep, she couldn't help but smile. Being born was hard work, and he'd had a tougher time than most.

Her smile faded as she remembered the thrill she'd felt when the colt was born, her feelings of joy and satisfaction at helping to bring him into the world. She couldn't deny that it had been one of the most gratifying moments of her life.

Involuntarily, her glance went again to Jack, who was still gazing at the sleeping foal. She couldn't imagine Nowell doing what Jack had done tonight, she thought, not for a minute. Nowell wouldn't have knelt on this trampled straw; he wouldn't have put himself in danger, or gotten himself dirty, or taken orders from her, as Jack had done. He wouldn't have done any of it, she realized, even if they'd shared a common goal.

Immediately, she became impatient with herself. Why should she expect Nowell to do any of the things Jack had done tonight? she asked herself. Nowell didn't know anything about horses, and he didn't care to learn. And why should he? Hadn't she herself declared long ago that horses were a part of her past she'd left behind? Why was she comparing him to Jack at all? The two men were as different as silk and steel, and a comparison wasn't fair to either of them.

It didn't matter anyway, she thought. She had the life she wanted; she'd worked hard toward her goal all these years. She wouldn't be back here now, if Aunt Tilda hadn't called her. This wasn't the kind of life she wanted, not at all, ever.

But it wouldn't be like that with Jack, an insidious voice inside her whispered.

Jack had money. And that's what it took, she thought with sudden bitterness: money. All the good will, all the best intentions, all the love of horses in the world didn't matter if that one essential ingredient was missing. Wasn't her father the perfect example of that?

Reminded of her father, she looked quickly at Jack. "I guess I'd better go and tell Dad about the new arrival," she said.

He glanced up. "Yes, I guess you'd better."

She didn't know why, but she started to say, "Jack, I wish—"

Just then, the lights came on. In the sudden glare, they both blinked, then Jack smiled briefly.

"Saved by the bell," he said. "Or in this case, the electricity. You don't have to say anything, Maggie. Let's just chalk it up to... the excitement of the moment."

They gazed at each other for a few awkward seconds, then she said, "Yes, I guess you're right."

"And I guess I'd better be going."

She had wanted to put some distance between them, but now suddenly, she didn't want him to go. "Why don't you come in with me to tell Dad? After all, you were part of this, too."

He shook his head. "No, I think this is a family moment. I know how eager Dan has been about this foal, and I think he'd rather hear it from you."

"But—"

They were standing by the stall door, and he touched her cheek briefly, a sad look on his face. She wanted to take his hand and press it to her lips, but she didn't dare. Heaven knew what that could lead to, and she felt so precarious emotionally that she didn't trust herself even to move. Her reaction to Jack, to that kiss, even to the horses here and the birth of this foal, made her feel so confused she didn't know what to do.

"Good-bye, Maggie."

"Good-bye?" she repeated unsteadily. "Don't you mean good-night?"

He gazed at her a moment longer, then he bent and kissed her cheek. "No, I think this is good-bye," he said, when he straightened. Even in the light, his eyes looked very dark.

"But Jack—"

He shook his head. "It's better this way, Maggie," he said quietly. "As you said yourself, you've got your life, and I've got mine. Our paths just don't...cross. Now that Never Forget has foaled, there's no real reason for you to stay on, and I know you're anxious to get back to New York...where you belong. That's what you said, isn't it?"

It was, but when he looked at her like that, she couldn't remember why she'd said it. Swallowing hard, she said, "Yes, I guess you're right." Then, like a fool, she held out her hand. "Thanks for all your help, Jack. I know Dad will tell you himself—he'll be as grateful as I am that you were here tonight."

Looking as though he wanted to push her hand away and hold her to him—a move she was desperately wishing he'd make—Jack briefly took her fingers in his.

"Good luck, Maggie. I wish you all the best."

When he turned and left, she waited until she heard his truck start. Until she heard him drive away, she hoped that he would come back and tell her—tell her what? That he loved her? That he couldn't live without her? That he didn't want her to marry Nowell Prescott and live a sterile, socially correct life in New York?

Close to tears, she checked on Never Forget and her foal for the last time, collecting all the paraphernalia they'd used and stowing it away. Then, her steps dragging when she should have been dancing in the aisles, she went into the house.

BELLE WAS in the kitchen, standing at the stove making a pan of hot chocolate, when Maggie came in. She took one look at Maggie's face and dropped the spoon. "Oh, no! Don't—"

"No, no, everything's all right," Maggie said quickly. Taking off her coat, she forced herself to forget about Jack and tried to smile. "Dad's got a foal," she said. "A colt."

Placing a hand over her chest, Belle closed her eyes briefly. "Thank heaven," she said. "When you came in, I thought..." Her eyes searched Maggie's face. "How about you? Are *you* all right?"

"I'm okay," she lied, sinking down into one of the kitchen chairs. She hadn't realized until now just how exhausted she was. "I'm just tired, I think. For a while, it didn't look good. But don't tell Dad, all right?" she added anxiously. "I don't want to worry him, especially since everything turned out fine."

"No, I won't tell him," Belle agreed. Worriedly, she came over to where Maggie sat. "Are you sure you're all right, Maggie? You didn't have a fight with Jack, did you?"

"With Jack? No, no, of course not," she said, wishing Belle didn't look so sympathetic. It made her want to burst into tears and sob out the whole story. "In fact, he was a big help. I don't know what I would have done without him tonight."

"I don't, either, to tell the truth. I was so relieved when I saw him drive in. Until then, I thought for sure I was going to have to tie Dan to the bed. With the lights out and all, he was frantic until I told him Jack was here to help."

"I was a little upset myself," Maggie admitted, pushing herself up from the table. "Well, shall we go tell him about the newest member of Gallagher Farm?"

Belle smiled. "After you, my dear. You're the heroine of the hour."

"Not me," Maggie said fervently. "For that honor, my vote goes to Never Forget."

Naturally, as soon as he heard about the colt, Dan insisted on getting up, getting dressed, and hobbling out to the barn. The women knew they couldn't stop him, so they didn't even try. But they did each hold on to an arm on the way, so he wouldn't stumble and hurt his back again.

"Let go of me, damn it!" Dan grumbled, trying to shake them off. "You're like limpets, I swear. A man can walk by himself!"

"Now, stop your moaning and groaning, Dan Gallagher," Belle threatened, "or we'll just go right back to the house."

Dan appealed to his daughter. "You wouldn't let her do that to me, would you now, Maggie?"

"I certainly would," Maggie answered firmly from his other side. "Now, stop it, Dad, we're almost there."

But once in the doorway of the barn, Dan paused himself. When they looked at him in surprise, he laughed self-consciously. "You won't believe it, but I'm nervous," he said. "I've been waiting for eleven months on pins and needles for this foal to get here, and now that he has, I'm almost afraid to look." Anxiously, he looked at Maggie. "Is he good, Maggie? Really good, I mean? Was he worth the wait? Tell me the truth now. I can take it, I swear!"

Maggie laughed. Gently tugging him forward, she said, "Why don't you see for yourself?"

The foal was still sleeping when they approached the stall, but he must have sensed someone was there, for he opened his eyes and looked up. Seconds later, he was on his feet—slightly more stable than he had been the first time, but still unsteady as he wobbled over to see who the new arrivals were.

Dan had forgotten his earlier nervousness. "Look at that chest!" he proclaimed proudly. "Look at the slope of the shoulder! Look at those straight legs, and those hocks!"

"Look at his color," Belle murmured admiringly. "He looks just like his mother, that lovely black-red, just like cherries. Isn't he beautiful!"

"Who cares about his color?" Dan exclaimed. "Why, from the length of those cannon bones, he'll be seventeen hands, easy, probably more, don't you think, Maggie?"

"Well, Dad, seventeen hands is pretty big—"

"Not for this fellow!" Dan boasted. "With those bones? He'll hit that before he's a yearling."

Maggie laughed. "I hope not."

"I do!" Dan declared. "Take a look yourself, Maggie! I'll bet his stride will be twenty-five feet, if an inch!"

"Another Secretariat, right?"

"He is beautiful," Belle said, giggling when the colt put his tiny muzzle up to the bars. Hesitantly, she reached through and touched the baby's silky nose, giggling again when he tried to get her fingers in his mouth to suck.

"Better watch that when he gets teeth," Maggie warned. But she, too, smiled at the sight. Glancing over at her father, who had lapsed into silence, she said teasingly, "Well, what do you think, Dad?"

She had expected him to rhapsodize, to start running on excitedly again about the colt's good qualities, real and imagined. What she hadn't expected to see were the tears in his eyes. His voice cracking, he said, "I think that he's the best thing we've ever produced at Gallagher Farm."

Moved herself, Maggie kissed his cheek. "I think so, too, Dad. Congratulations."

Embarrassed by his show of emotion, Dan dashed a quick hand across his eyes as he turned to look at the foal again. "He'll be a great runner, just like I planned," he whispered. "Oh, yes, this colt will bring glory to Gallagher Farm, you mark my words!"

Dismayed at what he'd said, Maggie looked across at Belle, who just shook her head. Realizing it was up to her, Maggie said, "Dad, pretty soon there won't *be* a Gallagher Farm, remember? You've got it up for sale." She paused. "Or have you changed your mind?"

"Changed my mind?" he repeated, giving her a quick glance. "No, no, of course not. It was just that I... I lost my head for a minute. It must be the excitement, I guess."

Maggie knew that wasn't all there was to it, and she felt uneasy as she looked from the colt to Dan again. He was gazing at the horses with a sad expression. Suddenly what should have been a night of triumph had lost its glow, and it was all her fault. Why had she felt so compelled to inject a sobering note of reality? Because she was tired of Dan's dreams, of his hopes . . . and failures? Or was it because she thought she'd had hers all figured out, and suddenly wondered if she was the one who was wrong?

Deciding she didn't want to pursue that line of thought, she said, "I think we should break out the champagne, Dad. What do you think?"

He turned slowly away from the stall. "I think I'd better get back to bed."

At once, Belle was concerned. "Are you all right, Dan?"

"I'm fine, just fine, woman," he said gruffly, and looked at Maggie. "By the way, where's Jack? Why didn't he stay around?"

Maggie couldn't meet his eyes. "I . . . uh . . . he had to go back and check things at home," she said lamely. "But he wanted me to congratulate you, too."

"I see," Dan said, clearly unconvinced. "Well. You'd better call the vet."

"I will, once the phone is working." Anticipating him, she added as he opened his mouth, "Don't worry, I put iodine on the colt's umbilical cord."

Not to be outdone, he demanded, "Did you make sure he got the colostrum?"

The colostrum was the first milk from the mother, the nutrient and antibody-rich first meal that set the tone for the foal's future health. "I did," she said. "Anything else, Your Majesty?"

"As a matter of fact, there is," he said. "When you get through with the vet, you'd better call a plumber. That rag you used for the pipe isn't much better than a bandage."

She didn't know how he had noticed, but then, it didn't surprise her. He always saw everything, even the smallest detail. "Yes, Dad," she said meekly. "I'll get on it right away."

When they came out of the barn, the air smelled clean and sweet, and high in the night sky, the stars twinkled through the last of the clouds scudding by. After hours of howling, the wind had died down to a gentle whisper, and they stopped for a moment to enjoy the quiet.

"Looks like the storm finally passed," Belle commented.

"Thank heaven," Maggie said, looking up. But uneasy again, she couldn't ignore the feeling that this storm was only a prelude to the one she could feel already stirring inside her.

CHAPTER NINE

I'D ADVISE YOU TO WEAR your armor, boy. Women like her eat guys like you for breakfast.

Floyd's warning echoed in Jack's mind as he dressed for the Kentucky Horse Breeders' fund-raiser. Frowning as he fitted the gold studs into his white shirt, he wondered if he'd made a mistake when he'd agreed to take Lilah Castlemaine to the event tonight. It wasn't that he was worried about handling Lilah; at the moment what really concerned him was what might happen if Maggie found out.

Then he sneered at himself. What made him think Maggie would even care? Now that Never Forget's foal was here, she would be leaving soon for New York again, to take up her interrupted life... to get married. He was a fool to think that the passionate kiss they'd shared changed anything; she'd made it perfectly clear that she regarded it as a mistake. A *big* mistake.

Even so, every time he thought of last night in the barn with Maggie in his arms, he felt an answering ache in his loins. Even with her hair plastered to her face and her cheek smeared with dirt, she was so beautiful that she'd taken his breath away. It had been all he could do not to pull her down with him on the straw and make love to her right there; if circumstances had been different, he might have done just that.

But then he had watched her, struggling in the lamplight to help the mare give birth, putting herself in danger so that the foal could be born, and he'd been so filled with admiration that he thought he'd burst. *Valor,* he thought. *Courage.* That's what she had. She'd been afraid—terrified, but she'd gone ahead and done what she needed to do no matter what she'd felt. He didn't know any other woman who would have been so brave or fearless. Especially not the woman he was with tonight, he thought abruptly. Lilah Castlemaine was no Maggie Gallagher and already he was regretting having agreed to the fund-raiser. He'd thought it was a good idea at the time, and some part of him knew it still was. He might not like Lilah, but through her he could meet many of the top people in racing.

But tonight, racing seemed far from his mind. As he shrugged into his black coat, all he could think about was Maggie. If only he had more time, he thought, and then shook his head. *Time* wasn't the problem; it never had been.

"Don't think about it," he muttered. But as he went out to his car—a racy, late-model Porsche painted the color of champagne—he still wished it was Maggie he was taking out tonight and not Lilah. With another heavy sigh, he got in the car and headed out the driveway to do his duty.

Lilah was staying with "Daddy" while she was in town, and as Jack headed toward the Castlemaine farm, coyly named CastleKeep, he found himself thinking about the past. Years ago when he and his family worked for Leo, it was his job to go up to the back door of the house for instructions about what the boss wanted done in his fields. Needless to say, given his lowly position, he'd never been invited into the house proper, but the back entrance was imposing itself, with a big service porch and an even larger kitchen beyond. He still remembered the single glimpse he'd had of the mammoth pantry in that house; its contents alone could have fed his family for a year, if not more.

He'd always felt like a servant going up to the "big house" as it was called; the only thing that made it bearable was the cook the family had at the time, a big, handsome black woman called Delia, who always had a treat for him. When he thought of her tonight, he smiled. He couldn't remember a time he'd gone away empty-handed after seeing Delia; she'd always press some fresh-baked delicacy on him no matter what he said.

"Now, you just take this, Jack," she'd say, giving him half of a pie, or a dozen cookies in a napkin. "You work hard, and you deserve it."

His mouth already watering, he'd protest half-heartedly, "I can't eat all this!"

"Yes, you can," she'd answer comfortably. "I know boys, and you're all hollow from stem to stern. Go on now, just don't eat it so fast you make yourself sick."

"I'd never get sick on your cooking," he'd say fervently.

She'd laugh, pushing him out the door. "Go on, now, you old flatterer you! And just in case you're interested, come Thursday, I'm makin' burgoo."

Burgoo was the Kentucky state dish. Delia had told him in detail that it was made from chicken, beef, veal, onions, celery, carrots, turnips, tomatoes, okra, potatoes, cabbage, butter, black pepper, corn and claret. And something else "special," Delia would add with a twinkle in her eye. She took pride in her stew.

Smiling at the memory and wondering what had ever happened to Delia, Jack turned off the road the locals called "Millionaire's Mile," and headed toward CastleKeep. It wasn't hard to find: perched on top of a hill, it was so brightly lit that it outshone everything else for miles around. When he was young, it had seemed so big, so rich and elegant, dominating all the other farms by sheer size. But as he drove up the long, curving driveway tonight, he stared at the house and wondered why he'd felt such awe.

He couldn't deny that the place was imposing, but in an area of equally glamorous homes, CastleKeep seemed gaudy, and too self-consciously pretentious. It might be the biggest house around, but he much preferred his own understated home—or even Dan Gallagher's comfortable farm.

Trying to brace himself for what he was sure was going to be a difficult night, he drove up to the front door, where the illumination was so bright that night almost turned into day. Floodlights spilled out across the carefully manicured lawns, capturing the topiary in their beams, and inside the house every single window was ablaze. In an era of growing concern about conservation, it was an appalling waste.

Deciding it didn't matter where he parked, since there was space under the portico for at least twenty cars, Jack pulled the Porsche to one side and got out. As he did, he caught a glimpse of Lilah's red Ferrari parked carelessly nearby. The car's front wheels had jumped the curb and were lodged squarely in an exquisite flower bed, crushing everything underneath. Shaking his head at the sight, he climbed the wide marble steps to the towering double front doors. Wishing the evening were over, he rang the doorbell.

A hollow, reverberating *gong!* sounded; seconds later, the door was opened by a man who was obviously the butler. Dressed in a gray suit with white shirt and gray tie, the man looked down his nose at Jack. Some things never change, Jack thought. "Good evening," he said. "Jack Stanton to see Lilah Castlemaine."

"Yes, you're expected, Mr. Stanton," said the man, bowing stiffly. "If you'll wait in the front room—" he gestured "—I'll have someone inform Miss Castlemaine that you're here."

"That won't be necessary, Albert," Lilah said, from the top of the stairs.

At the sound of her voice, both men looked in that direction, and Jack saw the grand staircase for the first time. Under the sparkling light from the Baccarat chandelier high overhead, the staircase was an awesome sight, sweeping up to the second floor in a graceful arch, forty feet wide at the bottom, only slightly narrower at the top. The carved and polished banister was a work of art, an intricate design of flowers and leaves and vines, and if he wasn't mistaken the stair runner had to be pure Aubusson. Where the carpet didn't cover, the polished oak underneath gleamed like silk.

But even in the midst of such grandeur, it was Lilah who was the star. Posing at the top of the stairs, she was a vision in red tulle and sequins. Her long gown fit like her own skin, a strapless affair that was made for an hourglass figure. Instead of sleeves, on either arm was a froth of crimson net; to complete the ensemble, she was wearing a matching pair of high heels that thrust her forward even more. Her more-than-generous breasts looked ready to pop right out of her tight bodice, and at the sight, Jack realized he was staring.

Lilah knew exactly the effect she was creating. "Good evening, Jack," she said. Rolling her hips from side to side, she sashayed down the stairs. When she finally reached the place where he was standing, mesmerized in spite of himself, she raised herself up on tiptoe—breasts straining against the fabric—and gave him a quick kiss.

The kiss broke the spell. "Good evening," he said, trying not to be obvious about backing away. Remembering his manners, he added, "You look lovely tonight."

"Why, thank you, Jack," she purred. "It's so nice when a man notices the effort a woman puts into her appearance."

He'd moved a step away, but she came toward him again on a cloud of musky perfume, her long, blond hair done up in some complicated arrangement atop her head, a few tendrils strategically placed around her temples and on her neck. Placing her hand on his arm, she drawled huskily, "I'm sorry Albert was a bore. I told him I'd be right down. I do believe I'm just going to have to ask Daddy to speak to that man."

"Don't bother on my account," Jack said. He'd been so preoccupied with Lilah's stage entrance that he hadn't even noticed the butler disappearing. Regretting this evening more with each second, he offered his arm. "Shall we go?"

Lilah gave him a feline smile. "Oh, we must go in and say goodbye to Daddy before we go, Jack, darling. When I told him who was taking me to the fund-raiser tonight, he was so surprised. 'Jack Stanton?' he said. 'That boy who used to work for me?' "

When Jack saw the malicious glint in her eyes, he was thrown for a moment into the past. Lilah had always had a way of cutting to the quick; he remembered their school days when she would deliberately say something to remind him of their different stations in life. She'd turned even more spiteful after he had rejected a couple of blatant passes she'd made. He hadn't had the time or interest to become part of her crowd, but from that time until they graduated, it had been war on her part.

He'd thought those days were over, a part of the past that had been, or should be, forgotten. Now, seeing the look in her hard eyes, he wondered.

Then he dismissed it. Lilah hadn't been able to hurt him then, and she couldn't now. "I doubt that your father is interested in discussing old times," he said mildly. "But of course I'll go in and say hello. It's been a while."

Another flash from her eyes. "Yes, it has. In fact—"

But just then Leo Castlemaine himself appeared. Puffing on a giant cigar, the master of the house emerged from what Jack judged to be the library. Dressed also in black tie, Leo stopped when he saw them standing in the entryway.

Jack saw right away that one thing Leo Castlemaine had done since he'd last seen him was grow older. He'd always been a big man, but the extra poundage he'd added in the time Jack had been gone made him even bulkier. The fact that he was almost completely bald now added to the impression of a fat, waddling pasha, but as Leo started toward them, Jack saw that his eyes hadn't changed. Light blue, like ice, they were as cold and calculating as they'd always been. He looked exactly what he was, a powerful, ruthless man who didn't give a damn about anyone but himself.

And perhaps his daughter, Jack amended, as Lilah immediately ran toward Leo, her stiletto heels sounding like miniature machine-gun fire on the black-and-white tiles of the huge entry.

"Daddy!" she exclaimed. "We were just going to come looking for you!"

To Jack's surprise, Lilah gave her father a kiss full on the lips. Despite looking pleased at the gesture, Leo immediately blustered, "Here now, here now, Lilah! You'll get lipstick all over me!"

Laughing gaily, she spun around for his inspection. "What do you think, Daddy? Do you like it? You should. It's a new Bob Mackie, and it cost you a fortune."

"Very nice," Leo said, giving her an admiring and appreciative once-over. "But why am I paying for yet another trinket of yours when you've got a fleet of ex-husbands who should be supportin' you?"

"Oh, Daddy, you know you're the only man in my life!"

"Hmmph," Leo growled. He glanced under bushy eyebrows at Jack, who so far hadn't spoken. "Is this the young man you were telling me about?"

Pouting slightly, Lilah turned toward Jack and motioned him forward. "Hello, Leo," Jack said, deliberately putting them on a first-name basis as he held out his hand. "It's been a long time."

Leo squinted, taking Jack's measure for a moment before he returned the handshake. "I hear you bought the old Tidleman place," he said. He shook his head ruefully, as though Jack had been a fool and he didn't want to tell him. "Bad piece of land, there. That's why it sat for so many years."

"Oh, I don't know," Jack said easily. "I've already found two artesian wells, so irrigation won't be a problem. And I've relocated the barns to take advantage of the summer breeze, and still have protection from the wind in winter."

Leo squinted again. "Ain't much good without horses."

"That's true. But now that the place is more or less workable, I'll be looking for stock."

Lilah had been ignored long enough. Putting a hand on her father's arm, she said sulkily, "Now, Daddy, let's not get started talking about horses, or we'll be here all night. You and Jack can discuss all that boring old stuff like bloodlines and racing times when we get to the fund-raiser."

Instantly diverted, Leo smiled at his daughter. "All right, little girl," he said fondly, patting the hand of his thirty-five-year-old daughter. "You go ahead now. I'll see you there."

Reaching up, Lilah gave him another kiss. "Don't forget," she murmured. "Jack and I are going to a late supper."

Leo looked significantly at Jack. "Don't you keep my little girl out too late, hear?"

Thinking that wasn't going to be a problem, Jack nodded. "Don't worry, Leo. I'll take good care of her."

"You'll be the first, then."

"Oh, Daddy," Lilah said, but she fluttered her eyelashes at him before she took Jack's arm. "Shall we go, darlin'?"

THE FUND-RAISER WAS being held at one of the new all-glass tower buildings in downtown Lexington. Expensive cars filled the parking lot behind the tower when Jack and Lilah arrived; more could be seen lining the narrow street in front.

"It looks like you have a good turnout tonight," Jack commented as he helped Lilah from the car.

"Oh, yes," she said carelessly. "Everybody knows the media will be here, and they're hoping to see their pictures in the society pages tomorrow morning. Still, it should be vaguely entertaining. I hear old Annabelle Sheffield of Finish Line Farm is going to be here." Her voice turned mocking. "The grand old dame of racing, they call her. Hmmph! My daddy could teach her a thing or two."

Jack refused comment. Like everyone else involved in the sport, he was well acquainted with the Sheffield name and reputation. The Sheffields had been in racing until Annabelle's husband, Grover, had died the year before. Their Finish Line Farm had produced more stakes winners in the past decade than any other breeding establishment in the country had, and together the couple had won three Eclipse awards as the nation's leading owners.

But Annabelle had lost heart after her beloved husband died, and the sporting community had been shocked earlier this year when she had suddenly announced that she was selling all the stock and getting out of Thoroughbred racing forever. A special sale was being held at Keeneland a week hence. Jack had received the catalog and intended to go. More than a hundred horses were going on the block, and among them were three of the best mares and fillies in the country. He wanted to bring home at least two of them, if not all three.

"Was your father surprised when Mrs. Sheffield announced she was getting out of racing?" Jack asked Lilah as they started inside.

"Daddy surprised?" Lilah repeated with a toss of her head. "No, he just said it was about time. The woman is older than God, you know. Even before old Grover died, she had health problems, and they both should have retired about a century ago."

"If they had, we wouldn't have had some of the best distaff racers in the country."

Lilah looked at him impatiently. "There's not a filly in the world can match a colt."

"Obviously not true. One of their fillies, Blazing Glory, won the Derby five years ago, and another horse of theirs, Eternal Rhythm—"

Lilah interrupted him with a toss of her head. "Everyone agrees it was an off year," she said flatly. "Why, my Daddy's Farington could have outrun her hobbled, so there!"

Jack gave up. Taking Lilah's arm, he ushered her inside.

The room where the fund-raiser was being held was ablaze with light when they walked in. Along the walls someone had pinned banners of racing colors from the various farms, but the bright silks couldn't compete with the glittering dresses of sequins and beads. The women stood out like peacocks among the more somberly dressed men in their black and white, jewels sparkling in their ears and on their fingers, wrists and throats.

Jack had never seen so many rare gems. Diamonds shot sparks; emeralds glowed; rubies shimmered. There was so much gold, the assemblage could have resupplied Fort Knox. The air virtually reeked of money and power and influence, and just for a moment Jack had a vision of himself as a boy in the tobacco fields. Although it had been years, he could still feel the ache in his back and hands so stiff he could hardly move his fingers. The image vanished in a moment, but it was enough to remind him how far he had come.

A few heads had turned their way when Lilah and Jack came in. Lilah clung possessively to Jack's arm, obviously enjoying the curious—and in some cases, avid—expressions of the women when they saw how handsome her escort was.

"Let me introduce you to a few friends," she purred. "Let's see . . . where shall we start?"

But before they could move out of the doorway, a tall man with graying hair detached himself from the crowd and hurried over.

"Jack Stanton!" he exclaimed, pumping his hand. "I had no idea you'd be here! Why didn't you tell me?"

Jack smiled. He'd met Phillip Glazier a few years ago in California, when Glazier's company, a firm that specialized in disaster control, contacted him about supplying equipment after the catastrophic 1989

San Francisco earthquake. Together, they had joined forces to aid the city and had been friends ever since.

"What are you doing in Kentucky?" Jack countered. "The last I heard, you were off to South America, or some other exotic locale."

Glazier grinned. "Yeah, well, I came back. Had to see my filly run at Santa Anita Racetrack."

"I didn't know you were into horses."

"You know how it is," Glazier said with a shrug and a twinkle in his eye. "Have to do something with all that money I get for sitting on my rear. I looked around and thought that I could lose it just as fast with horses as I could with the stock market, so here I am, proud owner of Roarin' Rosie—among others."

Remembering his manners, Jack introduced Lilah, who held out a languid hand. "Pleased to meet you," she murmured.

"The pleasure is mine," Glazier said gallantly. "Although I'm new to racing, I've long been an admirer of the horses from CastleKeep Farm."

"Oh, really?" Lilah said, looking pleased. She slanted her eyes at him. "I'd like to return the compliment, but I'm afraid I've never heard of—who was that filly you named? Rambling Rose?"

"Roarin' Rosie," Glazier corrected her, not in the least offended. "And I'm not surprised that you haven't heard of her. She was just a twenty-thousand dollar claimer I bought a while ago. Hardly big time." He added modestly, "You might be more familiar with Flying Condor, who just won a futurity out at Santa Anita." He winked. Either he knew Lilah by reputation, or he had already taken her measure. "Of course, that was only a hundred-thousand-dollar purse, but he's still young, so we're starting him out slow."

"Congratulations," Jack said, hoping to forestall whatever nasty comment he was sure Lilah was about to make.

Diverted, Phillip grinned at him. "Thanks, good buddy. Say, I heard you were getting into the business. Bought any horses yet?"

"No, I've been busy doing some rebuilding..." Jack started to say. Just then there was a stir, and when they all looked around, a diminutive, elderly woman with a definite regal air was making her way through the crowd toward them.

Even though he was new to racing, Jack would have recognized her anywhere. Barely five feet tall, Annabelle Sheffield was now in her nineties. She and Grover had built Finish Line Farm nearly sixty years before. Their contribution to racing was incalculable.

As always, Annabelle was unfailingly courteous. "Hello, my dear," she said to Lilah when she reached the place where Lilah and Jack were standing. It was obvious from the look she gave him that she'd come to talk to Jack, and Phillip stood back respectfully.

Not even Lilah had the nerve to be other than civil. "Hello, Mrs. Sheffield," she said, immediately turning to Jack to introduce him.

"I know who Mr. Stanton is," Annabelle said. Ten years ago, she had been afflicted by a palsy. Her hand shook slightly as she held it out, but when Jack took it, her grip was strong and warm.

"It's an honor to meet you, ma'am," Jack said.

Annabelle smiled. No one would have guessed her great age; her hand might have a tremor, but her mind was still sharp. "The pleasure is mine. I've been waiting to meet the man who bought the Tidleman place. Bert is an old, dear friend of ours—Grover's and mine. He wasn't the same after his wife died, but he tells me you did him right in the sale—" she paused, her eyes on him "—when you could have taken advantage of an old man."

"I can't take credit, Mrs. Sheffield," Jack said quietly. "All I did was pay a fair price for the farm."

"You did more than that, young man. And I won't forget it." She started to turn away, then looked back. "Do call me Annabelle. All my friends do. And please, come to see me soon, at the farm."

Jack knew there weren't a dozen people in the room privileged enough to call this woman by her first name. Aware of the honor just bestowed upon him, he said, "I'd be delighted... Annabelle. And you must visit Fieldstone Farm one day as well."

"It would be my pleasure."

The old woman lifted her hand in farewell. Then, obviously tired, she started slowly toward the door, a small entourage eagerly following. As soon as she was gone, the noise swelled. Under cover of the sound, Lilah said, almost enviously, "Well! How does it feel? You've practically been knighted by the old witch, and you don't have a horse to your name!"

Jack was too pleased by what had happened to take offense. With a smile, he said, "Give me time."

"Oh, and is that—"

But they were interrupted by what became a constant flow of people eager to introduce themselves to Jack. The queen of racing had bestowed an honor upon him more precious than gold. He could have worked *years* for this cachet and not reached the level Annabelle had elevated him to with a single conversation. Long before the evening was over, he considered it a triumph. Who would have believed that a boy who had once labored in someone else's tobacco fields would tonight be rubbing shoulders with the upper crust of racing? He could have laughed aloud with sheer delight.

The night passed in a whirl. Jack was enjoying himself so much that it was a while before he noticed that Lilah had been gone quite some time. Earlier, she had excused herself to talk to someone she knew across the room, and when he looked at his watch, he was surprised to realize she'd been gone almost an hour. Reluctantly deciding it was time to go and look for her, he excused himself from the group that had surrounded him and started circling the room.

Everywhere was talk of racing, and as he passed by various knots of people, he heard intriguing snippets of conversation.

One group was discussing certain bloodlines known for their meanness, and someone was saying, "Nasrullah was so mean, they say he used to hold a grudge. He'd go for people he hadn't seen in years if they'd once done something he didn't like."

Yet another group of people were debating the famous Triple Crown battle between Affirmed and Alydar. The heart-stopping stretch runs between the two colts were the stuff of which legends were made, and as Jack stopped a moment to listen, someone said, "People didn't understand that Affirmed just wouldn't be beat. Once in the lead, he wouldn't let another horse pass him, no matter what. Alydar was almost a hand taller but nothing was going to get by that little horse. And nothing did, did it?"

Jack remembered the thrill of those races. Many horsemen considered that Triple Crown year as one of the greatest tests of heart two colts had ever endured. As thousands cheered themselves hoarse, Affirmed, the little fifteen-hand-two-inch colt, battled his way first to the finish line in all three races. Refusing to give up or give in to his bigger opponent, he edged out Alydar every time, emerging triumphant at the end with racing's crowning glory and a place in history.

Wishing he had time to listen to more, Jack remembered his errand and continued in his search for Lilah.

He found her at the bar. As soon as he saw her, he knew she'd drunk too much. Her eyes at half-mast, she was leaning against the bar barely able to hold herself up, let alone hold the drink she clutched in one hand. Sighing inwardly because he didn't want to leave yet, he knew he had to do the gentlemanly thing and take her home.

"Come on, Lilah, it's time to leave," he said as he came up to her.

Her head bobbing a little, she managed to turn and look at him. It took her a second or two to focus, but when she did, her eyes turned malicious. "Well, if it ishn't the golden boy," she slurred. "Did you finally remember me?"

"I never forgot you, Lilah," he said, although he realized guiltily he had. "You said you had some people to see. I had no idea you wanted a drink. Why didn't you tell me? I would have gotten one for you."

Drunkenly, she waved the glass back and forth. "Oh, but I didn't want just *one.*"

Concerned that she would spill the glass she was waving unsteadily about, he reached out and tried to take it from her. Frowning, she jerked it back. The amber liquid splashed out, trickling down her low-cut bodice right between her breasts. An ice cube followed, ending up perched precariously on the soft shelf of her bosom, and she looked at it in surprise.

"Hey, thas cold!" she giggled. Looking up at Jack, she thrust herself forward. "Why don't you get that—with those luscious lips?"

He'd had enough of this. People were already looking at them curiously—and in some cases, knowingly. "Stop it, Lilah," he said, finally succeeding in taking the highball from her hand. Reaching out, he plucked the ice cube out of her cleavage before it melted completely, throwing it in the glass.

"Bartender!" Lilah called, turning to the man behind the bar. "I'll have another. Set 'em up right here!"

The bartender glanced at Jack who shook his head. "I think you've had enough, Lilah," he said. Taking her arm, he tried to get her to move. "Come on, let's go home."

"I don't wanna go—" she started to say, but just then a calculating look came into her eyes, and she swiveled her head up to look at him. "Wanna go to bed?"

"No, I want to get you home. You're drunk, Lilah."

"Drunk?" She seemed to find the idea hilariously funny. "I'm not drunk! What's the matter with you? I'm perfectly fine—see?"

Jerking her arm out of his grasp, she tried to walk what she perceived was a straight line. Her ankle turned on the second step, and she was just starting to collapse like a rag doll when Jack grabbed her. In her ear, he said, "I'm not going to carry you out to the car, Lilah, so get yourself together."

"Oh, Jack," she said, looking up at him with glazed eyes. Throwing her arms around him, she said, "I wanna be carried."

Aware that more people had turned to watch the spectacle, all he wanted to do was get her out of here before she made an even bigger scene. Grasping her tightly around the waist, he half lifted her, half dragged her out a side door.

"Oh, Jack, I don't feel very good," she moaned, when they got to the car.

He stopped in the act of unlocking the Porsche. "Are you going to be sick?"

"No, I...everything's just...spinning..."

He caught her just as she started to fall, but instead of collapsing against him as he expected, she wrapped her arms around his neck and pressed her mouth to his.

"Kiss me, Jack," she said, opening her mouth and trying to force her tongue past his teeth. "Come on, you know you want me. Kiss me, damn it!"

She was like a leech; he could hardly get her off. Barely suppressing a sound of revulsion, he managed to pry her away. Holding her at arm's length, he said, "You're drunk, Lilah. And I'm not—"

"You're not going to take advantage of me, is that it?" she asked. She laughed shrilly. "You don't have to worry about that, Jackie. No man takes advantage of me because I've never held anything back. It was that way in high school, and it's that way now. So what's the problem? Don't you find me attractive?"

Wishing he'd never heard of Lilah Castlemaine, he glanced toward the back door of the building. The last thing he wanted was for someone to come out and hear her talking like this, and he was about to tell her just to get into the car when he looked back at her, and froze. For a moment, he couldn't believe his eyes.

"What are you doing?" he demanded.

She looked up in drunken surprise at his outraged tone. During the few seconds he'd been distracted, she'd managed to pull the bodice of her gown down to her waist and was struggling with the rest of the tight material. She wasn't wearing a bra, and as she posed for him, she slurred, "I'm showing you what I have to offer, what do you think?"

He was appalled. "Put that dress back on!"

"Oh, Jackie, you don't want that, do you?" she whispered, coming toward him with little mincing steps. The parking lot lights illuminated her upper body, and despite himself, he caught his breath. Pushing up against him, she forced him back toward the car, reaching down for his hands so she could bring them up to her bobbing breasts.

Abruptly, Jack snapped out of his daze. "I mean it, Lilah," he said, jerking his hands away and reaching for the car door. "Enough is enough. Now get dressed. I'm taking you home."

"Oh, you're no fun at all!" she exclaimed, suddenly angry and not sounding drunk at all. Reaching down, she pulled the top of her dress up. "You're just like you were in high school, just an old stick-in-the-mud!"

"That may be true, but even if I were so inclined, I'd hardly take you up on your offer in a parking lot."

Salvaging her pride, she tossed her head. "Who says I'd want you anyway? Give me a cigarette."

"I don't smoke."

"Fine. Then I'll find someone who does."

She started to turn away, but he grabbed her by the arm. "Get in the car, Lilah."

She tried to free herself and almost fell. "I won't."

He clenched his jaw. "I'm going to take you home."

"I'll go with my father."

"Not when you came with me."

She stopped struggling. "Only if you let me drive."

"Are you crazy? You're in no condition to drive!"

"Yes, I am. I'm fine now. Give me the keys."

He had no intention of surrendering the keys, even though she did suddenly appear perfectly sober. Wondering if her drunken behavior had just been an act, he opened the door on the passenger's side of the car.

Her head lifted. "I told you, I won't go with you, and you can't make me!"

He had never in his life left a woman stranded, but tonight he looked at her set face, her angry slash of a mouth and malicious eyes, and slammed the car door shut.

"You're right," he said, going around to the driver's side and opening that door. "I'm sure you can find a ride you'd enjoy more."

When he started to get into the car, she screeched, "You're not going to leave me here!"

He stood up again. "Don't make it sound like I'm leaving you in the middle of a desert, Lilah. I offered to take you home, you refused. I'm not going to wrestle you into the car, not when you have friends inside who will be glad to give you a lift."

Her eyes fairly blazed. "I've never been so insulted in my life!"

"I'm sorry, Lilah. It's your choice."

"We'll see about that! Oh, you'll be sorry you did this, Jack Stanton. You'll be sorry, I swear!"

And with that, she whirled around and started back inside. Her heel caught on something—causing Jack to start forward automatically to help—but she righted herself, glared back at him and jerked open the door. Pausing before she went into the building, she turned to shout at him.

"I mean it, Jack! You shouldn't have turned me down. You're going to be sorry for this!"

Thinking that the only thing he was sorry for at the moment was that he had accepted her invitation, he got into the car. Lilah disappeared inside, but even after she was gone, he had to sit a moment to get himself together. He hated ugly scenes, and this one with Lilah ranked right up there at the top. He had no idea what she meant when she said he'd be sorry, and he didn't care. Right now all he wanted to do was go home and forget this night had ever happened.

Or forget this part of it, he thought as he drove slowly back to the farm. For a while, he had enjoyed himself tonight, and of course the high point of the evening had been his conversation with Annabelle Sheffield. Even now, it all seemed part of a dream he'd conjured up because he desired approval from these people so much; the thought that the owner of Finish Line Farm had deliberately sought him out made him proud.

But the closer he got to home, the more the glow faded. He didn't understand why he felt almost depressed until he turned in at the gates to his own farm and glanced in the direction of the Gallagher place. He couldn't see it from here, but as he pictured it in his mind, he knew what was wrong with him.

He hadn't wanted to admit it before, but he might as well now. All evening he'd been wishing that Maggie was with him instead of Lilah Castlemaine. He might as well confess it, if only to himself. It was no good hiding something he'd known for a long time, anyway. The truth was that, as thrilled as he was to have been singled out by Annabelle Sheffield tonight, he would have been even more proud to have had Maggie Gallagher on his arm.

CHAPTER TEN

NEVER FORGET'S FOAL was a week old, and Maggie still hadn't left for New York. She wanted to go; she fully intended to, but how could she leave when Dan still needed her here to run the place?

Concerned about Dan's complaints that his back still bothered him, she and Belle had taken him back to the doctor, who had examined him thoroughly and couldn't explain his continuing pain. It wasn't like her father to act the invalid, and the fact that he claimed he could hardly get out of bed worried Maggie so much, she asked to speak to the doctor privately.

"I know my father," she said when she and Dr. Davis were alone. Belle was helping Dan out to the car, and she only had a few minutes before her father would begin wondering what had happened to her. "If he says he's in pain, I believe him."

"I believe him, too," the doctor said. He was a kind-looking man, with deep-set brown eyes and a gentle smile. "The fact that I can't find any *medical* reason for his pain doesn't mean it isn't there."

Maggie frowned. "I don't understand—" she started to say. A thought occurred to her and she looked at him indignantly. "Are you saying he's a hypochondriac? Because if you are, I assure you, he's not. Dad's the most stoic man I know!"

"I'm not saying that at all—although I have to add that for hypochondriacs, their so-called imaginary pain is very real to them," he said, and held up his hand when she started to protest again. "What I am saying about your father is that injuries like his can be very painful long after we in the medical field can find any cause. The only thing we can do now is wait."

"Wait! For how long?"

"For as long as it takes."

"You don't understand," she insisted. "I can't stay here forever. I have to get back to New York!"

He was sympathetic, but there wasn't much he could do. "Then I suggest that you find someone to help out at the farm while your father convalesces. Until he has no more pain, I don't want him exerting himself. We don't want it to become chronic, do we?"

Maggie agreed, of course, but that didn't solve her problem. She couldn't leave her father when he was in this state; she'd never forgive herself if something happened to make his condition worse. She had seen how painful it was for him to get in and out of the car this morning. Feeling a little desperate, she asked, "Can't you at least give him something to alleviate the discomfort?"

"I have. Bed rest, heat, and two aspirins every six hours."

"That's all?"

"That's all, Ms Gallagher."

Defeated, she went out to the car. They had agreed that Belle would sit in back with Dan, so Maggie was driving. As she slid behind the wheel, her father said, "I'm sorry, Maggie."

"For what, Dad?"

"For keeping you here when I know how anxious you are to get back to New York. I know you have to get on with your work—"

"The office is getting along just fine without me," she said. She'd called again and had spoken to both her secretary and her second-in-command. The orders and suggestions she'd given had smoothed out the immediate problems in the computer paper division, and everything else could just wait.

"And then, there's your wedding," Dan went on. Their eyes met in the rearview mirror and she felt guilty when he said, "By the way, when *are* we going to meet your fiancé? You keep saying he's going to come for a visit, but he hasn't yet."

Hastily, she started the car. She didn't want to discuss when Nowell might come; she had enough problems right now without worrying about that.

Sounding reasonable—she hoped—she said, "I can hardly ask him to come right now when you're not up to par, can I, Dad?"

"I understand, Maggie. But I'd like to meet him *before* the wedding, you know. And so would Belle."

"And I'd like you both to meet him. But not just yet, all right, Dad? Now, can we talk about something else? I've been wanting to discuss this, and now's as good a time as any."

"You're going to say you can't stay here much longer. I know. Well, I'm sure—"

"Dad, I don't want you worrying about getting well so I can leave. I've been thinking that since you're not supposed to be doing anything strenuous, maybe we'd better hire someone to take over. At least until you can—"

"Hire someone!" Dan exploded, right on cue. "Over my dead body!"

"But Dad—"

"No! I won't have some... some stranger mucking about in my business!"

"Now, Dan," Belle put in anxiously.

"Don't 'now, Dan' me, Belle! I've said it before, and I'll say it again. Before I allow someone else to take over the farm, I'll get up and do everything myself!"

As always when her father turned obstinate, Maggie could feel her temper slipping. "You're just being stubborn! What difference will it make if you get someone in for a week or two? What *damage* could they possibly do?"

"Damage enough!" Dan said irately. "No, Maggie, I won't have it!"

"Dan, calm down," Belle soothed. "There's no need to get upset."

"There is a need!" he shouted. "Gallagher Farm is mine—until I sell it, that is, and no one else is going to run it but me!"

Maggie was doing her best to remain cool. Through her teeth, she said, "You still can run the farm, Dad, even if you get someone in to help. Whoever it is will do what you tell them to."

"How do you know? How can you be sure? Suppose they steal me blind, and me flat on my back in that damned bed, unable to supervise?"

"Don't be ridiculous! Belle will be here—"

"Belle doesn't know anything about running a farm!"

"Well, thanks for the vote of confidence!" Belle exclaimed.

"You know what I mean, Belle, so don't go sounding all hurt and wounded," he said to her. "This isn't about you." He glared at Maggie in the rearview mirror. "It's about *me* running *my* farm!"

Maggie intercepted her father's look and shot back one of her own. "And what have *I* been doing these past two weeks?" she demanded.

"That's different. You're used to it. You know what to look for and what not. Belle—bless her heart—doesn't."

"I'm not the only one who knows how to run a farm, Dad. Why are you being so obstinate?"

Dan seemed about to reply angrily, but suddenly he changed tactics. "Please, Maggie," he said. "I know it's a lot to ask, but if you just stay another few days—a week at the most—I promise that if I'm not up to it myself, I'll . . . I'll . . ."

He couldn't say it. "You'll what?" Maggie said it for him. "Agree to bring in someone until you can?"

"Aw, Maggie—"

"Don't back out on me now, Dad," she warned, pressing her advantage while she had one. Trying not to think of what Nowell would say when he heard she'd extended her absence yet again, she said, "That's the deal. I'll stay a few more days—a week at most. Then, if the doctor doesn't clear you to go back to work, you'll hire someone to help. Agreed?"

His jaw tight, Dan looked out the window. Watching him through the rearview mirror, Maggie waited. She knew how bullheaded he could be, but so could she be. After all, she thought grimly, she'd learned at the knee of the best.

"Well, Dad?" she asked, when he remained obstinately silent.

He wouldn't look at her. "All right, all right, you win," he conceded ungraciously. "But I'm going to be well by then, you'll see!"

"I hope so," she said. Switching her glance over to Belle, who raised her eyes heavenward in exasperated relief, she added, "Because if you don't get back on your feet soon, it won't be your back that's giving you trouble, it'll be your neck."

"My neck?" Dan's chin shot out. "And what's that supposed to mean?"

"It means," she said tersely, "that if you keep it up, it's going to be a race between Belle and me to see who gets to wring it."

THE PHONE WAS RINGING when they came in the back door. Hoping it wasn't Nowell, Maggie answered because Belle was busy helping Dan get back to bed.

"Gallagher Farm," she said.

"Margaret! Thank heaven you're finally home. I've been calling for an hour. I thought I might have missed you."

Damn it, why did she always have to answer when Nowell called? Wishing she could just hang up the phone and pretend she hadn't heard it ring, she thought of all sorts of things to say, and finally ended up with a weak, "Missed me?"

"Of course, I—" Something in her tone must have alerted him because his voice rose. "You *are* coming home, aren't you?"

It was now or never. "I *was,* Nowell. But we just got back from taking Dad to the doctor and—"

Even the single word sounded ominous. "And?"

She plunged in before she lost courage. "And he said it will be another—" she couldn't say a week; it sounded much too long even to her "—few days, at least."

"What? What do you mean, another few days? How *many* is a few?"

"I know how it sounds, Nowell, but—"

"No, you *don't* know how it sounds, Margaret! Now, I've been patient long enough, don't you agree?"

"Yes, but—"

"Think back, and you'll remember that I didn't object when you said you had to go home for a day or so."

"No, you—"

"And did I protest when you said you had to stay on for a week?"

"Well, as a matter of fact, you—"

"Then it was *another* week, remember? And I understood that, too."

"Did you? I thought—"

"And now it's a few more days!" he roared. "Oh, this is too much! If you don't come back today, this very afternoon, I... I don't know what I'll do!"

She had never heard him so upset. Guiltily, she tried to calm things down. "If you're worried about the office—"

"It's not the office!" he shouted, completely distraught. "It's the wedding plans! You don't know what mother has been up to in your absence! I'm beginning to think the woman is stark, raving mad!"

She couldn't believe he was saying such things. Wishing she didn't have to ask, she shut her eyes and almost held her breath. "What do you mean?"

"What do I mean?" he cried. "I mean that now she's increased the guest list to five hundred, and she's negotiating for a ballroom at the Plaza, *that's* what I mean!"

Feeling as though someone had taken the stuffing out of her, Maggie sank into one of the kitchen chairs. This was much worse than anything she could have imagined her future mother-in-law would do. She knew she sounded plaintive, but she couldn't help it. "What are we going to do?"

"Do? *Do?*" he exclaimed, beside himself. "What *you're* going to *do* is fly back here immediately and talk to her!"

"Fly back!" She was aghast. "But Nowell, she's *your* mother—"

"She won't listen to me! She keeps telling me to stay out of it! According to her, I'm only a man who doesn't understand such things. She keeps saying that she's sure you'll approve. Women always want big, fancy weddings, whether they know it or not, she tells me. I suppose the next thing I'm going to hear is that she's ordered your gown from Paris. She was threatening to do it the other day. I think the only reason she hasn't is because she's not sure how long your train should be. She's wondering if twenty feet would be enough."

Appalled, Maggie jumped up. "Twenty feet! I'd feel like I was dragging a tent behind me! Nowell, you've got to talk to her!"

"*You* talk to her! Today! Tonight, when you get home!"

"But I can't come home today! I told you, I have to stay and help my father!"

He stopped, breathing hard. "Well, fine," he said finally. "In that case, I hope you have a better plan than I do!"

She thought quickly. "I'll call her."

He groaned. "You can't call her!"

Did she want to know this? "Why not?"

"Because she's gone to Albany to see the governor."

"The governor? Why would she—" She stopped, horrified. "Oh, Nowell, you don't think—"

"Yes, I do," he said grimly. "She's known him for a long time. She went to see if he can attend the wedding."

"Oh, no!"

"Oh, yes. So you see why you're urgently needed here."

Despite the situation, she noticed that he didn't say *he* needed her there. Telling herself that it didn't matter, that he was obviously just as upset as she was getting to be, she tried a different tack. "When will she get back from Albany?"

"She'll be gone a few days. We have relatives nearby, and she thought she'd visit since she was there."

Sagging in relief, she said, "Well, then, even if I came home right now, I couldn't do anything until she gets back. And by then—" she heard his quick intake of breath and knew he was about to protest, so she rushed on "—I'll have things under control here. You've been patient this long. Surely, you can give me that much time, can't you?"

"Margaret—"

"Please, Nowell. You know I wouldn't ask you if it wasn't absolutely necessary."

There was a silence. Then she heard a heavy sigh. "Very well. I know you have responsibilities." His voice rose. "But a few days more, no longer—agreed?"

"Agreed," she said, and added quickly, hoping he wouldn't hear, "I promise I won't stay longer than another week."

He heard. "Now it's another week!"

"At most," she told him hastily, and said goodbye before he could protest.

The phone rang again almost immediately. She hadn't realized how tense she was until she jumped at the sound. Hoping it wasn't Nowell calling back, she answered gingerly. "Gallagher Farm."

"Hello, Maggie," said a voice she also knew well. "Is this a bad time to call?"

"A bad time?" she repeated, her voice high. She nearly laughed hysterically. "No, why do you ask that, Jack?"

"Well, you sound a little frantic. Is anything wrong?"

Anything wrong? Her entire life had been turned upside down. "No, no, nothing's wrong. What can I do for you?"

There was a pause. Then he laughed. "That's my Maggie. Always direct and to the point."

His Maggie. Trying not to think how warm those two simple words made her feel inside, she said, "I'm sorry. I didn't mean to sound abrupt. We just got back from taking Dad to the doctor—"

"Oh? It's not bad news, is it?"

"No, he's—" she started to say, but stopped suddenly when a thought occurred to her. Jack sounded genuinely concerned, but as she recalled now, Nowell hadn't even asked about her father; he'd been more worried about his own problems. Brushing away the treacherous comparison, she said, "Well, he's still in a lot of pain, and the doctor wants him to stay in bed for another week."

"Is it serious?"

"No, I don't think so. Not if all he prescribed was bed rest and aspirin." Remembering it now, she frowned indignantly. "He was a big help."

She could almost hear the smile in Jack's voice. "In other words, he didn't give you any idea how to hold the man down for a few more days, right?"

She had to smile. Wondering why Jack seemed to make her feel better, when Nowell's effect on her was just the opposite, she asked, "Do you have any suggestions?"

"I could come over and hog-tie him to the bed."

She nearly laughed at the mental picture that presented. "Why don't we save that until we *really* get desperate? Can you think of something else in the meantime?"

"I've got a collection of racing videos. Maybe that would entertain him for a while. I could bring them over if you like."

She didn't have to be asked twice. "Would you? It would be a godsend!"

"I'll do it on one condition."

Immediately, she felt cautious. "What's that?"

"That you go to the Keeneland Special Sale with me tomorrow night. Annabelle Sheffield is going to put all her stock on the block and—"

Maggie's smile faded. "Yes, I know about the sale." She'd seen the announcement in the paper, but Dan had known about it long before. They both felt sad about the prospect of Annabelle leaving racing; they knew that when she did, it would be the end of an era.

Maggie hadn't thought about going to the sale, but now that Jack had asked, she wondered if she should. She had no intention of buying any stock, but it might be a way of paying tribute to a woman she had always admired.

Or maybe it would be a way of spending an evening with a man who intrigues you even more.

The thought came out of nowhere, and her cheeks reddened. She hadn't forgotten Jack's kiss the night Never Forget's foal was born; every time she thought of it—and she thought of it far too often—she was unnerved by her passionate response. Her only excuse was that it had been an emotional moment. After all the tension and strain, who wouldn't have wanted a release?

Then she thought: a release? Who was she kidding? It had been much more than that, and she knew it. For those few precious seconds in Jack's arms, with his warm lips on hers and their bodies pressed tightly together, she had forgotten everything but the sensation of being with him. Nothing had mattered except Jack and the passion he had aroused with one simple kiss.

Nowell never made you feel like that, the same insidious little voice whispered again.

Her face burning, she pushed the thought away, telling herself that she'd never given Nowell the chance. And besides, Nowell wasn't Jack. As she'd repeated to herself again and again, it wasn't fair or right to compare the two men.

"Maggie?"

She blinked. "I'm sorry, Jack, I was just... thinking."

"About coming with me to the sale?"

Definitely not. She had to refuse. It was madness to go anywhere with him, even to a very public place like Keeneland. After what had happened, she knew that if she spent any more time with him, she'd be playing with fire.

No, she couldn't do it, she instructed herself. She had an obligation to her fiancé, to...to *Nowell,* she told herself fiercely, appalled when she momentarily forgot his name.

Tell him you can't go, she ordered herself. *Make up some excuse. Now. Do it!*

"I'd like that, Jack," she said. "What time does it start?"

THE KEENELAND Special Sale for the stock of Finish Line Farm was an all-day event that was scheduled to last well into the night, when the horses regarded as the cream of the crop went on the block. After Maggie—foolishly, she told herself at least a dozen times—agreed to go, she found herself even more involved than she intended to be. In addition to inviting her to go with him, Jack also asked her help.

"Oh, Jack, I don't know," she protested weakly. "It's been so long since I even looked at a sales catalog—"

"We'll ask your Dad's advice," he said blithely, unaware of her inner turmoil. "It'll give him something to do, right?"

How could she argue with that? Trying not to think she was getting in over her head, she invited him over and was glad for Dan's sake, at least, that she had.

Dan had been in the doldrums, but when Jack appeared carrying videos, studbooks and the sales catalog, he immediately brightened and began supervising everything from his bed. He approved one horse, disdainfully rejected another, carefully considered a third and then a fourth and more. Jack seemed to enjoy himself, too, discussing bloodlines and racing times with a man who had devoted his entire life to the sport, and together the two men had a ball.

Watching from the sidelines, Maggie contributed a remark or two, but as she'd said, she'd been out of the business too long to be familiar with the horses offered for sale, so she spent most of her time covertly watching Jack.

She knew how Dan was when he began talking about horses, but she was fascinated by the change she saw in Jack when he discussed the subject. His face lit up, his eyes glowed, he became so involved that he even forgot the time. When he talked about racing, he was like all the other horse people Maggie had known. Completely involved, he was in love with the horses who ran like no other creatures in the world, because racing was in their blood, and it was what they did best.

And what did she feel? she wondered, through the lively discussion that followed. Disturbed because she didn't know the answer, she sat back and tried to be inconspicuous.

Once, Jack looked up. "Is something wrong, Maggie?"

Troubled by her thoughts, she'd gotten up and gone to the window. Turning to look at him, she said, "No. I'm just getting cross-eyed from reading all that black print."

The black print she was referring to was just that: dark, heavy print in a sales catalog that was an indication of how well-bred a particular sale horse was. The more black print there was, and the higher it was on the page listing pedigree and performance, the more valuable the horse.

"You sure that's it?"

How could she tell him it wasn't that at all? Could she admit that watching him made her heart beat a little faster, that listening to his voice stirred a response in her she didn't trust? How could she say that seeing his hands holding the catalog made her long for the touch of those hands on her body, exciting responses no other man had ever aroused in her before?

"Of course. What else could it be?" she said, and excused herself quickly to make coffee.

CHAPTER ELEVEN

FEELING EVEN MORE unsure of herself when it was time for the big sale on Saturday night, Maggie nevertheless dressed carefully. It had been a long time, but she knew this would be a formal affair. Racing's elite was going to gather to pay homage to one of their own, and since she hadn't brought anything appropriate along, she had to make a quick trip into town to buy something.

To her surprise, she found the right gown in the first store. The emerald-green sheath she chose had a slit up to the thigh, with elegant beading on the shoulders and bodice. Matching high heels completed the ensemble, and as she got ready that night, she had to admit that after days of dressing in jeans and cotton blouses, it was a treat to dress up. She even decided to do something different with her hair, styling it into a sophisticated twist decorated with flowers. Before Jack was due to arrive, she pirouetted for her father and Belle, who was sitting beside Dan on the bed, and they both clapped.

"You look lovely, Maggie!" Belle said, her eyes shining.

Dan had a tear in his eye. "Aw, Maggie," he said softly, "you remind me of your mother."

Touched, Maggie bent down in a cloud of light but heady perfume and kissed his cheek, whispering,

"That's the best compliment you could have given me."

Jack came a few minutes later, his face lighting up when she met him at the back door. His voice sounding a little hoarse, he said, "You look... beautiful."

"You don't look so bad yourself," she replied, but underneath the green bodice, her heart was beating a little faster than it had been earlier. He looked so handsome in his tuxedo that she wanted to...

Hastily thrusting the thought away, she said, "Let's go in and say goodbye to Dad and Belle."

Duty done, they departed on a wave of well-wishes and encouragement from Dan to buy only the best. A stream of cars was turning into Keeneland's ivy-covered green gates when they arrived, and even though they'd come early, it was so crowded already that it took a while to park. Maggie was glad of the distraction; with Jack sitting so close to her in the Porsche, effortlessly handling the wheel and maneuvering the car, she was feeling a little breathless.

It's excitement, she told herself, trying to explain the fluttering in her stomach. *That's all it is, just excitement.*

"Excited?" Jack asked, when he finally found a parking space and stopped the car.

"Excited? No, why do you say that?" she asked nervously.

He pointed. She looked down at the catalog she had unconsciously rolled into a tight tube in her clammy hands. Embarrassed, she quickly smoothed it out. Hoping he'd believe the excuse—or at least not pursue it, she said, "It's been a long time since I attended one of these sales. That must be it."

"It must be," he agreed, and then made her feel even more light-headed when he took her arm after helping her out of the car. Together, they followed the flow of people inside, and as they sat down in their reserved seats, she took a deep breath and ordered herself to calm down.

She had forgotten just how thrilling these sales could be. Just as she and Jack got settled, there was an electric hum of anticipation that swelled into applause when Annabelle Sheffield walked in. Looking surprised and a little disconcerted at the attention, the owner of Finish Line Farm lifted her hand in a graceful acknowledgment, then sat down. As if that were a signal, the announcer and auctioneer with their assistants came out and the sale began.

The sale followed the usual procedure. As each horse was paraded in the show-ring for the crowd's approval, the announcer provided a quick review of pedigree, racing performance, history and any other pertinent details. The horse stayed in the ring until the gavel came down, and the auctioneer announced a floor price to begin the bidding. As the man concluded his opening remarks tonight, he sent out his tuxedoed assistants into the aisles of the Sales Pavilion. They were there to pass along a bid that might be raised by a nod, or even a tug at an ear.

"And now," the auctioneer said excitedly. "Lot Twenty-Two!"

With that, a nervous bay colt was brought into the ring, the number "22" taped to his hip. Frightened by the lights and the noise, the young horse jumped around his handler while the bidding began. The price started at fifty thousand and climbed rapidly until it reached well into six figures.

Bang! The gavel came down for the last time, and the auctioneer cried, "Sold to Merilee Mason, of Merry-Go-Round Farm!"

The next seventeen lots went just as quickly, Jack buying five mares himself for the beginning of his own broodmare band. Like everyone else, he was anxious to get to the high point of the sale, the last five horses. Among them were two mares and a filly he had already discussed with Dan and Maggie. The cream of the crop, the prize of the sale, was the brilliant distaff runner, Eternal Rhythm, who two years before had been named Horse of the Year. Then there was the incomparable Hidden Danger, the current three-year-old filly leader. And finally, a lovely mare called Fair Warning, who before being retired, had won over four million dollars in purses. Jack was determined to have all three.

The first horse of the top five was named High Caliber. He was a beautiful colt with a fiery red coat and a perfectly placed star. The floor price on the "coming-two"-year-old colt was two hundred thousand, but as Jack shifted in his seat, obviously prepared to enter the bidding war, Maggie forgot she was only here as an observer. She thought he might have seen it already, but if he hadn't, she wanted to warn him.

Leaning close, she whispered, "Are you sure you want to bid on him?"

He looked at her in surprise. "Well, I was, until you asked," he said. "Why, what's wrong? We discussed this horse, and Dan said—"

"I know what he said, but he hadn't seen this colt. Take a look at his pasterns, Jack. He's too straight. He'll break down."

Jack looked at her a moment, then he turned to stare at the colt. The display ring was deep with shavings; the horse's feet were buried almost to the fetlock. Obviously wondering how Maggie could see the colt's ankles, he glanced at her again.

"Are you sure?"

She shrugged. "It's up to you. But if it were me... I'd pass."

Jack seemed indecisive; already the bidding had started, rising at a furious pace. One of the assistants, having observed their whispered conversation, moved closer in case one of them signaled a bid. Hopefully, he looked their way, then moved off in disappointment when, after a moment's hesitation, Jack shook his head.

Jack had dropped out, but others in that glittering audience wanted the colt desperately. The price escalated so rapidly that soon the tote board blazed with numbers in the seven figures. When the gavel came down the final time, High Caliber had been sold for just under one million two hundred thousand dollars.

Smiling at Jack's woebegone expression, Maggie leaned over and said, "Don't worry. You've still got four more."

Jack gave her a skeptical look. "Any more advice?"

Smiling again, she said, "Bid on Good Measure, if you like, but don't go over five hundred thousand. He's not worth it. I don't care what the black print says."

Jack followed her advice, dropping out of the bidding on the next colt when it reached the half-million dollar mark. Then, as the auctioneer announced the appearance of Fair Warning, the great race mare who had won millions in purses before being retired, he looked at Maggie again.

"Now?" he asked.

He looked so wistful that she laughed. "Now."

Excitement ran high as Jack ran the bid on Fair Warning up to a million dollars. Now that he was actually in the fray, he seemed calm and composed, nodding his head once to make his bid when the auctioneer turned his way, sitting back in his seat until the next round. In the show-ring, the regal bay mare paraded calmly back and forth beside her handler, as though she were above this sort of thing, but in the audience, in her seat beside Jack, Maggie had never been more nervous.

Finally, she couldn't stand it any longer. Leaning over, she whispered in his ear, "How much are you willing to spend on her?"

"As much as it takes," he said, turning back in time to nod once to the auctioneer's assistant, who by this time was practically standing right on top of him.

Immediately, the aide leaped into the air, frantically waving his program. "Yes!" he cried, letting the auctioneer know Jack had raised the bid.

But across the Pavilion, another offer was made, and then from someplace behind them, another. Maggie thought she would faint with excitement before the gavel finally came down at one million twenty-five. As the papers were brought for Jack to sign, she gripped his arm.

"Congratulations!" she gasped.

He grinned. In his element, he signed the papers with a flourish, but before he could say anything, it was time for Lot Two, the three-year-old filly leader, Hidden Danger.

Heads were turning by this time; people were whispering when they looked at Jack. And with good reason, Maggie thought, as the elegant chestnut filly was brought out. She had calculated it herself, at this point in the sale, Jack had spent almost two million dollars. It seemed incredible, even to her. The thought flashed through her mind that her father probably hadn't spent that for horses in his entire life, and as she glanced quickly at Jack, she wondered why she didn't feel jealous.

Before she could answer the question, the bidding, which had started at five hundred thousand, had quickly escalated to a million. Unlike her stable sister, Fair Warning, the three-year-old filly in the ring right now was still in race training, and it showed. Accustomed to a set schedule, she knew something was different tonight, and whether it was the noise of the crowd, the bright lights, or the auctioneer's voice booming out over her head, she became so excited that her handler had trouble holding her.

Once, her auburn coat gleaming under the hot lights, she reared and struck out. Her eyes fierce as she came down on all four feet again and blasted out a shrill, challenging whinny, she drew an admiring sound from the crowd. Watching with shining face, Maggie thought that this horse was one of the most beautiful animals she had ever seen.

"Oh, Jack," Maggie breathed, her eyes glowing. "She's magnificent!"

Jack agreed. This time when the red-faced, perspiring aide raced down the aisle with the papers for him to sign, the amount on the bottom line was one and a half million dollars.

Grinning, Jack bent over and gave the stunned Maggie a brief kiss on the lips. His own eyes bright, he promised, "It's not over yet."

And it wasn't. The highlight of the evening was yet to come, Lot Number One, the mare who, two years before as an undefeated three-year-old, had been named Horse of the Year. Easily snatching up an honor almost exclusively awarded to the colts, this brilliant distaff runner had burst upon the racing scene like a bolt of lightning. In race after race, she had demolished all comers—fillies, colts and geldings—streaking to the finish line first in seventeen of seventeen races.

When the announcer called, "Lot Number One," the crowd suddenly became still. Even the auctioneer's voice sounded reverent as he took over the microphone and whispered into the hush, "And now, ladies and gentlemen, we come to the high point of the evening, Lot Number One. In her career, this mare has more than captured her rightful place in racing history. In race after race, she's proved her mettle by outrunning, out*classing* every other horse pitted against her, male or female."

Enthralled, the crowd was completely silent as his voice rose, beginning to tremble with excitement. "Ladies and gentlemen, I'm honored to present the pride of Finish Line Farm, the glorious, the phenomenal, the incomparable... *Eternal Rhythm!*"

As though she knew she deserved all the accolades heaped upon her by the wild applause of the crowd, Eternal Rhythm burst into the show-ring like a star. Almost dragging her handler after her, she reached the center of the stage and suddenly stopped. Every muscle quivering, she lifted her head and looked out, standing like a queen.

Under the hot lights, the mare's coat gleamed like black diamonds; her polished hooves seemed to shoot off sparks. Never had a horse looked so splendid, Maggie thought, not even the volatile Hidden Danger. Even to Maggie's experienced eyes, Eternal Rhythm was the embodiment of all a Thoroughbred should be.

The crowd went wild. Even the most sophisticated and jaded leaped to their feet, deafening the Pavilion with frenzied applause. It was five minutes before the announcer could speak above the wild tumult; another few minutes before the perspiring auctioneer could start the bidding.

"We start, ladies and gentlemen," he said reverently, when he could be heard, "with... one million dollars."

In the audience, Jack turned to Maggie. "What do you think?"

Maggie tore her eyes away from the magnificent horse on stage. Her eyes were brilliant. "You must have her!"

He nodded. "I agree," he said, and paused, searching her face. "For you."

"For me! Oh, no, Jack—"

Her protest was lost in the rising excitement of a new bidding war. Eternal Rhythm was the most valuable horse present, and everyone in the audience knew it. The bidding was fast and furious, and the glowing numbers on the tote board clicked upwards almost faster than the eye could follow. Frenzied assistants raced back and forth, turning back to shout out bids; waving their programs in the air, they feverishly scanned the audience so they wouldn't miss some faint signal.

Finally, after a wild flurry that made Maggie feel breathless and light-headed with excitement, the bidding was down to four people, then three...then two. Only Jack and Leo Castlemaine, sitting on the far side of the Pavilion, were still engaged; with the numbers standing at one million one-seventy-five, everyone else dropped out.

"We've got one-one-seventy-five, one-one-seventy-five, one-one-seventy-five," the auctioneer gasped into the sudden, intense quiet. It was Castlemaine's last bid, and he glanced across at Jack. One of his assistants stood near Jack, ready to leap into the air if Jack so much as twitched his nose, and in the sudden silence, the auctioneer leaned down over the podium. As if pleading with Jack, he said, "You're not going to let this magnificent horse go for a paltry one million one hundred and seventy-five, are you?"

There were smiles even in the tense audience, and as though she'd understood the question, up in the show-ring, Eternal Rhythm stamped her foot. There was an outbreak of laughter at that, and the auctioneer used his handkerchief to wipe his sweating face. Then he said into the quiet as he looked at Jack, "Yes? No? What's it going to be now?"

Beside Jack, Maggie didn't dare move, not even to look at Jack, who was sitting calmly beside her. She knew how much he wanted this horse, and yet he seemed suddenly to have changed his mind. Trying not to feel disappointed that he'd dropped out, she waited tensely as the auctioneer stared hopefully their way before reluctantly turning back to the other side.

"All right." He sighed heavily into the microphone before beginning his rapid patter again, going faster and faster until Maggie could hardly understand him. "We've got one-one-seventy-five, one-one-seventy-five, one-one-seventy-five. Going once!" Banging down the gavel, he looked expectantly at Jack. Tension seemed to leap and sizzle around the room, but Jack just sat there.

"Going twice!" Another bang on the podium. Jack just looked on. At the other side of the Pavilion, Leo sat back in his chair, looking smug and triumphant.

Staring back at Jack, the auctioneer began to chant. "It's up to you, up to you, up to you, make it two million and give this filly her due. It's up to you, up to you..."

He waited hopefully again. Still no sign from Jack. Finally, with a sigh that seemed to come from his soul, the auctioneer lifted his gavel a third time. In the millisecond before it started to descend for the last time, Jack gave the barest nod.

Instantly, the assistant whirled toward the stage, screaming out, "Two million here! Two million here!"

The crowd went wild again. If Maggie hadn't known it was all an act, she would have been worried that the auctioneer was having a heart attack. Clutching his chest, he jumped up and down before he whirled toward a furious-looking Leo Castlemaine and started in on him. "Two million one, two million one, what do you say, what do you say, what do you say?"

But Leo had said enough this night. With a disgusted wave of his hand, he lumbered to his feet and walked out. The auctioneer swept the audience again, but Jack had won.

"Sold for two million dollars to Mr. Jack Stanton of Fieldstone Farm!" he shouted into the uproar.

Everyone was on their feet, Maggie and Jack included. "Oh, Jack, you were wonderful!" she cried. And without realizing it, threw her arms around him and kissed him with all her heart.

Jack put his arms around her and pulled her tight into him, answering her with a pressure she felt build right through her. She wanted to cling to him, but there wasn't time. People were crowding around; there were papers to sign. Refusing to let go of her waist, Jack signed the contract he was presented with a flourish. When he looked at her again, his handsome face was flushed with victory and excitement—and something else. Something she was feeling herself.

"I couldn't have done it without you, Maggie," he said, his eyes shining. "Thanks."

She wanted to say he'd done it himself, but the words wouldn't come. With his arm still around her and that look in his eyes, she was trying to comprehend the sudden tumult of emotion she was feeling inside. It didn't matter. For the next few minutes, Jack belonged to the crowd. Now that the sale was over, and everything was official, they were surrounded by well-wishers. Even if she'd wanted to, she couldn't leave to get herself together; Jack kept a tight grip on her waist, holding her by his side as though afraid she would disappear.

Then, as she watched him accepting all the congratulations and signing more documents and papers arranging for care of the horses now that they belonged to him, Maggie realized she didn't want to leave. She wanted to be part of this, wanted to share this night of triumph with him . . . wanted to touch his face, to melt against him, to kiss him again, and again. Dismayed by the thoughts and feelings that assailed her, she closed her eyes briefly. When she opened them again, Jack was looking right at her. He smiled and without warning, her heart took flight again.

Oh, Jack! she thought, dismayed. *What's happening to me?*

It took almost half an hour to make their way out of the Sales Pavilion to the fresh night air. They were standing on the steps outside, Jack accepting another round of best wishes from latecomers, when Lilah Castlemaine appeared. Elbowing people aside, she marched up to them, her expression belligerent, her eyes furious.

"Well, I hope you're happy, Jack Stanton!" she cried.

"I don't know what you mean," Jack said politely.

"You know damned well what I mean!" Lilah shrieked. "You cheated Daddy out of that mare!"

Various knots of people were still standing about, discussing the thrilling aspects of the sale. When Maggie saw them turning curiously at the sound of Lilah's shrill voice, she wanted to put her hands over her eyes to blot out the sight.

Oh, not tonight, of all nights! she cried silently. She hadn't seen Lilah Castlemaine for years, but as far back as she could remember they had never liked each other. Against her will, images of her girlhood came racing back to her: herself at the backside of the track, compelled to help her father, while Lilah, spoiled and pampered by *her* father's money, lorded it over her. She could still feel the shame she'd felt then, dressed in jeans and muddy boots, dirt under her fingernails, hair in a ponytail, while Lilah paraded everywhere wearing expensive clothes and ordering her father's trainer around.

Although she tried not to let it show, Jack must have sensed something; when he turned to look at her and saw the look on her face, his own expression tightened. Turning back to Lilah, he said, "As far as I know, your father was as free as I was to bid on any of the horses."

Lilah clenched her fists. She was dressed all in white tonight; the sequins on the tight bodice of her dress shot sparks under the floodlights when she took in a breath. Her eyes glittering as she looked first at Jack, then at Maggie, and back again, she hissed, "I should have expected it! You always were jealous! Well, it won't work, I'm telling you! No matter what you plot and scheme, you'll never be like us—never!"

Maggie didn't know what came over her, but she couldn't remain silent. "I think you've said enough, Lilah—"

"I think you've said enough, Lilah," the woman mimicked savagely. Her eyes looked like black pits. "You always did think you were so superior, Maggie Gallagher—you, who didn't have a dime! Oh, I remember seeing you when we were kids, with your snooty nose in the air. Well, let me tell you something, *Maggie.* We all used to laugh at you, did you know that? We used to call both you Gallaghers—you and your father—also-rans. Yes, we did. You always were second-best. Why, I—"

As Maggie turned white, Jack stepped protectively forward. "I think you'd better go."

His tone was so quietly fierce that even Lilah was momentarily silenced. Openmouthed, she looked up at him; he stared implacably back. She looked at him with hatred for a moment longer, then she tossed her head.

"Oh, I'll go," she said with a shrill laugh, to save face. "But don't think I'm going to forget this, Jack. You're not so much yourself, you know. No matter how you dress it up now, no matter how much money you spend on horses, we all know that you're the son of a tobacco sharecropper who once worked for my father. Nothing changes that, and nothing ever will!"

With that, she turned on her heel and swept away. Her dramatic exit was marred somewhat when she caught her heel in the grass lining the path; stumbling slightly, she cursed, but she didn't look back.

The excitement over, the rest of the onlookers melted away. Left alone with Maggie, Jack muttered, "I'm sorry that happened."

"So am I," Maggie said. Alarmed at how shaky she sounded, she took a deep breath. "It's obvious that *she* hasn't changed."

Jack shook his head. "No, I'm afraid not." Then seeing the pain in Maggie's face, hearing it in her voice, he put his arm around her. "It's not true what she said, Maggie."

She couldn't look at him. "Oh, yes, it is."

Placing his hand under her chin, he turned her head so that she had to meet his eyes. "It doesn't matter what Lilah says or thinks," he said quietly. "The important thing is what you believe. You don't think that you and your father were second-rate, do you?"

She jerked away from his grasp before he could see the shame in her eyes. The worst thing about Lilah's accusation was that, no matter how cruel, Lilah had only said what Maggie herself had been thinking for years.

Feeling guilty and ashamed, she shook her head. "I don't know what I think anymore," she said.

He was silent a moment. Then he said, "I think I'd better take you home."

She didn't argue. The evening, with its emotional highs and lows, had drained her. What should have been an exciting climax to this glittering night had fallen flat and they were both painfully, achingly, aware of it. They were quiet on the way back, and when she tentatively asked if he wanted to come in for coffee, he shook his head.

"No, I don't think it's a good time, Maggie. I'm sorry."

"So am I," she said, wanting to cry. "I didn't mean to ruin the evening."

"You didn't ruin it. Lilah did."

Trying to forget her own feelings, she put a hand on his arm. "Don't let her ruin it, Jack. You're on your way now. And... and no matter what else happened this evening, I want you to know that I was proud to be with you, proud that we shared this night. I'll never forget it—never." Then before he could respond, she got out and ran into the house.

CHAPTER TWELVE

THREE DAYS LATER, Maggie sipped at a cup of coffee in the kitchen while she waited for the farrier to arrive. Her feelings about Jack and Nowell were still as confused as ever. And a nagging question had arisen, demanding an answer. Had she become engaged to Nowell just to prove she had completely left her old life behind?

Not that she'd had time to think about it, she thought in exasperation. Dan had been ecstatic about what Jack had done at the sale, but the excitement seemed to give him new energy. The very next day he was back at the helm again, trying to run the farm from his bed. He'd kept Maggie too busy to think, much less work out her problems, and after running back and forth receiving orders and carrying them out, she was already exhausted this morning and the day hadn't even started.

Wearily, she put down her cup and reached for the rubber band that had held the morning paper together. Needless to say, she hadn't had time to read the paper for days.

With a baleful glance at her father's closed bedroom door, she pulled her hair back into a ponytail and wrapped the rubber band around to hold it in place. The Margaret Gallagher she'd been in New York would have died before being seen like this, but the plain old Maggie she'd become here couldn't muster the energy to care. A ponytail kept her hair out of her face, and she had the feeling that the afternoon wasn't going to be any easier than the morning had been. She was scheduled to help the farrier trim the feet of some of the horses, and she was already preparing herself for some hard work.

She was just reaching for her coffee cup when Belle appeared, closing Dan's bedroom door behind her. "I can't believe he's been quiet for a whole minute," Maggie said. "What did you do—slip him a mickey?"

Laughing, Belle sat down. "I told him he had to lay off for a while and rest. That, or we'd leave him here alone while we went into town dressed in our best to see what kind of time we could scare up."

"The way I look today, *scaring* is the operative word."

"Don't be silly. You look just fine."

"Thanks," she said dryly. She was well aware of how she looked, but she couldn't do anything about it now, with Hank coming in a few minutes. Gratefully, she looked at Belle. "I can't tell you how glad I am that you're here to keep Dad occupied. If it was just him and me, I'd have strangled him long before now."

"That's because you and he are so much alike."

"Me, like Dad?"

"Don't look so horrified," Belle said calmly. "You know it's true. You both know your own minds."

"Do you think so?" Maggie replied, suddenly glum. "I used to believe I did, but now I'm not so sure."

"What do you mean?"

She hesitated. She hated to drag Belle into her problems, especially when she hadn't fully sorted them out herself, but as she had already discovered, the other woman was a good listener, and she needed to talk to someone about her doubts.

"It's Nowell," she said reluctantly.

Belle already knew about the problems Maggie was having with Nowell about her staying on so long. She asked sympathetically, "Did you quarrel again?"

"Again? It seems as though that's all we do lately. Last night, he told me that if I'm not home soon, he's going to come down here and take me back to New York himself." She had shuddered at the thought, but now she felt indignant. "Can you imagine? You'd think we were back in the Dark Ages!"

Not bothering to hide her smile, Belle asked, "What did you say?"

"After I'd recovered from my shock, you mean? I told him it wasn't necessary for him to go to so much trouble, that I was perfectly capable of coming home all by myself."

"And what was his reply?"

Maggie pursed her lips. "In a tone only Nowell could use, he said, 'And when will that be, my dear? Soon, I hope.'"

Belle laughed. "You have to admit, he has been patient."

"Yes, he has. It's just—"

Maggie stopped, fiddling with her coffee cup. Seeing her expression, Belle leaned forward. "Just what, Maggie? From the look on your face, it's more than just arguing over the phone about coming home." She hesitated. "Maybe you don't want to talk about it."

"It's not that. It's just that I'm not sure what the problem really is. Maybe it's just me. It seems that lately I'm having doubts about everything."

"We all go through that at times."

"But I've been going through it too long. I *have* to decide what to do, but every time I try to think about it, I become more confused than ever. Things were so *clear* before," she said intensely. "I knew what I wanted to do, and how I was going to do it. After all, I'd planned it for years. But now..."

"Now?"

Restlessly, Maggie got up and fetched them more coffee. Setting the pot back on the stove, she leaned against the counter for a moment. At last, she said, "When I first came down here, I'd intended only to stay a day—two at the most. In fact, I didn't even want to come. Now, it's been several weeks, and when I should be itching to get on a plane and go home, I..."

Belle said it for her when she hesitated. "You don't want to leave."

Unhappily, Maggie shook her head. "No, I don't. I can't understand it, Belle. Sometimes I think that even if Dad didn't need my help anymore, I'd think of an excuse to stay on—for a while, anyway—maybe longer." She frowned in frustration. "I know I'm not making much sense. I don't want to go, and I can't stay. I never expected the farm to exert such a hold on me."

Belle was silent a moment. Then she said quietly, "I know it sounds trite, Maggie, but sometimes coming home can be a comfort. Especially if you're starting to feel overwhelmed by something else that's going on in your life."

"Are you saying I'm trying to avoid my problems back in New York?"

"Only you can judge that. I hate to say it, and it probably isn't any of my business, but could it be that you're having doubts about marrying Nowell?"

"Nowell? Of course not." She answered quickly, but shook her head. "I don't know. I don't know what I think anymore. You'd think that if I was sure, I'd be anxious to get back home—not feeling that home is here, at the farm."

"Is that what you're thinking? That the farm is home?"

"It's ridiculous, you know. For years now, I told myself I'd be glad when Dad finally sold the place. I thought I meant it. I *did* mean it. Now I don't know what I think. Before, I convinced myself that my only memories of the farm were painful ones, and I wanted to put them all behind me. But I'm not so sure of that, either."

Her voice quiet, Belle said, "You must have had good memories, too, Maggie, or you wouldn't feel so torn."

"I do. I *do* have good memories—now that I'm back. Oh, I just don't understand it, Belle! I thought I had it all worked out!"

Belle smiled. "Sometimes life is like that—you think you have it filed into neat little boxes. Then something unexpected comes along, and you have to dig through it all again to find the answer and everything gets all torn up."

Maggie looked at her in surprise. "You do understand!"

"Of course I do," Belle said with a laugh. "You're not the only one who's ever felt that way. I had a few moments about my relationship with Dan, if you want to know the truth."

"But you worked it out," Maggie said enviously.

"Yes, and so will you."

"Do you think so?" she said, as a truck rolled into the yard. Glancing out the window, she was almost relieved to see that the farrier had arrived. "I wish I could be so—"

"Maggie!" Dan called just then from the bedroom. "The farrier's here!"

Rolling her eyes heavenward, she muttered, "Give me strength." Then, because she knew Dan would continue calling her until she answered, she raised her voice and said, "I know, Dad! I'm on my way!"

"Do you have the list?"

Sighing in exasperation, Maggie marched into Dan's bedroom. "Dad, you know I hate shouting through doors—"

"Then don't do it," Dan said, holding out a piece of paper. "I made a list."

"You already gave it to me."

"I forgot a couple of horses."

"You mean Le Rouge and City Squire?" she asked innocently, naming the two horses she had discovered he had inadvertently omitted from the trimming schedule.

Dan sat back with a strange look on his face. "How did you know?"

"I know the horses, too, Dad. After all, I've been leading them back and forth from pasture to barn for weeks now. Did you think I wouldn't notice which needed the farrier's attention and which didn't?"

Squinting at her, he said, "I don't know what I thought, Maggie. I guess I should have realized how thorough you are."

She couldn't be annoyed after that. Bending down on impulse, she gave him a quick kiss on the forehead. "I was taught by the best, wasn't I?"

"I don't know about that," he muttered. But he reached for her hand when she started to move away. "Maggie—"

She stopped. "Yes, Dad?"

His eyes searched her face. "Did I tell you how grateful I am, Maggie? No, I mean it. I know I don't say it enough, but I really appreciate all you've done since you came home. I don't know what I would have done without you."

She flushed at the compliment. "Oh, you would have managed somehow. You always do."

"Yes, but it wouldn't have been the same. Maggie, about that foal—"

He fell silent. "Yes, Dad, what about it?" she asked when he didn't say more.

But Dan seemed to have changed his mind again about what he wanted to say. Giving her hand a little shake, he pushed her toward the door, saying gruffly instead, "Better not keep Hank waiting. Oh, and tell him to take a good look at that Grand Cru filly. Her left front's getting a little clubby and I want her set down on the heel."

Maggie didn't say she'd already made a mental note of the problem. "Okay. Anything else?"

Again, Dan hesitated. Then he shook his head. "Give him my regards," he muttered. "Tell him I'm sorry I can't help him today."

"He understands, Dad."

Dan looked at her in annoyance. "Does everybody in the entire state know what a damn fool thing I did?" he demanded.

Hiding her smile, Maggie said, "Oh, I don't think *everybody* knows, Dad. I'm sure there's a few people who were out of town when it happened and haven't heard yet how you let a couple of hay bales get the best of you."

"Out! Out, before I get out of this bed and—"

Belle appeared in the doorway. "You're not going anywhere, Daniel Aloysius Gallagher," she said serenely. "So stop shouting. It's time for your vitamins."

"I don't want any vitamins!"

"Well, you're going to take them whether you want to or not."

Smiling, Maggie left them to the argument, having no doubt who would win. Thanking Providence again that Belle was here to handle their difficult patient, she went outside to greet the farrier.

"Hi, Hank," she said, coming down the steps. "You all ready for a tough day at the office?"

Hank Dunbar was a big, burly man in his mid-forties who had been shoeing horses for almost twenty-five years. More broad than he was tall, he looked strong enough to wrestle a horse to the ground. But Maggie, who had known him for a long time, knew that he had a gentle hand. He'd rather cajole a fractious horse into behaving than physically subdue it. The fact that he could shoe or trim anything on four legs was another factor, and she was glad he'd made time for them today.

Hank had been getting something from inside his truck. Pulling his head out, he turned around and grinned at her. "I take it we're doing some youngsters today. Maybe I should get my armor on."

"Maybe we both should," Maggie said, smiling in response. "You ready?"

"As ready as I'm ever going to be." Taking his heavy leather shoeing apron out of the back of the truck, Hank belted it around his considerable middle, picked up his tools and said, "Let's go."

Maggie had the horses she wanted trimmed ready for him, some in the front paddock, others still confined to their stalls. They elected to do the paddock horses first, then they moved into the barn.

"At least it's cooler in here," she said, taking a handkerchief out of her pocket and wiping her perspiring face. Outside, the spring morning had long ago turned warm, and after nearly two hours of wrestling young horses, she and Hank were hot, dirty and tired. Trimming feet was tough business even if the animals behaved and not all of them did. The farrier took it all in stride, wiping his dripping face with a big bandanna.

"Would you like to stop for a minute and have something cool to drink?" she asked, thinking longingly of some iced tea herself. After so long in the hot sun, she was ready for a rest and didn't mind admitting it.

But Hank said, "How many more do we have to do?"

She calculated. "About seven."

"Then let's get to it."

Stifling a sigh because she knew he was on a schedule, she said, "You're the boss," and led the way to the first stall.

"How's your dad?" Hank asked, as they took a breather after getting six more of the horses trimmed. The final horse was the two-year-old colt, Le Rouge, and Maggie had saved him for last because she suspected he'd be the most difficult. At the question, she made a face. "Let's just say we *all* wish him a speedy recovery."

He grinned. "I take it he's not a good patient."

"The worst."

"He's just used to activity. I remember the time I broke my leg and was off for eight months. Mona and I just about got a divorce, I was such a son of a—so bad."

Maggie shuddered. "If Dad's out for half that long, we'll all lose our minds."

"You're staying that long?"

"Oh, no," she said quickly, grabbing the halter and opening Le Rouge's stall door. Slipping inside, she added, "I've got to go back to New York."

Hank's reply was lost when the colt immediately started to give Maggie a hard time. Acting as though he'd never seen a halter before, the two-year-old rolled his eyes and reared up when she reached for his head.

"Here, now!" she muttered, trying not to get into a battle before absolutely necessary. "What's the matter with you, Red? You've done this ten thousand times, at least."

To her annoyance, the colt jerked away from her and whirled around to the other side of the stall. Watching from the doorway, Hank said, "You want some help?"

"Not yet. I think I can get it."

It took her three more tries before she finally became exasperated enough to grab one of the colt's ears to hold him still while she slipped the halter on. Still lounging in the doorway, Hank said, "We're going to trim this guy, right? Tell me you don't want front shoes on him today, please."

Panting slightly from her exertions, Maggie grinned over her shoulder at him. "What if I told you I want him shod all around?"

"Then I'd tell you I was getting too old for this job and you could call someone else," he replied. But he smiled to show her that he didn't mean it, and picked up his tools. Pulling up his shoeing apron, he came into the stall.

Le Rouge was still acting up; as though Hank were a monster of some kind, he backed away from the farrier, dragging Maggie with him.

"Easy, fella," Hank murmured, as Maggie gave a sharp tug to the lead rope to hold the colt still. Coming slowly up to the horse, he ran his hand along the colt's quivering shoulder. Patting him lightly, he faced the colt's rear, smoothed his hand carefully down the horse's leg and reached out to pick up a hind foot. Immediately, Le Rouge fired out with both hind feet.

"Stop that!" Maggie cried, giving the rope a much sharper jerk to get the colt's attention. She looked at Hank. "Sorry. I don't know what's gotten into him."

"No problem," Hank replied, reaching for the same hind leg again. This time he held on tightly when Le Rouge tried to jerk his foot away. Grunting with the effort of holding a thousand pounds of horse by one hoof, he added, "We'll get it done, but I can't guarantee it'll be pretty."

"I don't care what it looks like," she said between her teeth, as the colt tried to rear again. "Just do what you can."

Thirty minutes later, after chasing Le Rouge around the stall, Hank doggedly holding on to a hind foot, Maggie being dragged around despite digging her heels into the straw, the farrier finally managed to get both of the colt's hind feet trimmed.

"Let's take a break for a minute," Maggie gasped. Sweat was running down her face, between her breasts, in rivers down her back. Le Rouge's struggles had stirred up enough dust to choke them, and as she brushed straggles of hair back from her hot face, she was ready to scream.

Panting himself, Hank straightened. Holding his tools—the knife, nippers and rasp—in one hand, he wiped his other forearm across his face. "No argument here. Lordy, what's the matter with this fellow today?"

Glaring at Le Rouge, who looked a little the worse for wear himself at this point, Maggie said, "I don't know. Maybe we should wait until next time to trim his front feet."

Looking as though he'd prefer to do just that, Hank shook his head. Drops of sweat flew off his face as he did, but he hitched up his leather apron again, took a firm grip on his tools and said, "No, let's get it done."

Thirty seconds later, they were into the fray again. After Hank had struggled unsuccessfully to get hold of one of the colt's front feet before Le Rouge reared and struck out, Maggie called a halt once more.

"I've had it," she said grimly. "We're going to put a twitch on him right now."

To the uninitiated, a twitch—a pincher-like instrument that was placed on the horse's upper lip—seemed cruel and unnecessary. Like anything else, in the wrong hands it could cause inordinate pain. But used properly, a handler could adjust the pressure immediately in response to the horse's behavior, saving both the animal and the people trying to work with it, injury, time and energy.

Maggie didn't like to use a twitch unless it was absolutely necessary, but in this case she judged that it was. There was nothing wrong with Le Rouge. He was just being stubborn. If he'd been frightened or sick or injured, she would have handled his behavior another way entirely.

"Hold him, will you, Hank?" she asked. "Dad keeps a twitch in the tack room. I'll be right back."

Leaving the horse with Hank, she dashed down to the tack room, grabbed the twitch and hurried back. As she did, she thought she heard a car in the yard, but she didn't have time to check. Determined to get this task done, she entered the stall again.

In her youth, she'd attached a twitch to horses dozens of times without thinking. As the colt started to back away from her out of sheer obstinacy, she grabbed his lip, slipped the implement on and tightened it just enough to get his attention. To her satisfaction, Le Rouge stopped abruptly, looking surprised.

Seeing that the horse was secure, Hank grabbed his tools. "This is going to be the fastest trim job in history."

"At this point, I don't care if all you do is run the rasp around the edge of his foot. I'm...going...to make him stand...still if it's...the last...thing I do."

Her last sentence came out in gasps, for despite the twitch, the instant Hank reached for a foot, the colt started to struggle. Hank was an experienced pro; Maggie knew what she was doing, too. Now that they'd come this far, neither of them wanted to let the horse win, so they clung determinedly to him as the battle escalated.

"You got him?" Hank shouted.

"I got him!" Maggie cried. She wasn't going to let the colt go if she had to go down with him.

Dust began to rise in giant clouds from the struggle; Le Rouge was so outraged that he whinnied in frustration. The other horses in the barn joined in, whether in sympathy, or encouraging the rebellion, Maggie couldn't be sure.

"Almost there!" Hank shouted, as they all careened into the wall. He wasn't going to let go of the foot he had; Maggie wasn't going to let go of the colt, and they were both being thrown around like human tetherballs.

"Are you all right?" she yelled back, over the noise and dust and confusion. She didn't know how Hank could possibly see what he was doing; dust and sawdust filled the air, and she felt as if she was about to choke. She opened her mouth to ask him again, but just then, the colt jerked back, hitting one of the stall walls with his full weight. The noise reverberated through the entire barn; it sounded as though the whole place was coming down.

One of the basic tenants of horsemanship was never to lose one's temper, but Maggie lost hers now. Coughing and choking from the dust, her hair flying out of her straggling pony tail, hardly able to keep on her feet because of Le Rouge's struggles, she started to shout, "Stand back! I'm going to kill this—"

The end of her sentence was lost when the colt reared up a final time. Maggie refused to let go either of the twitch or the halter rope, so she went right up with him. Trying to get her off, Le Rouge flung his head to one side, swinging her like a mouse at the end of a string. As she went flying through the air, she heard Hank's amazed and appalled shout, and had just enough time to catch a glimpse of someone standing in the aisle as she came sailing out of the stall.

Why, that looks like—

She didn't have time to complete the thought. Flailing her arms in a vain effort to keep her balance, she came stumbling out backward—right into the arms of Olivia Prescott. They flew back together, both struggling to stay upright, but Maggie's velocity was too great. Her feet went out from under her and she went down, right on her backside.

It was a nightmare, she thought blankly as she looked up, openmouthed, into her future mother-in-law's shocked face. Breathing hard, one hand to her breast, Olivia was holding on to some stall bars at the other side of the aisleway, looking as if she couldn't believe her eyes.

Uninjured, but shocked beyond belief, Maggie's glance went wildly to the man who had leaped forward to help his mother. When Nowell glanced back at her over his shoulder, he couldn't have looked more stunned if he'd found her attacking the rented limousine outside with a wrecking bar.

"Maggie!" Hank shouted, interrupting her trance. Still inside the stall, he had grabbed Le Rouge. "Maggie, are you all right?"

She couldn't just sit here, in the aisleway, on her rear, like this. "How nice to see you again, Mrs. Prescott," she panted, as though they had met at the Galt House for tea. Quickly, she reached up to push her hair out of her face. When she felt the tangles, she knew it was no use. Jumping up, she quickly brushed the dust off the seat of her jeans.

Nowell was looking at her in utter stupefaction, and by this time, Olivia looked ready to pass out. "You'll have to excuse me," Maggie added politely. "But we're having a little disagreement in there. I have to help settle it. It won't take long, I promise. Please... make yourselves comfortable."

And before she could think about what an absolute, utter fool she was making of herself, she turned resolutely and headed back into the stall.

"Maggie?" Hank asked.

"Never mind," she said tensely, grabbing on to the halter rope. The twitch had fallen off and she didn't have time to look for it. Giving Le Rouge a look that froze him to his bones, she said, "Just get the last foot done. I don't care how you do it."

By the time Maggie emerged from the barn again, Olivia had refused Belle's invitation to come inside and was collapsed in the back of the limousine. Outside, a rigid Nowell paced beside the car's open door, while the driver had tactfully removed himself to a position a few yards away to study nonexistent cloud formations.

Hank had come out with Maggie. He took one look at the scene, gave her a sympathetic glance and disappeared into the house to wash up and get paid. That left her to face Nowell and his mother alone.

She hadn't taken time to freshen up—at this point, she was so sweaty and dirty and bedraggled that it would have taken two days—but she had stopped to wash her face in the tack room. Appalled by the sight of her reflection in the mirror, she'd scraped back her hair into another ponytail, tucked her torn shirt in as best she could and taken a deep breath before she went out to face the music.

"Hello, Nowell," she said, as she approached the car. She'd decided she'd just have to make the best of it. "I wish you would have called."

He looked at her as though he'd never seen her before. "Yes," he said, sounding choked. "I'm wishing that at the moment, as well."

She had to do it. Bending down, she peered into the darkened interior of the car. Olivia Prescott was sitting in the far corner, a handkerchief to her nose, as though she'd smelled something foul. When Maggie looked in, she shrank away even farther.

"Hello, Mother Prescott," Maggie said calmly. "This is a nice surprise."

Olivia merely closed her eyes and turned away. "Nowell?" she murmured, distressed.

Nowell had obviously been cued. When Maggie straightened and looked at him, he cleared his throat. "Margaret," he said stiffly, "I'm willing to...to overlook this incident if you return with us immediately to New York. In fact, I'm prepared to pretend it never happened. We need never speak of it again."

A devil seemed to have taken her over. The look Olivia had given her just now made her do it. "Speak of what?" she asked innocently. She looked in the direction of the barn. "Oh, you mean that little dispute we just had? But it was nothing. Things like that happen all the time."

Nowell flushed. "Not to my...not to anyone *I* know! Really, Margaret, where's your pride? Your sense of self? I can't believe what I just saw in there! I mean, for heaven's sake, don't you have *help?*"

"As a matter of fact, we don't," Maggie said. She was beginning to enjoy this. She'd always thought she'd die of embarrassment if Nowell and his mother saw the farm as it really was, but now she didn't even care. Even better, the person she'd been before would have writhed with shame to have been caught in such a predicament, but the one she was now saw the humor in it and almost wanted to laugh.

Almost. When she saw how genuinely distressed Nowell was, she suddenly felt sorry for him. He was who he was; it was she who hadn't been true to herself.

"I'm sorry, Nowell," she said. "I don't want you to be upset."

"Well, I *am* upset!" he exclaimed. "I mean, I never...I never..." He glanced around and shuddered. "When you said your father raised racehorses, well, I thought...I thought..."

"I know what you thought," she said, wondering why she didn't feel the old ache of shame and guilt. "And I'm sorry for that, too. I know you thought Gallagher Farm was on a par with the other famous farms around."

Miserably, his eyes met hers. "Well, you did say—"

"I know." Her glance was steady. "As I said, it was my fault."

"Nowell," Olivia said from the car. From the querulous trembling of her voice, she sounded on the verge of a breakdown—she, who was one of the most formidable women Maggie had ever met. "Nowell, I want to leave now."

"Just a minute, Mother," Nowell said. He looked at Maggie. "Well?"

"Well, what?"

He stiffened. "Please don't be difficult, Margaret. I don't know what's come over you here. You're not yourself. But Mother and I are prepared to wait here while you...er...change into your traveling clothes. Then we can all go to the airport and fly home again—" his glance flicked nervously around the yard "—where we belong."

His eyes came back to her, reflecting his concern when she didn't answer. Suddenly, the weeks of indecision and soul-searching seemed to be coming to a head. She thought of Jack on the night of the sale. She could see his flushed face, the triumph and excitement in his eyes. And when she remembered how she had felt when he had kissed her, and how close he had held her, as though he was afraid she might run away, she knew Nowell could never make her feel that way, not if they were married a lifetime.

It's not his fault, she thought sadly: it's mine. She'd thought she could fit into his world; for years, her only goal had been to make herself do so. But she realized now that she didn't belong there with him, any more than he was suited to be here with her. Their backgrounds were too dissimilar, their beliefs and truths too far apart. Right now she wasn't sure where she fit in, but she'd dwell on that later. She couldn't marry Nowell, no matter what she thought he could give her. She was ashamed that she'd even considered the idea.

"I'm not coming with you, Nowell," she said quietly.

"Not...coming?" he repeated blankly. "But...but what do you mean?" Abruptly, he became angry. "But of course you're coming. Don't be ridiculous,

Margaret! We have plans. We're going to be married!"

Maggie looked down at her engagement ring. It seemed propitious that she was wearing it; usually when she worked in the barn, or with the horses, she left it in the house. But this morning she'd been too preoccupied to remember to take it off, and as she pulled it from her finger, she felt for the first time since she'd accepted it that she could breathe freely again.

Holding the diamond out to him, she said, "I can't marry you, Nowell. I'm sorry, but I can't."

Shocked, he looked down at the ring. "What do you . . . this is outrageous! Of course you can . . . Margaret, you don't mean it!"

"Yes, I do," she said, pressing the diamond into his hand. Softly, she added, "You know we're not right for each other, Nowell. We never have been. Oh, we work well together, I can't deny that, but as for marriage . . . I'm sorry. I realize now that we'd just make ourselves miserable and what's the point of that?"

"What's the point?" he repeated. He looked at her as though he'd never seen her before. "But I . . . I care for you, Margaret! You know I do. I wanted you to be my wife!"

It flashed through her mind that he hadn't said he loved her, but then she realized that was typical of Nowell, too. But none of that mattered now. "And I thought I wanted to be your wife, too. But it just wouldn't work, Nowell. You're Larchmont, Sag Harbor, Upstate New York, while I—"

"But you said your father is going to sell the farm, Margaret," he said desperately, giving another quick glance around. Though he tried to hide it, she could see the disapproval in his face as he continued quickly,

"And when he does, you need never come back here again!"

She looked at him sadly. Without realizing it, he was proving her point. "I'm sorry, Nowell," she said again. It seemed the only thing she was capable of saying. "I have to stay here a few days longer, but I know you need me at the office—"

She'd hurt him, so she couldn't blame him when he reacted angrily. In an effort to salvage some of his pride and save face, he drew himself up angrily. "We'll have to see about that, Margaret!"

"Yes, we will," she agreed calmly. She really doubted that they could work well together after this, but she couldn't just run out on the company. There were other divisions, in other states, and something would work out.

"Goodbye, Nowell," she said. "I really am sorry it turned out this way."

He looked almost ready to cry. "Goodbye, Margaret," he said, his voice choked. Turning jerkily toward the limousine, where the driver had already leaped to the door, he brushed the man aside angrily as he got inside. Just before the chauffeur closed the door, Maggie saw Nowell reach for his mother's hand. Olivia, of course, hadn't said goodbye.

Maggie waited until the big car disappeared, gingerly negotiating the pits and ruts in the Gallagher driveway as it slowly drove away. But long before the car was gone, she was breathing more freely than she had in weeks. Relieved that it was all over, she went inside to tell her father and Belle she wasn't going to get married after all.

JACK CALLED that night after supper. Trying to get Nowell's hurt expression out of her mind, Maggie had cooked dinner, and then as extra penance, announced she'd do the dishes. She was just finishing up when the phone rang.

"Hi," Jack said when she answered. "Is this a bad time?"

For a second or two, she thought he already knew that she'd broken her engagement. Then she told herself it couldn't be when he added, "It wasn't important. I can call back."

"No, no, it's fine," she said quickly. As always, her heart had given a little stumble and then a leap when she heard his voice. With wonder, she realized she could feel this way now, without feeling guilty as well. She wasn't obligated anymore, and the thought made her feel almost giddy. Reaching for a chair, she sat down. "What can I do for you, Jack?"

"A big favor, if you're so inclined."

She wanted to tell him about Nowell, but she didn't know how. "What kind of favor?"

"I know it's a lot to ask, but there's a sale coming up, and I wanted to ask... I mean, I know you're going back to New York soon, and might not have time...but if you do, I was wondering if you could go with me and advise me about a couple of horses I want to buy."

If she didn't know better, she'd think he was nervous. But that couldn't be, she thought. Jack Stanton nervous? After what she had seen at Keeneland, the man didn't have an anxious bone in his body.

Forcing her thoughts away from a sudden mental image of Jack's body, she tried to keep her mind on the conversation. Casting back, she tried to remember if she'd seen another sale coming up, but she couldn't recall reading about one.

"A sale?" she repeated. "I don't think—"

"It would only be for a day—and a night," he added quickly. "As I said, I know it's a lot to ask, Maggie, but I thought we made a pretty good team at Keeneland, and I value your advice."

"Thank you, Jack. I—" Suddenly, she realized what he'd said. "What do you mean, a day and a night? Where is this sale, anyway?"

"Oh, didn't I tell you?" he said, too innocently. "Er... it's in Maryland."

"Maryland!"

When her voice rose, he said hastily, "It's not like it's at the other end of the earth, Maggie. The trip will only take a couple of hours, and we don't even have to stay the night if you don't want to. I thought it would be easier, but if you'd prefer to come home the same day, we could do that with no problem."

She didn't know what to say. "Oh, Jack, I—"

"I promise it'll be strictly business, Maggie. I don't have an ulterior motive, I swear. If you want, we can even take a chaperon. Your Aunt Tilda, for instance."

Maggie burst out laughing. "Boy, you *must* be sincere if you could suggest that, Jack. She'd be worse than a duenna."

"Then you'll come?"

"I'll think about it. When is the sale?"

There was the slightest of pauses. "The day after tomorrow."

Smiling to herself, she said wickedly, "You don't believe in putting on *too* much pressure, do you?"

"I thought if I didn't give you much chance to think about it, you'd say yes."

"You're pretty sure of yourself."

"It's all a facade," he said, although she didn't believe it for a minute. "Will you at least think about it? And I was serious about a chaperon. I wouldn't want your fiancé to think—"

This was the opening she'd needed. "I'm not engaged anymore, Jack. Nowell came to visit today and I—we—decided not to get married, after all. I returned the ring, and he went back to New York."

Jack was silent a moment. Then, solemnly, he said, "I'm sorry, Maggie, I mean it. This must be a difficult time for you, and here I am pressuring you to go look at some horses for sale. Please forgive me. If I'd known, I wouldn't have asked. Is there anything I can do?"

She would never get over how thoughtful he could be. Her heart swelling with gratitude—and another feeling that was becoming all too familiar where Jack Stanton was concerned, she said, "As a matter of fact, there is."

"What? Anything."

She knew he meant it. Smiling, she said, "Tell me what time the flight leaves."

CHAPTER THIRTEEN

"HAVE YOU EVER been to Baltimore?" Jack asked Maggie two days later, when they were on their way to Maryland.

She'd been staring out the plane window, but at the question she turned to look at him. "Don't you mean 'Bawlamer'?" she teased, pronouncing it the way the natives did.

Then, without realizing it, her face changed, and she turned to look out the window again. "Yes, I've been here. Even though Dad never had a horse running in the Preakness, we used to come sometimes. When we had the money, that was."

Remembering how much her father loved it here, and how few times they'd been able to afford it, Maggie felt a renewed sense of shame at how she'd acted back then. She'd been bitter and angry with Dan throughout much of her teens, accusing him of caring more about the horses than about his daughter. Now that she was older, and seeing things more clearly for perhaps the first time in her life, she thought that she couldn't blame him if he actually had preferred the horses; they had certainly treated him much better than she had.

"You look as though you'd rather not remember it," Jack said.

She shook her head. "It isn't Maryland, it's me. When I think of how awful I was back then when I had to help Dad—"

"What do you mean?" Jack said, sounding surprised. "I remember that you were always at the barn, or at the track helping out. You were your father's right hand!"

"Yes, but I resented it."

"Hey, I resented the hell out of having to work in those damned tobacco fields. There were times when I wasn't a very nice guy myself."

She turned to look at him again, a smile curving her lips. "You? I can't believe that."

"Believe it," he said sardonically. "Sometimes when I look back..." It was his turn to shake his head. "I guess the only comfort is that no matter what we felt, we did what we were supposed to."

"Small comfort at times, when you feel like you let someone down."

"You didn't let your dad down, Maggie," Jack said. "It's written all over him how proud he is of you, and he loves you more than life itself."

"I love him, too," Maggie said softly. She was thinking of Dan and how sympathetic he'd been when she'd told him and Belle that her marriage was off. Awkwardly patting her shoulder, he'd told her it was a shame, and that she must feel awful.

But that was just it, she thought: she didn't feel awful at all. It was clear to her now that Nowell had been the wrong choice, and when she realized how close she'd come to marrying him, she shivered. He'd probably make a wonderful husband for the right woman. It was just that that woman obviously wasn't her.

"What are you thinking?" Jack asked.

She might as well tell him. "I was thinking about Nowell."

He hesitated a moment, then he asked, "Are you having second thoughts about breaking off your engagement?"

"Oh, no. It was for the best and I know it. I think some part of me always realized that we weren't really suited for each other, but I didn't want to admit it." She glanced down at her clasped hands. "I thought he was offering the kind of life I wanted, but I know now it was a mistake."

He leaned closer. "What kind of life was he offering, Maggie?"

Although she tried, she couldn't hold his eyes. Glancing down again, she said, "Safety, stability, maybe just serenity in a turbulent world. I don't know, Jack. Until a few days ago, I thought I had every detail of my life planned." She sighed. "Now, I just don't know."

"But you are going back to New York?"

"I have to—if only to decide where to go from here. After all, I still have a job there—a career. I was an executive at Prescott Paper before Nowell and I got involved. One shouldn't have anything to do with the other."

He looked doubtful. "It shouldn't, but it might. Usually these things do."

"I know. But if it's a problem, I'll just have to decide what to do then."

"You like it that much?"

"Yes, I do. I'm good at my job, Jack."

"I have no doubt. But then, I know you're good at everything you do."

She wasn't sure what to say. In fact, she didn't know if she wanted to pursue the conversation or not. It was difficult for her to think when he was sitting right beside her like this. Since he had insisted on getting first-class tickets, the seating was generous, but he was still far too close. She had been keenly aware of him ever since he had picked her up this morning, and for an instant, as the plane touched down and the powerful engines went into reverse thrust, throwing her back against the seat, she started to panic.

She shouldn't have come with him; it wasn't right. But she'd thought at the time—had she thought? She couldn't be sure now—that she could handle it.

But whenever Jack touched her, as he had in the most innocent ways during the trip—a hand under her elbow as they crossed from the parking lot to the airport, taking her luggage from her hand despite her insistence that she could carry it herself, passing her a magazine or a pillow—it was as though a current passed between them. If she felt this way in the airport or on the plane, how was she going to feel in the car, alone with him?

Or tonight, she thought suddenly, when they stopped at a hotel before they headed back tomorrow? Oh, what a fool she'd been to believe she could carry this off without something happening!

His words still hung in the air between them. "You're good at everything you do."

Trying to speak lightly despite her racing pulse, she said, "Thanks for the compliment, Jack, but I'm taking one thing at a time right now. And right now, we have some horses to look at."

Taking his cue, he immediately changed the subject. "I'm not sure about one or two of those mares at

Sweetbrier Stud. Do you think they're worth looking at?"

Relieved that they were talking about something other than *her* plans, she said, "I don't think it will hurt. I have to admit, I'm more interested in the sale horses at Fullermore Farm, but Sweetbrier is on the way, so we might as well stop."

"Whatever you say. As we agreed, on this trip, at least, you're the bloodstock agent."

Inadvertently, he'd voiced one of her concerns. "I wanted to talk to you again about that. I really don't think I'm qualified. It's been a long time since I was involved in horses, and even then, I was just a young girl."

His blue-gray eyes held hers. "You've got all the experience I want, Maggie. I trust you."

"But what if I make a mistake?"

"Then I won't pay you commission."

He was impossible, and she had to smile. Surrendering gracefully, she changed the subject again. "Speaking of horses, how have those you bought at the Keeneland Sale settled in?"

"Just fine." He grinned and the smile transformed his handsome face in a way that caused something to stir inside her. "I had them vanned in, once the place was ready for them and they took over one of the barns as though they owned it. Especially the filly and those two mares. Like queens they are, demanding this, expecting that. I'm going to have to decide on a trainer soon. Eternal Rhythm and Hidden Danger should go back to the track. If they don't return to training before long, they're either going to take someone's head off, or jump out of their skins."

Maggie laughed appreciatively. "Welcome to the world of Thoroughbred racehorse ownership. Who do you like as a trainer?"

"Well, I wanted to talk to you and Dan about that. I was considering Luther Manning, if he's got room for them."

Picturing Luther, whom she had known years ago, with his brisk, no-nonsense manner and his immaculate, efficient stable, she nodded approval. "He'd be a good choice, all right. And as for having room—with the caliber of horses you want to bring him, he'd put them up in his house if he had to, just to get them under his wing. That's the least of your worries, Jack. I wouldn't give it a thought."

"That's because you know what you're doing," he said. "Me, I'm just a neophyte."

She looked at him as the flight attendant announced that they were free to deplane. Beginning to gather her things, she said, "I don't know about that. It seems to me you're doing just fine."

THEY DIDN'T HAVE TIME to discuss anything else until after they had rented a car and were on their way out of the city. Jack was driving and she had the map, but once she got them onto U.S. Highway 1 toward the two farms they intended to visit near Bel Air, she sat back with a sigh. "I hope this is right. It's been a long time since I was here last, and then Dad and I never went farther than Laurel and Pimlico Racetracks. I'd hate for us to get lost."

Jack looked across the seat. Instead of the sports car he usually drove, he'd rented a luxury car because it had more room. With the sleek Lincoln purring under them, he said, "If we do get lost, we'll see some pretty country."

"And maybe end up in Pennsylvania," she said dryly.

"With Chesapeake Bay in front of us?" he teased, obviously not worried about it. "I don't think so, Maggie."

They didn't get lost. An hour later, after visiting Sweetbrier Stud and deciding that the horses weren't quite what Jack was looking for, they headed up the road to Fullermore Farm. At the end of the drive was an elegant three-story brick house with a trilevel stone barn behind, and as they drove into the yard, Maggie pointed with delight.

"Look, Jack!"

To their right were the stallion paddocks. As Jack stopped the car, two of the horses were running back and forth along the fence line, racing each other. They were separated not only by wire and fence, but by about six feet of grassy path. There was no danger of them actually meeting face-to-face, but they were acting as though they were in fierce competition right beside each other on the track. Galloping hard, they both neighed shrilly to impress the mares—and to warn any colt within earshot that the big bosses were still very much around—before reaching the end of their paddocks, turning, and racing back again.

"I'm impressed," Jack said with a grin, watching the stallions showing off.

"Unfortunately, the mares aren't," Maggie retorted, indicating the broodmare band. All the mares were grazing; as she and Jack turned to look, one lifted her head and glanced indifferently at the big boys before dropping down to graze again.

Jack and Maggie were still smiling at the sight when a man emerged from the barn. Seeing them, he waved and came over to introduce himself. He was the owner, Stewart Fullermore, the man they'd come to see. After making the usual polite small talk, he led them into the barn and began showing them the horses he had for sale. All were mares, two of which Maggie liked immediately. But as the men fell into a deep conversation about the merits of each, she was distracted by the sight of a colt out in the paddock.

"Excuse me," she murmured, going outside to get a better look.

Although they weren't the same age, this youngster reminded her of her father's new foal at home. Dan was proud of that colt, and Maggie reflected he had reason to be. Even at two weeks old, the son of Never Forget had a look about him that indicated a future champion.

Dad finally caught the gold ring, she thought, but instead of being happy for him, all she felt was sad. Why did it have to happen now, when he was going to sell the farm? Why couldn't it have happened years ago, when he needed a winner? And then: *Would you have stayed if that colt had come along then?*

She didn't want to think about that, she decided with a frown. Still, she couldn't deny her feelings of satisfaction and pleasure when she watched her father's new colt playing out in the pasture, his mother protectively nearby. And every time she saw the foal dig in his heels and take off, she felt a thrill of pride. But was it because she was responsible for his being here in the first place—or was it something else, something deeper, inside? Maybe she was meant to be with the horses, she thought. Maybe, as Dan said, racing was in her blood as much as it was in his.

Deeply disturbed by those thoughts, she was about to go inside when the men came out. "I see you like the looks of that colt," Fullermore commented.

"Yes, he's got a nice line and good bone," she said.

Fullermore looked pleased. "Thanks."

His arms on the top rail of the fence, Jack had been staring at the yearling. Turning to face the farm owner, he said, "Too bad I'm not in the market for a stallion. He'd be a good prospect."

Fullermore's eyes gleamed momentarily, then his face deliberately went blank. "I could make you a good deal."

Watching him, Maggie almost smiled. So did Jack. "I'm sure you could," Jack said easily. "But as I said, I'm not ready to buy a stallion yet. What say we get down to business about those mares?"

Seeing that Jack wasn't going to bite, Fullermore decided to quit while he was ahead. By the time Jack and Maggie left the farm an hour later, Jack was the proud owner of two more mares. As they got into the car, Maggie congratulated him. Delighted with the outcome himself, he looked at her as they drove back down the winding driveway and took the road back to Baltimore.

"I think a celebration is in order, what about you?"

"I think you're right," she said with a smile. "The champagne's on me."

"You're on. I'll stop at the first nice place we see."

They found a beautiful little inn just outside the city. The terraced garden with a trellis bridge entranced Maggie, and outside, under a domed pavilion, was a pond filled with exotic goldfish. Tables tucked here and there amid lush greenery afforded privacy, and as they sat down beside a trickling little waterfall that added to the elegant ambiance, Maggie said, "It's beautiful, Jack."

And it was. By this time, it was late afternoon and the sun was bathing everything in a golden light. But suddenly, even though they'd forgotten to have lunch, Maggie wasn't hungry. All too aware of Jack right beside her, she was questioning if this was a mistake when Jack ordered champagne.

"Oh, no, I said I'd buy the champagne," she exclaimed.

"We'll settle up later."

She wanted to settle up now. Wondering why she was suddenly so nervous, she reminded herself this was a simple drink to celebrate, and that was all. Nothing had to happen unless she wanted it to... and did she? Every time she looked at Jack, she felt a quivering sensation in the pit of her stomach.

To her relief, the waiter came just then with the champagne. After he'd gone again, Jack raised his glass. Maggie quickly lifted hers.

"Congratulations, Jack," she said. "I know Fieldstone Farm is going to be a big success."

He didn't drink as he was supposed to. His eyes on her face, he said softly, "I couldn't have done it without you, Maggie."

She flushed. "Don't be silly. I didn't do anything."

"You gave me advice."

"You bought the horses."

"But I might have bought the wrong ones, or none at all if you hadn't been there. It was the same the night of the Keeneland Sale. I guess that means we make a good team."

This was dangerous territory, and she quickly touched the rim of her glass to his. "Here's to Fieldstone Farm," she said.

His eyes crinkled. "I'll drink to that."

They both drank. The champagne tickled her nose when she took a sip. Appreciating the sensation despite her growing apprehension, she put the glass down. "You really have come a long way, Jack."

He sat back with a happy sigh. "I'd be a fool to deny it, but it sure took me a long time to get here."

She'd been wanting to ask, and now seemed to be the time. Toying with her glass, she asked, "Why did you come back to Kentucky? You were doing well in California, and if you wanted to race horses, you could have done it there."

"Yes, but I knew the territory here."

"I'm serious, Jack. Why did you come back? You remember the way the other kids used to laugh at us. What Lilah said the night of the sale is a perfect example of how they all felt."

A shadow crossed his face. "Lilah and her father aren't the only owners around. And as for what happened when we were in school—of course it bothered me, don't think it didn't."

"You could have fooled me. You always seemed to take everything in stride. You used to joke about it yourself, in fact. I heard you, many times."

"What was I supposed to do, Maggie? Admit that I hated never having any money for dates? Or worse yet, that I wouldn't have been able to take a girl anywhere even if I could have scrounged up a few dollars? I didn't have a car until I was almost twenty."

She couldn't help herself. "Floyd did."

He looked away. "Floyd was different. He always was."

She heard the edge in his voice and knew she shouldn't pursue it, but some compulsion made her go on. "Yes, he was," she said. "I remember him well. I hope he's changed."

"What do you mean?"

"You said you've made him your manager. I know it's none of my business, but what does he know about running a horse farm?"

Jack shifted uneasily in his chair. "About as much as I do about owning racehorses. I told you, we're going to learn together. And until then, I'm going to hire someone to help."

"Oh?"

"Yes, for a while, I'd hoped it would be you."

"Me!"

"Don't sound so shocked. You'd be a natural. The perfect choice."

"Oh, no, I don't think so."

"I do. And Dan, for one, would love for you to stay."

Her voice suddenly sharp, she said, "Well, the whole idea is out of the question. I told you, I have a job to get back to, a life in New York." She saw his expression and knew that he was thinking of her broken engagement. She glanced away. "Besides, even if I wanted to, I couldn't stay. Dad's selling the farm to you, and—"

"He wouldn't sell if you weren't going to leave."

She didn't want to continue with this; it was too perilously close to thoughts she'd been thinking herself. Wondering if she was trying to convince herself as much as him, she said intensely, "If I stayed, I wouldn't have the money to run it, and that's not for me. Even if I wanted to—and I'm not saying I do—I couldn't live the way I used to when I was growing up. I hated our hand-to-mouth existence back then, having every spare dime, every nickel, every *penny* going to the horses. I swore I'd never live like that again."

"But it wouldn't be that way now, Maggie."

She didn't want to give him a chance to say what she thought he was going to say. "It doesn't matter. That part of my life is over."

"I can't believe that. You can fight it and deny it all you want, but the truth is that horses are in your blood. Don't forget, I've seen you with them. I saw how gentle you were with Never Forget, and what your reaction was when her foal was born. I saw how excited you were at the Keeneland Sale, and how you looked when Eternal Rhythm came out onto the stage. You're a born horsewoman, Maggie. Horses are part of you and always will be."

"But I don't want them to be!"

As soon as the cry was torn from her, she realized her error. She hadn't denied the truth of what he said, only the way she felt about it. Seeing the look on his face, she took a quick swallow of champagne. Angrily, she set her glass back down.

"I don't want to talk about this anymore, Jack."

Instantly, he reached for her hand. "I'm sorry, Maggie. The last thing I want to do is make you angry."

"I'm not angry!" But she was. Angry that he had put into words things she did not want to think about.

"Okay, my mistake. Look. Maybe we should leave and look at a few more horses before it gets dark."

She wasn't ready to forgive him. "I don't think you need me, Jack. You're doing just fine on your own."

"I don't want people to think I'm a complete rookie at this. I'd hate to look like a fool."

"I don't think you've ever looked like a fool in your life."

"Don't be too sure. As I remember all too well, I was a fool once with you."

She couldn't be coy; she knew what he was talking about. Distracting herself by looking at the little waterfall trickling merrily beside their table down into the fishpond, she said, "It was a long time ago. We were very young then."

"So you do remember that night on the river."

It was useless to pretend she didn't. Abandoning her pose, she turned to him again. She had been wanting to say it for years, and this was her opportunity to put the issue to rest.

"You know I remember. I've thought about that night a thousand times since. About what I said, about what I *could* have said...about what I really wanted to say and didn't. I know I hurt you, Jack, but I didn't mean to."

He was silent a moment. "And I know I shouldn't have pressed you like that, Maggie. But I couldn't help myself. I didn't want you to leave. I was so crazy about you that I—"

"Don't tell me this, Jack...please."

"I have to." Leaning forward again, he put his hand on her arm. "I've thought about that night a lot, too, Maggie. I've thought about it too many times to count. I wanted to say so many things to you, but you weren't ready to listen. It was driving me crazy because I knew if you left, I'd never see you again—at least not for a long, long time." He paused. "And I was right, wasn't I?"

She didn't know what made her say it. Maybe it was because she felt guilty, or because she wanted to explain, or perhaps because she'd been regretting her hasty words ever since. "It wouldn't have worked, Jack. Not then."

"And now?" he asked, his eyes on her face. "Would it work now, Maggie?"

She didn't want to look at him; she couldn't look away. "I don't know, Jack."

He reached for her hand. She didn't seem to have the strength to move it away. When his fingers clasped hers, she closed her eyes. His hand was warm, solid, comforting, strong. She wanted so much to turn her hand up and lace her fingers with his, but she couldn't move. She could hardly breathe. Her heart was thudding away like a trip-hammer, reminding her with every beat how much time had been lost.

"Answer me, Maggie," he said quietly. "Please. I've waited years to hear you say it, once and for all. We're both grown-up now. We know our own minds—at least I know mine. I realize it's too soon after breaking your engagement to commit yourself, but I just want to know if there's a possibility, a chance that it would work now."

She didn't know what to say. She wanted to be able to trust her own feelings. She'd thought she was in love with Nowell, and that hadn't worked out; the last thing she wanted to do was rebound from that relationship into Jack's arms.

Swallowing hard over the lump in her throat, she said, "I don't know, Jack. I wish I could tell you, but I can't. I'm sorry. I just don't—"

"Don't say anymore," Jack said. A look of pain flashed through his eyes before he released her hand. "I'm sorry, Maggie, I shouldn't have pressed you. It's too soon. I wasn't thinking of you, but of myself."

"Jack—"

"Let's just forget it, all right? Pretend it never happened. We're here to talk about horses, and that's all we're going to do."

He reached for the menu the waiter had put by his elbow, but she put her hand on his arm. "Jack, don't be angry."

"I'm not angry."

Realizing she had hurt him again, she said in a low voice, "I'm sorry, Jack. It's just that too many things have happened lately. I need some time to think things through."

"I understand," he said. Making a determined effort, he smiled at her. "Like I said, let's just forget it, all right? Look, we didn't have lunch, so why don't we have an early supper. Then, if you want to, we can fly back tonight."

Suddenly, she knew that she didn't want to fly back—not tonight, anyway. She might not know what she wanted tomorrow to bring, but one thing she did know, and that was that she wanted to be with him... this night, at least. She wasn't going to let this opportunity pass, as she had the one so long ago.

She'd tried, but she couldn't deny her attraction to him any longer. He'd drawn her to him ever since she'd come home, and her feelings had intensified until every time she looked at him, she felt almost dizzy with longing. She knew he felt it, too; she could see it in his eyes, his face, the lines of his body. Even their brief quarrel hadn't dimmed her desire for him;

in some strange way, it seemed to have made her feelings for him even more intense.

You want him. You know you do, a little voice breathed into her inner ear. *So go ahead. Tell him how you feel.*

"Jack—" she said.

He looked at her over the champagne. His eyes suddenly seemed to change from blue-gray to midnight-black. Softly, he said, "You feel it, too, don't you, Maggie?"

She couldn't look away from him. Shakily, she answered, "You know I do."

Without another word, he got up. Reaching down, he pulled her to her feet. Together, they went inside to rent a room.

MAGGIE'S DAZED STATE lasted until Jack unlocked the door of the room they'd been given. She had a brief impression of floral wallpaper, gleaming antiques, a softly patterned rug on the floor, and a high, old-fashioned four-poster bed. Then Jack pulled her into his arms. As soon as his mouth came down hard on hers, she forgot her surroundings. For all she knew, or cared, she could have been in a tent in the middle of the desert.

"Jack, I...I didn't bring anything," she gasped, when they pulled away from each other for a moment, breathing hard.

His eyes looked nearly black as he gazed down at her. Hoarsely, he said, "I did."

She drew in a sharp breath. "You were so sure of me?"

He shook his head. Tenderly, without releasing his hold on her, he traced her jaw with one finger. "You can't blame a man for planning ahead, can you?"

She looked at him indignantly. "I'm not sure."

"Perhaps this will help to convince you, then...."

Reaching behind him, he locked the door. Then he pulled her into him again, against his suddenly trembling body, and when she felt the fierce heat of his desire for her, she forgave him everything. Wrapping her arms around his neck, she pressed tightly against him, raising her lips to his for another kiss.

"You don't know what you do to me...." he whispered, holding her close.

She knew what he was doing to her. Even through their clothes, the flame leaped, and when she took his hand and guided it to her breast, he put his head in the hollow of her neck and sighed in sheer bliss.

"I've dreamed about this for so long," he murmured hoarsely. "I never thought it would actually come true...."

Her breath was warm against his cheek. "I've dreamed about it, too," she whispered. "But, Jack—"

Alarmed, he drew back. "You haven't changed your mind, have you?"

She shook her head. "No. I just...after thinking about it for so long, I...don't want to disappoint you."

"Disappoint me?" He looked at her tenderly, then he laughed. "Never, Maggie. You could never disappoint me, no matter what."

"But we're no longer the teenagers we once were," she said.

His eyes were like blue stars. "Thank God for that," he said, and pulled her over to the bed.

With his arms around her, Maggie gave herself up to pure sensation. Drawing him closer, she breathed in deeply, taking in a heady mixture of soap and faint after-shave and something else that was essentially him, a scent that could never be duplicated by any chemist, but one she would remember a lifetime.

Loathe to leave each other even to undress, they took turns removing garments one by one, delighting in new sensations of sight and touch. Maggie was wearing a blouse and slacks; when he removed the blouse, and then her bra, he just stood there looking at her in wonder. Almost reverently, he reached out and touched one breast lightly before cupping it in his hand. Closing his eyes with delight, he breathed in a shaky breath.

"You're so beautiful," he murmured at last, opening his eyes and looking down at her again. "So beautiful...."

Then it was her turn. When she took his shirt off and saw his broad chest, she sighed and pressed her cheek against him. His hands went to her back, caressing her, touching her, arousing feelings she'd never imagined feeling, even with him. Before she knew it, she was unbuckling his belt with sure fingers, pulling his slacks down over his trim hips, taking his erection in her hand as he groaned with pleasure.

"My turn," he said, his breath coming in gasps, his eyes widening when she stepped out of the pool of her slacks on the floor and stood before him, naked. He reached for her and pulled her close, and they stood for a moment, reveling in the sensation of skin against skin.

Then, with a smile, she reached out and pulled the covers down off the bed.

As she had known he would be, Jack was a wonderful lover. She had expected him to be experienced, and he was, but even she wasn't prepared for the passion he aroused in her with his kisses, and caresses, and the careful attention he paid to her every desire. One magical moment led to another, and then another, until finally even his expert touch wasn't enough. Their bodies were slippery with the sweat of passion; their harsh breathing filled the room. His hands and his lips were hot and demanding—but no more demanding than hers.

She couldn't get enough of him; kissing him, running her hands through his thick hair, touching his face, kneading the strong muscles of his back and shoulders and long legs, was heaven. His hands on her aroused her to fever pitch; his mouth on hers, his tongue circling her breasts and teasing her nipples, drove her almost wild. She wanted all of him, wanted to feel him deep within her as they moved together in the timeless rhythm of all loving creatures. Finally, she couldn't bear the anticipation any longer.

"Jack!" she gasped, taking him and guiding him inside her.

His answer was a half moan, half groan. Burying his head in the crook of her shoulder, he held her tightly and together they rocked back and forth, lost in blissful sensation.

Once, just before she was transported to another plane where the only reality was the pleasure that was lifting her higher and higher, claiming not only her body but her mind, he pulled back and looked down at her. She could see the sheen of perspiration on his forehead, could see how dark his eyes had become with passion.

"Oh, Maggie," he whispered. "I never thought I'd get a chance to say this, but I love you. I love you with every beat of my heart...."

Then he lowered himself down onto her again, and as evening shadows purpled the walls and the last of the sunset faded, Maggie was swept away. When he drove into her, thrusting harder with every answering rise of her hips, she clutched his perspiring back with her own slippery fingers, kneading his taut buttocks, wrapping her legs around him to pull him deeper and deeper inside her. Arching her back, she lifted her aching breasts for him to kiss, and he obliged with a gasp, bending his head and sucking one swollen nipple, then the other, until she couldn't bear it any longer. Sensation drove her to a frenzy; with a cry she couldn't hold back, and with one final arch, she spun into another dimension of pure pleasure. Her body wasn't her own; it had become ethereal, a being that could fly.

Jack came with her, a hoarse cry of triumph ripped from his throat. Fiercely, he kissed her a last time, then he laughed aloud before he collapsed in a spent heap beside her.

THEY MADE LOVE twice more before the clock struck midnight, both of them marveling that the frenzied passion of their first encounter seemed to increase each time they came together. Finally, Jack reached for the blankets to cover them against the evening chill only to discover all the bedclothes in a pile on the floor. He sat up against the single pillow they had left.

"If I don't get something to eat, I won't be able to get out of this bed in the morning," he panted.

Laughing, she pulled the sheet up. "How can you think of food at a time like this?" she teased. But she was hungry herself, and when she looked at the clock, she was shocked. "We'll never get anything now. The kitchen must have closed hours ago."

"Not to worry," he said, taking a deep breath before dragging himself off the bed. "I'll go out and get something."

She looked at him in amazement. "You'd do that?"

He pulled on his clothes. "I'm a starving man. I'll do anything." Bending down, he kissed her, then cupped a breast briefly in his hand before squeezing it lightly. "Maybe you're right," he said, closing his eyes and enjoying the sensation. "Who needs food, anyway?"

But he went, despite her protests, and when he returned, he was carrying a bulging sack from which he produced four thick sandwiches, two boxes of crackers and a bottle of wine.

"My goodness," she said, gazing down at the largesse. "You don't intend to eat all this, do you?"

"No, you can have one of the sandwiches if you like," he said with a grin. Then he threw off his clothes and got into bed again.

MAGGIE FELT more confused than ever the next day on the way home. Was she in love with Jack? Every time she looked at him, she wanted to touch him, to feel his lips on hers, his hands in her hair and on her body. Maybe spending the night with him had been a mistake. Although they hadn't discussed the future, both of them pretending to be content just taking the present one step at a time, she was painfully aware that nothing had really changed except that she wasn't going to marry Nowell Prescott.

She didn't want to be in love with Jack, she told herself again and again. Love would make everything even more difficult than it already was. Jack wanted something she didn't and never would, and she doubted she could change even for him. It was as though they were on trains going in different directions. He was committed to Fieldstone Farm; it was where his future was.

And her future? She didn't know anymore. She just knew that after the passionate night they'd spent in each other's arms, she didn't know which would hurt worse: to go, or to stay.

"Oh, Jack," she murmured, reaching for his hand as the plane touched down in Louisville.

Wordlessly, he squeezed her fingers. When she turned to look at him, his gaze was just as troubled as hers. He knew the conflicts she felt, but as he'd murmured tenderly to her during the night, only she could decide what she wanted. He'd told her he loved her; he'd confessed that he wanted her to be his wife.

The decision, he'd said, would be up to her.

CHAPTER FOURTEEN

IT WAS LATE WEDNESDAY afternoon when Floyd was awakened by the ringing of the telephone. Jolted out of a sound sleep, he reached for the receiver before he realized what he was doing. Jack was away on a business trip, so he'd taken advantage of his brother's absence by catching a little shut-eye in the office. But the instant he recognized Lilah Castlemaine on the other end of the phone, he jerked his boots off the desk top and sat up straight.

"Jack's not here," he said, rubbing the sleep out of his eyes and reaching for a cigarette. He'd been told not to smoke in the barn, but he'd always figured that what his brother didn't know wouldn't hurt him.

"It's not Jack I want to talk to," Lilah purred in his ear. "Oh, I'm so glad I caught you, Floyd. Are you up to a little business proposition?"

Floyd squinted suspiciously through the smoke he'd just exhaled. "What kind of business? And why aren't you discussing it with Jack?"

"Because Jack wouldn't understand a deal like this. And I figured that if anyone would understand the opportunity I've got to offer, you would. I really think that underneath it all, you and I are two of a kind, don't you?"

"Huh!" Floyd snorted. "You and I are about as much alike as a nun and a call girl."

To his surprise, Lilah laughed. Throatily, she said, "I don't have to ask which category you put *me* into!"

It was the laugh that got him. Deciding that it wouldn't hurt just to listen, he said grudgingly, "You mentioned a business proposition."

"So I did. All right, here's the deal. I've heard of a certain horse for sale right now—and maybe more in the future, if this works out—who's going dirt cheap. Now I know you and Jack aren't the best of friends—"

"Who told you that?" Floyd bristled.

Lilah laughed. "No one had to tell me, Floyd! We went to school together, remember? I know how it was. Everybody always compared you to Jack. Why, if I were you, I'd hate him myself!"

"I don't hate him," Floyd muttered.

"Perhaps not, but I'll bet you can't help feeling a little envious that he's got more money than he knows what to do with, while you've always been...down on your luck."

"I'm not envious. He's just always had all the breaks, that's all."

"You see what I mean?" she said persuasively. "Well, I'm calling now to tell you how you can even the odds a little. You'll even be able to make a little on the side for your own account. How does that sound?"

Against his will, he had to admit that it sounded pretty good. Jack always *had* been lucky, where as *he* had always been at the train station when his ship had come in. It wasn't fair.

"Exactly what do you have in mind?" he asked cautiously.

"As I said, I know of a horse for sale right now. It's a real dog, won't run worth a damn. But the owner paid a pretty price for the useless old thing, and if he got, say, twenty-five thousand for it—more than it's worth right now—well, he's not adverse to leaving the purchase price blank on the receipt. In other words, someone could give him a check for whatever amount they wanted, and this guy would give the difference back in cash." She paused. "If you get what I mean."

Floyd got it, all right, and his eyes narrowed. "What you're saying, is that if someone buys the nag for twenty-five thou, gives a check for, say, thirty thousand, this guy will give him five thou in cash and put the full thirty on the receipt."

"That's right." She laughed huskily. "But why think small, Floyd? What's five thousand to Jack? You could make it five times that and he still wouldn't notice."

Floyd's eyebrows shot up. "You mean buy the horse for twenty-five and say he'd cost fifty? Oh, no, I—"

"What's the matter, Floyd?" she interrupted mockingly. "Don't tell me you're scared of your brother!"

"I'm not scared!" he insisted. Weakly, he added, "It's just that a . . . a hundred percent profit sounds a little indecent."

"Indecent?" She laughed merrily. "After all you've endured? Take a look around you, Floyd. Don't you think you deserve it?"

Involuntarily, Floyd glanced around. Everywhere he looked evidence of Jack's money gleamed, from the stainless steel fixtures in the barn to the new state-of-the-art computer Floyd had no idea how to use. Lilah was right, he thought with a fierce frown. Jack had more than he needed; he certainly wouldn't miss a measly twenty-five grand.

Then he thought of something and his eyes narrowed again. "Wait a minute. Just why are you doing this? I can't believe you'd want to split the profit."

Lilah laughed again, as though the very idea were absurd. "For heaven's sake, you think I'd want a piddly little amount of money like that?"

"Then what? I might not know much, but I know that people like you...and me," he added mockingly, "don't do something for nothing. What's in it for you?"

She wasn't laughing now. Her voice sharp, she said, "Never mind. I have my reasons for wanting to get back at Jack and they don't concern you. Just tell me, are you interested or not?"

Floyd looked around the office again. Through the open window, he could see the big house, all plate glass and chimneys and limestone accents. Beyond the house, he could see the acres of rolling pastures, enclosed now by miles of freshly painted white fences. And not ten feet away from him, secure in their luxurious stalls, were the horses Jack had bought at the sale, all five million dollars worth of them. Would Jack miss twenty-five thousand? No, Floyd didn't think so. In fact, he thought with a sudden gleam in his eye, he probably wouldn't miss ten times that.

Ignoring the ugly specter of betrayal that rose in his mind, he pushed away all thought of how much Jack had already given him, how much his brother trusted him, how many times he'd tried to help Floyd. Righteously convincing himself that this little business deal between him and Lilah couldn't possibly hurt Jack, who had so much he wouldn't even miss it, he stabbed out his cigarette and immediately lighted another one.

"I'm interested," he said curtly. "Tell me what to do and when to do it."

Ten minutes later, he came out of the office and shut the door behind him. Lilah's final admonition still echoed in his ears, and he frowned.

"Now, remember," she'd said before she hung up. "If Jack asks why you took it upon yourself to buy a horse for him, all you have to say is that you thought you were doing him a favor. You know, proving to him that you're really trying with this job as his farm manager. And for heaven's sake, don't mention me! The last thing we want is for him to get suspicious!"

Floyd agreed with that. With so much money riding on this, and maybe more in the future if it worked out, he was going to be quiet as a mummy. Still, he felt a little nervous about it as he started walking down the aisle. Jack wasn't stupid, far from it. If he even *guessed*...

"He ain't gonna guess," Floyd muttered to himself. And in any event, he didn't have time to think about it. He was supposed to take a check right away to the owner, who was waiting for him in town; as soon as the guy had his money in hand, he'd sign over the papers and the horse would belong to Jack. It was as simple as that.

But he still felt nervous at the other arrangements Lilah had made. For some reason, she didn't want the horse to be delivered here, to the farm; it was going to be transferred from the old owner's barn at the track to Luther Manning's stable there. Luther was Jack's new trainer, and Floyd was supposed to call him and tell him that Jack wanted the nag to run in the first race he could enter.

"Yeah, but what if Luther objects?" Floyd had asked Lilah uneasily. "I mean, you said yourself that this horse can't run. Won't Luther know that?"

Lilah dismissed his concerns. "It doesn't matter if he does or he doesn't. Luther works for Jack. He'll do what he's told."

"But—"

"Don't worry about it," she'd said sharply. "Now, look, Floyd, if you're getting cold feet . . ."

"I ain't getting no cold feet! It's just that I need to know what to say in case this Manning guy gives me some trouble."

"He won't," she insisted. "Trust me. Jack's an owner. An *important* owner. He's already sent Hidden Danger to Luther and promised him more, and with horses like that, Manning will enter a *pig* in a race if Jack tells him to. I know what I'm doing, Floyd."

He didn't like it, but he had to go along with her plan. More money than he'd dreamed about was at stake; nothing could go wrong.

But what if something did? Trying to ignore the churning in his stomach, he jammed his hands into his pockets. He had to leave right now or he'd be late, and as he started out, he was glad the crew had already gone for the day so he wouldn't have to explain anything. Except for Ralph Jorgenson, who lived in an apartment over the barn in order to watch over the horses at night, Floyd was alone on the place.

Well, not exactly *alone,* he amended, aware of stares following him as he walked quickly along. On each side of the aisle, horses watched him with their tiny brains and big stupid eyes. Each stall was fitted with a brass placard that identified the occupant, and Floyd stopped in front of the stall that held Eternal Rhythm. Not being interested himself, he couldn't have told one horse from the other without the nameplates; except for variations in color, they all looked the same to him.

All except this black demon, he thought, staying well back from the bars when she saw him and snorted. The instant he'd seen this creature flying out of the van, he knew she'd been misnamed. Devil Demon, that's what they should have called her. Even now he couldn't believe what Jack had paid for her. Two million dollars, he thought. *Two million.* In his book that was a lot of hamburger.

As though she'd read his mind, Eternal Rhythm suddenly pinned her ears back and came at the bars. She stopped just short of crashing into them, but Floyd leaped quickly back anyway.

"Here now, you witch, you stop that!" he shouted. In answer, the highly strung mare bared her teeth.

He knew what would happen to him if he gave into impulse and did what he wanted to her, so after glaring at her a moment, he hunched his shoulders and continued on his way. He'd never admit it, but he was afraid of that black horse; he didn't trust her because it seemed to him that she was always about half-ready to jump out of her skin. Jack said it was because she needed to get back into race training to dispel all that excess energy, but Floyd didn't agree. To him, what she needed was a quick trip on the knacker's wagon.

Two million, he thought again. No four-legged creature on earth was worth that much money. He'd said it before and he'd say it again: to his way of thinking, his brother had gone out of his mind.

Maybe it was because he was in love, he thought with a cynical grin. Jack had sure been happy since he got back from Maryland last weekend, and Floyd knew why. It was obvious that he and Maggie Gallagher had something going; a man would have to be deaf, blind and stupid not to know what was happening right before his eyes.

His smile faded slightly as he thought of how different Jack had been lately. There was a lightness about him, a joy Floyd hadn't seen in his brother before. Jack smiled more, and he laughed a lot quicker. There was a spring to his step, and he even seemed somehow younger.

Then he snorted derisively. *Love!* He'd seen the trouble a man could get into when a woman got her hooks into him. Three ex-wives and quite a few girlfriends had taught him to stay clear of getting entangled with females. They knew too much; they saw too many things. A man didn't have half a chance with women, not when they were determined about something. Oh, Jack was going to regret getting involved with that Maggie Gallagher, he thought. He remembered her from school, and if ever there was a determined female, she was one of them.

Floyd stopped suddenly right there in the aisle as an awful thought occurred to him. He'd only seen Maggie Gallagher once since he'd been here; she'd come over to see the horses, and when they'd met, he knew right away what she was thinking. It was plain that she thought he didn't belong here, and he'd felt his belligerence rising. What right had she to judge him?

But he couldn't forget that look in her eyes, and when he remembered how much she knew about horses, he felt a stab of uncertainty. Suppose Maggie found out what he and Lilah were up to? She'd tell Jack, and there'd be hell to pay before he knew it.

"Aw, how can she find out?" he muttered to reassure himself. He wasn't going to say anything, and he knew Lilah wouldn't. No, he was just getting antsy, that was all; letting his nerves get the best of him. Once he'd met this guy in town and completed the transaction, he'd feel better, he knew it.

BUT FOR SOME REASON, Floyd didn't feel better after he got back from town. It was dark by this time and as he let himself into the trailer, the first thing he did was head to the refrigerator. Beer always calmed him down, but as he reached for one, he reconsidered. His stomach was really churning, and he needed something stronger.

Slamming the door closed, he reached into the cupboard for a bottle of good old Kentucky sour mash. He didn't know what was wrong with him; he'd done the deal and it had gone smooth as could be. He had the money, and he should be out celebrating. But as he poured the first shot and drank it, he thought suddenly of Jack and shivered.

"Don't think about it," he muttered. "You're not hurtin' nobody."

But once he'd thought of his brother, he couldn't get Jack out of his head. It took the whole evening and the rest of the bottle to make him forget what he'd done, and Jack's accusing face was before him the whole time. Just when he thought he'd go crazy, he solved it by drinking so much, he finally passed out.

WHEN JACK GOT HOME from his business trip to Atlanta, the first thing he did was call Maggie. Disappointed when Belle told him she'd gone into town, he left the message that he'd call her later about dinner, and then headed out to the barn to check on the horses.

Maggie had laughed gently at his enthusiasm, assuring him that the newness of horse ownership would quickly wear off, but he doubted it. The success he'd enjoyed with his company didn't come close to the satisfaction of coming home to Fieldstone Farm. Seeing the horses and dreaming of those to come gave him a thrill he couldn't begin to describe.

Then there were his feelings for Maggie. Sometimes that night in Baltimore seemed like a dream; he was almost afraid to believe it had really happened. They hadn't had any time together since. A problem in the Atlanta office had required his direct intervention, so he'd had to go. But he was back now, and at the thought of seeing her tonight, his smile broadened into a silly grin.

"Hello, Ralph...Emil," he said, greeting two of the barn crew as he walked into the barn. They were busy cleaning stalls, and he was pleased to note that most of the horses had already been put out on pasture, including his special favorite, Eternal Rhythm. Seeing her out in the paddock reminded him how pleased he was that Luther Manning had agreed to take her. Her stable sister, Hidden Danger, was already at Luther's training stable at Churchill Downs, and he intended to call the trainer later tonight to get a progress report.

Whistling with sheer good spirits, he headed on to the office to talk to Floyd. He'd expected to see his brother hard at work, but when he got there, the room was empty. Coming out again, he called down the aisle, "Ralph? Where's Floyd?"

The barn manager poked his head out of the stall where he was working. "I don't know, Mr. Stanton. I haven't seen him this morning."

"He hasn't come down yet?"

"No, sir."

Frowning, Jack wondered if something was wrong. He knew Floyd was here because the purple Caddy was parked out front. Switching directions, he headed for Floyd's trailer. Through the open curtain, he could see the lamp on. Hoping Floyd wasn't sick, he knocked and called his brother's name. There was no answer.

"Floyd? Floyd, are you in there? Is something wrong?"

Had that been a groan he heard? He tried the door. It was unlocked, and he pushed it open.

"Floyd!"

Another sound, from the bedroom. Starting in that direction, Jack didn't notice the empty whiskey bottle on the floor until he accidentally kicked it. "What the hell...?" he muttered. The bedroom door was partially closed and when he pushed it open, he didn't know what disgusted him most: the sour smell of liquor, or the sight of Floyd sprawled across the bed, fully dressed, dead to the world.

Jack felt his temper rising. Floyd had promised him this wouldn't happen. Before he could stop himself, he reached down, hauled his brother to a sitting position and gave him a hard shake to get his attention.

"Wha...whatsa matter?" Floyd muttered.

"You! You're the matter!" Jack couldn't remember ever being so angry. Although they were almost the same size, he jerked Floyd up off the bed as though he were a doll and dragged him to the bathroom. Shoving him into the shower, he turned on the cold water and held him under the stinging spray until Floyd came awake enough to realize what was happening. Instantly, he filled the bathroom with howls of outraged protest.

"Hey! What are you...? Damn it, Jack...let me go!"

Jack didn't even answer. Mercilessly, he held his struggling brother under the water until Floyd was shivering. "You sober now?" he snarled.

Water running down his face and onto his sodden clothes, Floyd looked up angrily. "What do you think?"

"I don't want to tell you what I think. Just get dressed. I'm going to make some coffee."

Not trusting himself to say more, he left Floyd to climb out of the shower by himself. Heading toward the kitchen, he jerked the coffee canister toward him and tried to calm himself by counting out cups. But he was still angry when Floyd appeared ten minutes later, barefoot but dressed in dry jeans and a T-shirt. Lighting a cigarette with hands that shook slightly, Floyd looked warily at him and said, "I can explain."

Jack had been staring out the window trying to get a grip on his temper. "Fine," he said, a muscle leaping in his jaw. Right now, it wouldn't take much for him to kick Floyd off the farm. "Go ahead."

"Uh...you mind if I have some coffee first?"

Jack didn't even turn around. "Help yourself."

Armed with a cup and obviously wishing he dared add a little hair of the dog to go with it, Floyd sat down gingerly at the breakfast table.

"I know you're angry—" he started to say, and flushed when Jack glanced at him "—and you have a right to be. I know I promised I wouldn't get...I wouldn't do any heavy drinking, so I'm in the wrong. I guess I just got carried away."

Jack still wouldn't look at him. "That's putting it mildly."

There was a little silence. "Don't you want to know why?"

"No."

"Well, I'm going to tell you anyway. It was supposed to be a surprise, but I'd rather you knew than be mad at me. The truth is, little brother, I did something while you were gone—something you're going to like...I hope."

"Oh, and what's that?"

"I bought you a horse."

Slowly, Jack turned to look at him. "You did what?"

"Now, I know I don't have much experience—" Seeing Jack's expression, he went on hastily, "All right, I don't have *any* experience. But I wanted to show you I was *trying,* so I've been studying those books in the office, and when I heard about this horse being for sale, I checked it out. It seemed like a pretty good deal to me, so I...I bought it for you. You don't have to keep it, I guess. I can always call the owner and tell him I made a mistake. In fact, I think that's what I'd better do. It was a lousy idea. I'll call the bank and—"

Floyd started to reach for the phone, but Jack said, "Wait a minute." He came over to the table and sat down so they were face-to-face. "Tell me the truth, Floyd. Why did you really buy this horse?"

Floyd looked him right in the eye. "I know it sounds silly, but I wanted to prove that your faith in me wasn't misplaced. I know I haven't been much in the past, but you've given me a new chance here, and I wanted to show you how grateful I was. Now, I know you probably don't believe me... hell, if the shoe were on the other foot, I wouldn't believe me, either. But it's the truth. I swear it."

Jack sat back, a strange expression on his face. The part of him that knew his brother wanted to ask what his angle was, but another part, the one that *wanted* to believe in Floyd, told him to accept the story and be pleased that he'd made such an effort. He couldn't remember a time in their lives when Floyd had ever asked for, or even wanted, his approval, and Jack looked at him in a new light.

"Shall I call the bank?" Floyd asked. "Maybe it's not too late to stop the check and get back the fifty thousand."

"Fifty thousand?" Jack looked at Floyd, saw the uncertainty on his face and smiled. "It's okay. We'll keep the horse and see how it does."

Floyd stared down into his coffee cup. "Well, I don't think you'll be sorry," he muttered. "I got a good deal on the nag, and... and Luther's going to train it." Forcing himself, he looked up at Jack. "I guess you think that's pretty presumptuous, me putting a horse in training, but—"

"No, no, it's all right," Jack said. "If Luther agreed to take it, and he has room, I think it's fine." He smiled. "If the horse wins, maybe we'll split the purse."

"No, no, that's okay," Floyd said hastily. "I mean, you got to make your money back first. It still cost you fifty thousand."

Jack didn't bat an eye. "Well, we'll see," he said, holding out his hand. "I'm sorry I doubted you, Floyd. I know now that you're trying, and I appreciate it."

Floyd briefly took his hand. "Don't worry about it," he muttered. "It wasn't that big a deal. After all, you paid for it."

JACK DIDN'T FIND OUT how dearly he'd paid until later that night, when he and Maggie were having dinner. At the time, horses were the last thing he wanted to discuss; just being with Maggie after being away these past few days was thrilling enough.

But when he wanted to talk about *them*, about their relationship, she seemed to want to avoid any mention of it. During the drive to the restaurant, she chatted intensely about how busy she'd been, and how Dan seemed to be getting better; she told him how the new foal was growing, and how glad she was that she and Belle had become friends. She told him everything, in fact, but what he wanted most to hear.

He'd promised not to press her; he'd told her in Maryland what his feelings were and said that the next move was up to her. But as he watched her expressive face over dinner, thinking how beautiful her eyes were, remembering how soft her lips were, he began to wonder anxiously what the end of the evening would bring. He didn't like her not meeting his eyes; he was even more alarmed when she avoided all mention of their involvement. As the evening wore on, he felt sure she was trying to work up the nerve to tell him she'd decided to end it.

Finally, over coffee, he couldn't stand it anymore. If she was going back to New York, he wanted to know it. If she had decided she wanted him to buy Gallagher Farm after all so she wouldn't have any ties here, he wanted to hear it. Not knowing was worse than her saying it, and he was just about to ask her what she was thinking when she told him.

"Jack, there's something we should talk about," she said.

Instantly, his anxiety level shot sky-high. Her eyes were brilliant in the light from the little candle on the table; her face the most beautiful sight he'd ever seen. Wondering how he could love a woman so much, he said, relatively calmly, "Okay, what is it?"

"I've been thinking about the time we spent in Maryland," she said. "In fact, it's about the only thing I've been thinking about. I can't get it out of my mind, and yet..."

"And yet?"

"Jack, I know you want some commitment from me—"

"No, no, I don't," he denied hastily. He didn't like the way this conversation was going already. "You know how I feel, but I want you to have all the time you need or want, Maggie. I told you I wouldn't press you, and I won't."

"I know, and I'm grateful. But it isn't fair to you—"

"Oh, yes, it is," he assured her. "Trust me. I'll wait—however long it takes."

"But what if—"

This wasn't getting him anywhere. Her clasped hands were on the table and he reached out and covered them with one of his own. "When I told you that I loved you, that I've always loved you, I didn't say it to make you unhappy, Maggie, or to put pressure on you to make you feel the same way about me. That's the last thing I want, believe me. I told you how I felt because I thought you should know, and because I didn't tell you once before when I had the chance. I wasn't going to make the same mistake twice."

"But—"

"No, let me finish. Nothing would make me happier than if you loved me, too, but we're not kids anymore, and we both know that sometimes things take time and sometimes they don't work out. That's why I said I'd give you all the room you needed."

She started to say something, but he tightened his hand on hers. His eyes on her face, he said, "If you decide you don't feel the same way, well, I'll accept that." He smiled painfully. "I won't like it, but I'll accept it. So don't feel you have to make any excuses to me, Maggie—please. I'd hate that more than anything."

"Oh, Jack," she sighed. "I wish—"

"If wishes were horses, pigs would fly."

She smiled tensely. "Aren't you mixing your metaphors?"

"I hope so." As he'd intended, he'd lightened the moment. "Now, let's not talk about it anymore—not right now, at least. Okay?"

She hesitated. Then she nodded. "Okay."

He didn't want to return to such a treacherous subject, so he said the first thing that came into his head. "You won't believe this, but Floyd bought me a horse."

Successfully diverted, she looked at him in surprise. "A horse? *Floyd* bought you a horse?"

"I don't blame you for being startled."

"Startled? I'm astounded. I didn't think Floyd knew anything about horses and cared less."

"I know. It was a shock to me, too." He was trying his best to keep his mind on the subject, when what he really wanted to tell her was that he hadn't meant a word of what he'd said earlier. He didn't want to accept any decision she made about her future unless it had him in it, he thought. It had been a stupid thing to say and he was angry with himself for playing the martyr.

But he couldn't very well say he'd changed his mind after he'd foolishly promised—again—not to press her, so he continued doggedly with Floyd's story. "The horse is called Amber Isle. He paid fifty thousand, but that's not too outrageous. You won't believe this, but he put him in tr—"

Maggie looked up sharply. "What did you say the horse's name was?"

It was his first inkling that something was amiss. "Amber Isle," he repeated. "Why?"

Something flickered in her eyes, and she looked quickly away. "It doesn't matter. Go on."

"Go *on?* When you look like that? What's wrong, Maggie? What do you know that I don't know?"

"Nothing!" she exclaimed, and then saw the look on his face. "I mean... I'm sure there's been a mistake."

"What do you mean? What kind of mistake?"

She didn't seem to want to meet his eyes. "Nothing, Jack. It's a... wonderful story."

"No it's not," he said flatly. "I know you, Maggie, and you're hiding something. What is it?"

Obviously distressed, she took a quick sip of water. "I... I'd rather not say."

He was trying not to hear the alarm bells going off in his head. "What do you mean, you'd rather not say? You know how important Fieldstone Farm is to me, and if something's wrong here, I need to know it."

Slowly, she put down her water glass. "Dad was talking about that horse just the other day," she said reluctantly. "He told me the owner had it for sale for twenty thousand and couldn't *give* it away."

"Twenty...!" He couldn't believe it. Hoarsely, he said, "There must be some mistake."

She stared back at him. "Was the owner a man named Harry Lindstrom?" She saw in his eyes that it had been. "Then there's no mistake, Jack. I'm sorry, but it's the same horse."

Jack just looked at her. For a few seconds, he couldn't even speak. If Maggie was right—and he couldn't doubt her, for she knew her horses—then Floyd had pulled a fast one... again. At the thought, he felt a rage building in him, an anger so great he wanted to smash something. It wasn't the money; he could have written a check for five times that and not even counted it. It was what Floyd had done.

Why had his brother cheated him? What reason could he possibly have? Money? Jealousy? But he'd given Floyd every chance; he'd helped him in every way he could.

And how had Floyd repaid him? By lying to him, and cheating him, and making him look like a fool. That's what he'd done.

"Jack?" Maggie said anxiously. "Maybe I'm wrong. Maybe I made a mistake."

As though coming back from an explosive edge, Jack focused on her. Floyd had played him for a sucker. He'd never suspected it; Jack hadn't even doubted him. Embarrassed and humiliated, he didn't stop to think that this was the woman he loved; all he could think of was what a fool he'd look in her eyes if she knew how Floyd had tricked him.

He didn't know how he managed it, but from some depths he didn't know existed, he forced a laugh. It sounded hollow, but it was the best he could manage when he felt so murderous. "Maybe so, maybe not," he said, and shrugged with shoulders that felt like they weighed a ton. "It doesn't really matter."

Maggie blinked. "It...doesn't matter?" she repeated. "Jack, how can you say that?"

He laughed again. He was getting better at it—as long as he didn't think what he was going to do to Floyd when he got home tonight. "Because it's true. Hey, I know Floyd pulled a fast one, but that's just Floyd, you know? He never can resist playing a joke—"

"A joke! Jack, this is no joke. Floyd deliberately cheated you. I don't think you should treat it so lightly."

He should have been warned by the sound of her voice, but he was too preoccupied with trying to save what little dignity he had left.

"Listen, Maggie, it's no big deal. It's only money, and God knows, I've got plenty of that." He saw her face and knew he'd made a big mistake but it was too late now. Doggedly he went on making things worse. "Furthermore, Floyd is my brother. He's my problem and I'll deal with this as I see fit."

Without warning, Maggie shot to her feet. Her eyes weren't sparkling now; they were blazing with anger and her voice had an icy ring.

"I assumed that since you asked me to be your wife, my opinion would count for something. Obviously I was wrong. It's none of my business and it never will be. So you go ahead and deal with it, Jack. Just count me out." Without another word, she snatched up her purse, turned, and ran out of the restaurant.

"Maggie!"

Muttering a curse, Jack jerked out his wallet, threw a few bills down on the table and went after her. She was just climbing into a cab when he came bursting out the door.

"Maggie!" he shouted.

She didn't even look back.

SOME FRAGMENT of common sense told Jack it would be futile to go after Maggie right now. His face murderous, he turned his attention to his brother instead and made record time back to the farm. He had no idea what he was going to say when he got there; as he drove with hands clenched tightly on the wheel, he decided it didn't matter. Why waste words when action would suit him better?

The living-room lights were on in the trailer when Jack came driving up in a cloud of dust and gravel. Floyd was just reaching for a cigarette when Jack came bursting in; he took one look at Jack's face and held up his hands in surrender.

"I can explain," he said.

That was explanation enough for Jack. He reached down and jerked Floyd up off the couch by his shirt. With their faces only inches apart, he said through gritted teeth, "Get out. Get out before I kill you."

Floyd's eyes widened. But he couldn't escape for Jack was holding him by a fistful of shirt material. "Jack, I—"

"I trusted you," Jack said, his voice shaking with rage. "I *believed* you. What kind of a man are you?"

"The kind who's never had the breaks, that's—" Floyd started to say. But then he looked into his brother's eyes, and suddenly, without warning, the fight went out of him. "You're right, Jack," he said, his voice quiet. "I got no excuse. Will you let go of me a minute?"

For a few seconds, Jack didn't move. But finally, inch by inch, his grip on the front of Floyd's shirt loosened and he released him. Stretching his neck, Floyd stepped back. Shakily, he said, "I don't know about you, but I could use a drink."

Jack was breathing heavily. "Fine. Make mine a double."

Amusement flashed quickly across Floyd's face. "You don't drink."

"I do tonight."

"All right, then. While I'm getting the sour mash, why don't you take a look inside that envelope on the table."

Jack was still feeling the effects of his rage. Blankly, he looked down at the littered coffee table. Amidst the piles of magazines and overflowing ashtrays and beer bottles was a manila envelope. He reached down and picked it up.

Inside was a thick wad of hundred dollar bills. The money in his hand, he turned toward the little kitchen, where Floyd was pouring the drinks.

"What's this?" he asked hoarsely.

Floyd smiled briefly. It looked more like a grimace. "It's the money I got from the sale of that horse. You can count it if you like. The whole twenty-five thousand's there." He came into the living room, carrying two glasses. "It belongs to you."

Jack looked down at the money, then back to Floyd. "I don't get it."

Floyd sighed. Handing Jack one of the glasses, he said, "I don't either. Who would have thought that this late in life I'd develop a conscience?"

"You mean you're giving it back to me?"

"You know, you always were the smart one of the family," Floyd said, amused. "I remember Mama telling us you had a mind like a steel trap. Of course I'm giving it back to you. What am I going to do with it? I never had that much money at one time in my entire life. Who knows? I could go somewhere and blow it all in one place."

Jack frowned. "I still don't understand."

Dropping down onto the couch again, Floyd took a hefty swallow from his glass. He started to say something flip, but then he saw Jack's face and changed his mind.

"Hey, look, little brother," he said, "I knew it was wrong from the moment I told Lilah I'd do it. I thought I could go through with it, but I just couldn't. That there money just sat there, starin' me in the face, making me more nervous every minute, and I finally decided, hell, it just wasn't worth it. I mean, I'm not going to go getting all sentimental here and makin' us both embarrassed, but the truth is, you've been pretty good to me over the years, and I just couldn't stiff my own brother. Funny, isn't it? If it had been someone else, well, my conscience might not have been so inconvenient."

He'd meant the last as a joke, but when Jack didn't laugh, he looked anxious. "What?"

Slowly, Jack looked over at him. "You mentioned Lilah. What's she got to do with this?"

So Floyd told him about Lilah's plan. When he got to the part about her insistence on putting Amber Isle in training with Luther Manning, Jack smiled grimly.

"I didn't understand what that was all about," Floyd said. "Do you?"

"Oh, yeah, I understand, all right. You said the horse couldn't run. She wanted to make me look like a fool for buying the thing in the first place, and then putting him in race training."

"Oh," Floyd said in a small voice. "Hey, Jack, I'm sorry. Look, Luther just got the horse. I'll call him in the morning and tell him—"

But just then the phone rang. Looking surprised, Floyd picked up. He listened a moment, then a smile broke out over his face. "Just a minute, Luther," he said. "Jack's right here. Why don't you tell him yourself?"

When Jack took the phone with a puzzled frown, the horse trainer was almost beside himself with glee. "I can't believe it!" he enthused, after Jack had said hello. "Man, I thought you were crazy, but I guess you sure know what you're doing!"

"What are you talking about, Luther?"

"I'm talking about this new horse you sent me, this Amber Isle! I didn't think you were back yet, so I was calling to leave a message with your brother."

"What kind of message?" Jack said cautiously.

"Well, I thought this nag was a loser for sure, the way it ran for old Harry Lindstrom, you know. But just for the hell of it, we breezed him a mile today and you won't believe it. The blame thing did it in one-thirty-four and change! He wasn't even breathin' hard at the finish line. I think we've got a runnin' horse here, Mr. Stanton. Harry was using him in short races, but it seems to me the farther he goes, the better he likes it. I've entered him in the Sheffield Stakes this week, and I'll bet we got better than an even chance."

"Of being in the money, you mean?" Jack asked.

"Hell, no, Mr. Stanton!" Luther said gleefully. "I'm talking about *winning* the race!"

Feeling a little dazed, Jack hung up the phone. Floyd was waiting anxiously, and he said, "Luther thinks Amber Isle can run."

The two brothers looked at each other, then Floyd's face almost split with his grin. Lifting his glass in salute, he said it for both of them.

"Hot damn! Lilah is going to be gnashing her teeth."

Jack smiled, too. But as pleased as he was about this outcome, he had a far weightier problem to deal with. He'd made a fool of himself tonight where Maggie was concerned, and he'd probably lost her forever. That thought was more than he could bear. He felt an almost physical pain. Cursing his pride, he finished his drink and went up to the house.

It was hours before he slept that night, but long before morning came, he knew he had to get her back, to talk to her, to apologize. Without Maggie, nothing else mattered, not the company he'd built, not the farm of which he'd always dreamed, not the horses he'd just bought. It was all meaningless without her, and after coming so close after all these years, he wasn't going to give her up. Not without a fight.

CHAPTER FIFTEEN

MAGGIE HADN'T BEEN ABLE to sleep at all. When the taxi dropped her off after that horrible quarrel with Jack last night, she'd gone inside and straight up to bed, thanking Providence that Dan and Belle were busy watching television. This morning, heavy-eyed and out of sorts, she was up and dressed before the alarm went off. All during the long, endless night, she'd thought about what had happened and knew she'd been living in a fool's paradise.

There was no way she could consider marrying a man who, instead of discussing a problem, told her it was none of her business. Jack had changed—he had allowed success to go to his head. What had he said? Money didn't matter, he had more than enough. He was no different from people like the Castlemaines and the others who had looked down on those who had had to work for a living like her father.

Again and again, Maggie castigated herself. But why was she so disappointed and shocked? She should have seen the signs; the showpiece farm he was building, the horses he had bought. Jack had admitted that he wanted to join those high society circles she'd always despised. He had the money now, and with the stock he was acquiring, he'd command their respect, no matter what anyone privately thought.

Her eyes burning, Maggie went downstairs. Grabbing a cup of coffee, she glanced at Dan's closed bedroom door and then tiptoed outside. She didn't want to talk to her father or Belle. She was still so upset about what had happened that she had to be alone. She needed to think about what she intended to do now.

As always, when she'd been troubled in the past, she was drawn to the horses. A fast ride used to clear her head, so she pulled Freebie out of his stall and put him in the cross-ties. Taking a comb and brush, she started to groom him when she heard footsteps behind her. Pausing, she looked over her shoulder and saw Belle.

"Hi," she said, hoping that if Belle noticed, she wouldn't comment on Maggie's red eyes.

"Good morning," Belle said. Carefully, she added, "You're going for an early ride?"

Maggie returned to brushing Freebie down. "It's such a beautiful morning, I thought I'd take advantage of it while I could."

"I see," Belle said. She waited a moment, then she said, "Maggie, can I ask you something?"

"You know you can."

Belle paused again. "I know you went out with Jack last night. But when you came home and went right up to bed without stopping in to say good-night . . . well, I just wondered if everything was all right."

Feeling the sting of tears again, Maggie straightened and went around to brush out Freebie's tail. "Everything's—" she started to say, but suddenly her lip trembled and she couldn't lie. Mournfully, she looked up at Belle. "We had a fight last night. It was awful, Belle. I never want to see him again."

"But why?" Belle said, alarmed. "I thought right from the start that you and Jack were the perfect couple. I saw the way he looked at you that first day in the kitchen. And I saw the look on *your* face. You were in love with him even then."

"Oh, how could I be? I didn't even know him then!"

"Oh, yes, you did," Belle insisted. "Just like I knew Dan the first time I saw him. Oh, I don't mean that even before he told me I knew what toothpaste he used, or what his favorite flavor of ice cream was. I mean I knew what kind of man he was." She looked into Maggie's eyes. "And you knew it, too, about Jack, didn't you?"

Maggie's expression was bitter. "I thought I knew what kind of man he was. But I was wrong."

"Oh, Maggie, I don't think that's true."

"I do!" Abandoning all pretense of grooming the horse, Maggie threw down the comb and the brush. Scraping her hair back and dashing the last of her tears from her eyes, she added, "But it doesn't matter what he's really like, because I'm going back to New York."

"You don't mean that. You're just upset—"

"No, it's more than that. You know why I didn't want Jack to buy this place? It was because he tore down the Tidleman farm and built one to rival Finish Line itself. What was to prevent him from just...sweeping away everything here? Then who would have known, or cared, what Gallagher Farm had been?"

"Why, Maggie," Belle said softly. "I think you do love the farm."

"Of course I—" she started to say, and then stopped. "Of course I love it," she muttered, her face reddening. "I know I ran away before. I know I was a coward. But staying here these past few weeks made me realize that no matter how much I want to deny it, this place is still . . . home."

"You weren't a coward, Maggie. You were just young. You'd been hurt. You needed to go away so you could look at things in a different light."

"Yes, but I didn't have to reject my life here completely. I know I hurt Dad, and I'm sorry. But at the time—oh, it's no excuse, and I hate myself!"

Her face sympathetic, Belle put her arms around her. "I understand, because I've felt that way, too, in the past. I was bitter for years."

"I know you're trying to make me feel better, but I don't believe you were ever that way, Belle," Maggie said tearfully. "You're too happy. Too loving and kind."

Smiling faintly, Belle said, "Thanks, but I wasn't always this way—if I am now."

Wiping away tears again, she asked, "What happened to make you change?"

"You can only hate something for so long before it becomes an effort. When I realized I was only hurting myself, I decided I needed a whole new change of scene."

"What did you do?"

"I opened the atlas, closed my eyes and pointed. I vowed that wherever my finger landed, that's where I'd go for my new start."

"And you pointed to Lexington?"

"Well, actually, when I opened my eyes, I was pointing to Savannah, but I only had enough money to get me to Kentucky." Laughing at the memory, Belle continued, "I was working in a drugstore, saving up my money so I could go on, when one day in walked your father." She smiled at the memory. "After that, I'll tell you, Georgia was no longer on my mind."

Maggie didn't know whether to believe her or not. Sure Belle had spun the story to make her feel better, she said, "You're making that up."

Solemnly, Belle crossed her heart. "I'm not. You can ask your Dad."

"I just might."

"In the meantime, what are we going to do about you?"

Reminded, Maggie looked tearful again. "I don't know. I'll appreciate any suggestions." Then she couldn't help it. With a burst, she said, "Oh, Belle, sometimes I feel so ashamed. Looking back on it now, I hate the way I felt."

"I know. Sometimes feelings aren't pretty, but they're just feelings, after all. It's what you do with them that counts, isn't it?"

"But what if you don't know what to do with them?" Maggie asked plaintively.

Belle smiled. "You'll know when the time comes. All you have to do is follow your heart."

Before Maggie could answer, Dan called from the house, and Belle smiled. "Duty calls," she said with a wink. Impulsively, she reached up and gave Maggie a kiss on the cheek. "When the time comes, you'll know what's right," she said. "I did."

MAGGIE STILL wasn't sure what was right when her Aunt Tilda came that morning to visit. Once she had Freebie brushed down, she realized she didn't have the heart to go for a ride, so she led him outside and released him to roll in one of the paddocks. Preoccupied with her troubles, she hadn't heard Tilda's little Volkswagen rumble in; she was just heading toward the house when her aunt came out. She'd been inside talking to Dan and Belle, and she was smiling from ear to ear.

"You'll never guess!" Tilda said excitedly, when Maggie reached her at the bottom of the porch steps and gave her a kiss. She looked ready to burst with the news. "When Dan and Belle get married later in the year, I'm going to be matron of honor!"

Forgetting her own problems, Maggie smiled in genuine pleasure. "You are? That's wonderful!"

"It is! Belle just asked me, and of course I said yes."

Maggie couldn't resist. "But I thought you disapproved of this marriage."

Tilda drew herself up. "Why, Maggie Gallagher," she said haughtily. "Where on earth did you get an idea like that? I love Belle. I think she's the salt of the earth. And she's good for your father, you know." Lowering her voice conspiratorially while Maggie tried not to laugh, she went on, "I've never seen Dan so happy, not since your dear mother died. And it's about time, don't you think?"

"I do, indeed," Maggie agreed.

Tilda put a pudgy hand on her niece's arm. "You don't mind that Belle asked me to be in the wedding, do you, Maggie?" she asked anxiously. "Oh, I'd hate to think that your feelings are hurt because she asked me instead of you."

Impulsively, Maggie gave her round little aunt a hug. "I don't mind at all, Aunt Tilda," she said honestly. Belle had already discussed it with her, and she thoroughly approved.

"Oh, that's good," Tilda said, relieved. Then she looked anxious again. "Wait—since I've never married myself, does that make me a matron, or a maid, of honor?"

Maggie laughed. "I don't think it matters, Aunt Tilda. Just as long as you're there giving them your blessing."

"Well, of course they have my blessing!" Tilda sniffed, getting into her little car. "Honestly, Maggie, sometimes I don't know *where* you get your ideas!"

Shaking her head in fond exasperation, Maggie waved as Tilda tooted her horn and left. But her smile faded as she started the chores, and the morning seemed to drag because she still felt so indecisive.

She knew she had to go back to New York and talk to Nowell about her job, but she just couldn't do it yet. She'd called several days ago and talked again to her second-in-command, and things were still running smoothly... for now. But she couldn't put off returning indefinitely; it wasn't fair to Nowell or the people who worked under her. She had to make a decision one way or the other.

To stay or to go, that was the question, she thought grimly. Belle had told her to follow her heart, but she wasn't sure where her heart was telling her to go. And what, after all, had changed? Even if she wanted to stay, she couldn't—not if Dan and Belle were to go to

Florida. Her father would never sell the farm if he thought there was a chance she wanted it, and he couldn't retire without the money the sale would bring. Just because she was having second thoughts, she couldn't force him to choose; it wasn't fair to him or to Belle.

With a sigh, she thought that maybe she should just go back to New York after all. Once she talked to Nowell, she'd know where she stood as far as her job went, and she could make any changes then. She was foolish even to think about keeping the farm when she didn't have the money to run it. And she couldn't ruin her father's bright plans. She should just tell everyone she would be leaving tomorrow.

And what about Jack?

She didn't want to think about Jack. After what had happened between them, it was obvious that he was another part of the past that should have stayed behind her. No matter what Belle said, Maggie had been a fool to think she and Jack could somehow work things out.

With these glum thoughts on her mind, she took Never Forget and her colt out to the pasture. She was standing by the fence, watching the foal run around in circles, expending all the energy he'd stored during the night, when her father joined her. For a man who'd spent the past few weeks flat on his back, he looked astonishingly fit.

"What are you doing out here?" she asked with a worried frown. "You're supposed to be in bed."

"I'm tired of trying to run everything from a pillow," he said, casually putting a booted foot on the fence's bottom rail. Watching him carefully, Maggie saw with astonishment that he didn't even grimace at the movement. "Besides," he added, not looking at her, "I'm fine now. Fit as a fiddle."

"What is this?" she asked suspiciously. "A miraculous recovery? Yesterday you could hardly move. Today you're sauntering around. Come on, Dad—what gives?"

"Never could fool you for long, could I, kiddo?" he said. "But can we talk about it later? Right now, I got something else to say."

"What?"

Instead of answering right away, he gestured toward the horses she'd just put out. The colt was playing with a rock, pushing it along with his nose, trying to toss it into the air. Smiling at the sight, Dan turned back to her.

"Have you thought of a name for him yet?" he asked. "You helped him to get here, so you get the honor, you know."

Smiling herself, at the foal's antics, she said, "I know. And I have thought of one. Given the name of his sire, Worth Waiting For II—and the fact that he's undoubtedly the best thing this farm has ever produced, I think we should call him . . . Worth the Wait. What do you think?"

"I think it's a fine name," Dan said, smiling. "It suits him."

"Is that what you wanted to talk to me about?"

He hesitated a moment, but then shook his head. Painfully, he said, "Maggie, I know you've always thought I was second-rate—"

Stricken, she protested immediately. "That's not true, Dad! I never—"

"Yes, you did," he insisted quietly. "And perhaps you were right. We never did have any big winners here at Gallagher Farm, and maybe it was my fault. Maybe I just didn't know enough, or work hard enough—"

More agitated and upset with every word, she put a hand on his arm. "No, I won't listen to this! No one could have worked harder than you, Dad. And you've forgotten more than most of the trainers nowadays ever knew."

"Thanks, but it isn't true," he said sadly. "Otherwise, we would have been a lot farther down the road than we are now. Anyway, I always wanted to make it up to you."

She couldn't bear seeing her father this way. Fiercely, she said, "You don't have anything to make up to me, Dad. If anything, it's I who should be apologizing to you!"

His eyes were bright as he looked into her face. "Aw, Maggie, you've got nothing to apologize for. No father could have asked for a finer daughter than you."

She couldn't disguise her bitterness—and her self-loathing. "Oh, yes, so fine she ran away right out of high school."

"You had things to do, Maggie. I never begrudged you that." His glance went to the horses again. Bored with his previous diversion, the colt was trying to engage his mother in a game of tag. As they watched, Never Forget pinned her ears at her son, and the foal scooted off.

Dan looked at Maggie again. "I've been wanting to say this for a long time. And now that I'm about to sell the farm and leave here, I want to get it off my mind."

Whatever it was, Maggie didn't want to hear it. Avoiding her father's eyes, she looked at the colt again, and suddenly saw him in her mind's eye as the stallion he would grow up to be. She was certain that, like his sire, he would one day take his place in the record books. She knew it as sure as she was standing here.

That's the colt who should be the foundation stallion for Jack's Fieldstone Farm, she thought, and felt an almost physical pain. It wasn't meant to be; it never had been.

"He's yours, Maggie," Dan said quietly. "Worth the Wait. I want you to have him."

Quickly, she turned to him. "Mine! Oh, Dad—"

"No, hear me out, please. I know you want nothing to do with horses or the farm or anything that reminds you of racing, and I guess after what I put you through growing up, I can't blame you. But whether you keep him or sell him, I want you to have him."

"Dad—"

He put his hand on her arm, the look on his face making her fall silent. "For once I want to give you something special—something to prove to you before I got out of the business that all these years haven't been wasted. I planned real careful, Maggie, and that colt out there is my legacy." His blue eyes were bright with pride and pain. "He's a gift to you from me."

Maggie didn't know what to say. Tears filled her eyes, and then spilled over onto her cheeks. She tried to speak and couldn't. Her throat working, she threw her arms around her father and hugged him close as she sobbed.

After awkwardly patting her back, he pulled out his big bandanna and shoved it in her hand. "Now, now, don't go blubbering," he said. "Especially when I got another confession to make."

Maggie took the big handkerchief. Wiping her eyes, she said tearfully, "Another confession?"

"Remember what I said about not being as bad off as I claimed?" he said, looking sheepish. "Well, the truth of the matter is that I could have been up and about a few days after I put my back out."

She looked up. "What are you saying, Dad? Are you telling me your injury was just a sham?"

Seeing the look in her eyes, he said quickly, "Now, now, don't jump the gun like you always do. I had my reasons."

"What reasons? What reason could you possibly have for letting me think that you were hurt? Oh, Dad, how could you?"

"I could because I love you," he said, reaching for her arm again as she turned away. "Listen to me, Maggie. At least hear me out. I know it was wrong, but I wanted to give you one last chance to see if *you* were doing the right thing."

"The right thing! What does that mean?"

"Now, Maggie, you know you wouldn't really have been happy with that fellow in New York."

She reddened. "You don't know that! Just because it didn't work out—"

"And why was that?" he said reasonably. "I never met the man, Maggie, but I knew he wasn't for you. Living in some mansion, stiff and proper as could be, never having any *fun*...well, that wasn't my Maggie."

"Oh, I see. And without knowing *anything* about Nowell, you just decided he wouldn't be right for me. Honestly, Dad, sometimes I could—"

"Hold on there. Did I say one word against your fiancé until you broke the engagement? Tell me, Maggie. Be honest now."

She opened her mouth to reply, then closed it again. Grudgingly, she admitted, "Well, no, you didn't." Then she looked at him sternly. "But to *fake* an injury! That's low even for you, Dad!"

"Yes, well, I didn't fake the accident. I just took a little longer to recover than I needed to because I wanted you to stay until you knew what you were doing. Because with the farm for sale, this would be our last chance. Would you have stayed just because I asked you to?" he asked, and then answered his own question. "No, you wouldn't have. You'd have been off to New York again in a flash, and then where would I be?"

"With your nose in your own business, that's where!"

"Now, Maggie, don't be mad at me. Besides, Belle thought it was a good idea, too."

"Belle was in on this?"

"Not at first. Now, don't get in a tizzy until I have a chance to explain. We both thought that if you had a chance to compare life here with what you had in New York, you'd be sure of what you wanted, don't you see?"

"And what makes you think I didn't know what I wanted?" she demanded.

"Well, it was just a guess," Dan said. He flushed. "After all, you *are* my daughter. I know you as well as anyone, don't I?"

She didn't want to admit that he did. Frowning, she said, "Go on."

"Well, Belle didn't like it at first, I'll be honest with you about that. But I promised her that if, after staying here for a while and running the place, you decided you still wanted what that Nowell fellow could provide, well, then I'd give my blessing and behave myself at your wedding." He looked at her keenly. "But I didn't think you'd choose that kind of life, Maggie, and you didn't, did you?"

She couldn't hold his eyes. "Oh, Dad, I don't know. Things aren't so easy as that."

"But your roots are here, right in this place."

"And what about *your* roots?" she suddenly demanded. "I never thought you'd leave the farm. It's been your whole life!"

Tenderly, he put his arm around her and drew her close. "It's time for a change for me, Maggie. I have to admit it, these Kentucky winters are hard on me now, and I want to see what Belle and I can do where it's warm. Besides—" he smiled "—if I really get to missing the horses, there's always Aqueduct Racetrack down there in Florida."

She felt so torn. "Dad, even if I wanted to—"

"Don't say it, darling, please. I've seen how you took to the farm again, Maggie, and if you want to stay, we can swing something. I don't have to sell the whole place, just part of it. What do you say?"

Feeling more comfort in her father's arms than she had in a long time, Maggie forgave him his little deception and laid her head wearily on his shoulder. "I don't know what to say," she sighed. "You're exasperating beyond belief, but I love you in spite of it." Still worried, she lifted her head. "But Dad, you can't just sell pieces of the farm. For you and Belle to retire, you have to sell all of it."

"Maybe we can work something out."

They both turned at the sound of the new voice behind them, and when Dan saw Jack standing there, he looked at Maggie and gently disengaged his arm. Murmuring something about seeing how Belle was getting along without him, he waved and walked quickly away.

Left alone, Jack and Maggie stared at each other for a few tense seconds, then Maggie abruptly turned away to stare out at the horses in the pasture.

"What do you want?" she asked coldly.

"To talk to you."

When she didn't reply, Jack came up to the fence and leaned against it, too. Still, she wouldn't look at him. She hated to admit it, but she didn't trust that she could do so without losing what little control she had left. She'd tried since last night to convince herself that it was all over between them, but with him right beside her, she knew she couldn't put him out of her life as easily as that. No matter what he'd become, she couldn't hate him.

Still, she told herself, she had to try. "I don't have anything to say to you, Jack."

"Then let me talk." Gently, he took her arm and made her face him. Even the simple touch of his hand threatened to destroy her fragile self-control, and she would have jerked away if she'd been able.

"I'm sorry, Maggie," he said simply. "I didn't mean those things I said. I only said them because I was embarrassed."

"Embarrassed?" She wanted to send him away but she couldn't. It was the look in his eyes; she had to believe him.

He reddened, but made himself continue. "Yes, and I was also humiliated that Floyd had taken me in so easily. I didn't want to admit that I was such an easy mark, Maggie. It made me look stupid and foolish, like I didn't know what I was doing. So I tried to play it down."

She started to say something, but he continued. "I don't have any excuses. I know I'm new at this, Maggie, and that even if I'm in it a hundred years, I'll never know as much as you and your dad. But I wanted you to think I did, so you... you'd be proud of me and see me in a new light."

She didn't know what to say. Even if she had known the words, she couldn't have said them anyway. No man had ever spoken to her like this. Jack had been so devastatingly honest that she had to be honest, too.

Without warning, she thought of the night of the sale. She could still see the happy look on his face, the joy and excitement in his eyes. There had been no pretense about Jack that night; he had been genuinely thrilled and delighted. And when she remembered the way he had kissed her, and held her, and how he had wanted to share that proud moment with her, she was even more ashamed.

She hadn't realized it until now, but she had blown this thing out of proportion—jumped to wrong conclusions—so she'd have an excuse. Loving Jack frightened her; it forced her to choose. And she'd spent so much time running away from this place that she hadn't wanted to face just what she had left.

"Maggie?" he said anxiously. "Do you believe me?"

She could hardly look him in the eye. Painfully, she nodded. "Yes, I believe you," she said, her voice low. "I'm sorry."

"It was my fault. But I'll never exclude you again, I promise. I don't want this to come between us, not when we've found each other again." His eyes were bleak. "Not when I waited all these years. Not when I've dreamed so many dreams."

Now was the time to tell him she'd decided to go back to New York. She wanted to say it, but the words wouldn't come.

Jack grasped her arms, holding her in front of him. "Maggie, please! Don't you know how much I love you? I'll never stop loving you! I want you to be my wife, my partner, my friend..." He laughed shakily. "I want you to be the manager of our farm. The manager of your own farm, if your dad will still sell it to me after this."

Before she could answer, he went on intensely. "But most of all, I want to be with you. I love you more than life itself, Maggie, and if you ask, I'll sell Fieldstone Farm and all the horses and never look back."

"You... you'd sell your farm?"

"And everything else. Nothing else matters but you. If you're not with me, it's all meaningless."

Suddenly, she recalled Belle's words. Maybe it was time to stop leading with her head, and go with her heart. But it wasn't that easy.

"Don't keep me in suspense," Jack pleaded, agonized. "Just say the word and I'll do whatever you ask. But tell me before I go crazy. I can't stand much more of this."

"Dad will have to sell the farm if he and Belle are going to go to Florida," she said shakily.

"I'll buy it," Jack said. He said it so quickly she knew he had already thought about it. Could it be that he understood her better than she did herself? He smiled at her confusion. "It will be my wedding present to you."

"You're giving me the farm?"

"I always intended to. I thought... after all these years, it should stay in the family."

"Oh, Jack," she sighed. In one stroke, he'd banished all her objections. Thinking that she loved him so much it hurt, she said shakily, "Then, I've got a wedding present for you. Dad gave me the colt, Jack, and I'm giving him to you. He'll make a fine addition for us at Fieldstone Farm, don't you think?"

Jack didn't react for a few seconds. It was almost as though he didn't dare to believe it. But as Maggie started to smile, he threw back his head and laughed.

"You mean it!" he shouted. Grabbing her again, he swung her jubilantly around. "Does this mean you've said yes?"

"Yes, Jack," she said. And then, laughing for joy herself, she said it again. "Yes. Yes! *Yes!*"

As Jack pulled her fiercely into him and gave her a kiss, the colt out at pasture suddenly gave a shrill whinny and took off. Looking as though he had wings on his heels, he was a beautiful sight as he ran, and they both turned to watch.

Jack's voice was choked as he held Maggie close. "I think," he said, "that that colt will be the foundation stallion for Fieldstone-Gallagher Farm."

Proudly, Maggie noted the name change. "I think so, too," she murmured.

And then, as the colt whinnied again and raced away toward a future that Maggie finally felt was secure, she looked up into Jack's handsome face and laughed with sheer happiness.

"He took a long time to get here, my darling," she said. "But like all good things—" she reached for Jack's hand "—he was definitely worth the wait."

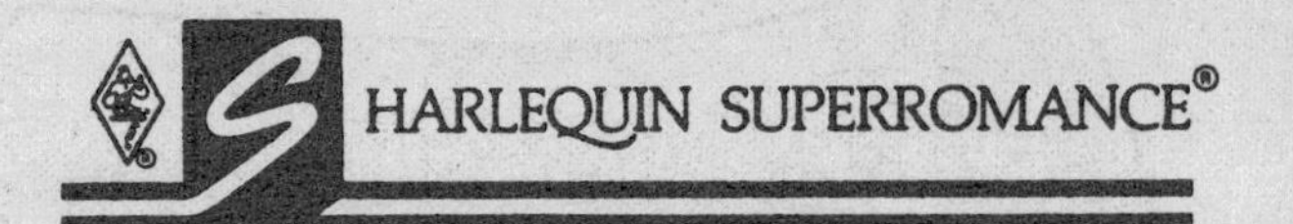

COMING NEXT MONTH

#546 AFTER THE PROMISE • Debbi Bedford

Despite all his knowledge and training, Dr. Michael Stratton could only stand by helplessly as his small son, Cody, battled for his life. But something good might come of this—Cody's illness had thrown Michael and his ex-wife, Jennie, together. While others worked to heal his child, Michael could heal his marriage.

#547 SHENANIGANS • Casey Roberts

Paul Sherwood was a man with a mission: to take over ailing cosmetics giant Cheri Lee. Lauren Afton was a woman with a goal: to save her mother's self-made empire. Lauren knew she was a match for Paul in the boardroom, and she had a sneaking suspicion they'd also be a pretty good match in the bedroom....

#548 THE MODEL BRIDE • Pamela Bauer

Model Jessie Paulson had been on the jury that convicted Aidan McCullough's father of murder, yet now the verdict was beginning to haunt her. Aidan, too, was haunted by his father's conviction. Not only had it uncovered a past best left buried, it was standing in the way of his future with Jessie.

#549 PARADOX • Lynn Erickson
Women Who Dare, Book 5

Emily got more than she bargained for when she decided to start a new life in Seattle. Her train crashed and she woke up to find herself in the year 1893, at the home of rancher Will Dutcher. Trapped in time, Emily had to discover a way to return home. But how could she abandon the man she loved?

AVAILABLE THIS MONTH:

#542 WORTH THE WAIT
Risa Kirk

#543 BUILT TO LAST
Leigh Roberts

#544 JOE'S MIRACLE
Helen Conrad

#545 SNAP JUDGEMENT
Sandra Canfield